*Bad Luck Bridesmaid*

# Bad Luck
# *Bridesmaid*

A Novel

Alison Rose Greenberg

ST. MARTIN'S GRIFFIN
NEW YORK

First published in the United States by St. Martin's Griffin, an imprint of St. Martin's Publishing Group

BAD LUCK BRIDESMAID. Copyright © 2021 by Alison Rose Greenberg. All rights reserved. Printed in the United States of America. For information, address St. Martin's Publishing Group, 120 Broadway, New York, NY 10271.

www.stmartins.com

Designed by Gabriel Guma

Library of Congress Cataloging-in-Publication Data

Names: Greenberg, Alison Rose, author.
Title: Bad luck bridesmaid : a novel / Alison Rose Greenberg.
Description: First edition. | New York : St. Martin's Griffin, 2022.
Identifiers: LCCN 2021035254 | ISBN 9781250791597
    (trade paperback) | ISBN 9781250791603 (ebook)
Subjects: LCGFT: Romance fiction.
Classification: LCC PS3607.R4468 B33 2022 | DDC 813/.6—dc23
LC record available at https://lccn.loc.gov/2021035254

Our books may be purchased in bulk for promotional, educational, or business use. Please contact your local bookseller or the Macmillan Corporate and Premium Sales Department at 1-800-221-7945, extension 5442, or by email at MacmillanSpecialMarkets@macmillan.com.

First Edition: 2022

10  9  8  7  6  5  4  3  2  1

To Max and Zoey
You're worth moving mountains for.

# One

I knew right before the violinist's fifth loop of Ben Folds's "The Luckiest" that I was, in fact, the opposite. I was zero for three. I did nothing to disguise my resting this-is-awkward face, helplessly peering down at a crowd of two hundred impatient strangers stuffed into the small, ancient church. I felt the heavily contoured "honey, *now* you have a jawline" foundation melt down my cheeks. The church's two ceiling fans were no match for Georgia's August humidity, and while the makeup artist had promised I would emerge looking like a "dewy Instagram filter," my face resembled something closer to a sad clown's. Not helping was the ambitious flower crown digging into my skull. Was I not a bridesmaid after all, but actually a thirty-one-year-old boho flower girl?

I adjusted the folk horror film dangling over my eyes and took in the Gothic sanctuary. Light cascaded into the room through stained-glass windows, which depicted scenes from the Bible—or possibly a toga party gone wrong. The bride, Rebecca, had clocked a disconcerting number of hours on Pinterest, and it showed. Rustic Chic Jesus was *thriving*. Vines of eucalyptus lined the aisle, with white orchids and light pink peonies dancing on the twigs. Cascading towers of white candles set in mason jars lit a pathway to the altar, arched in a display of orchids. It was all so beautiful. It was all so unnecessary.

Our bride was Gone Girl.

*Once is happenstance. Twice is coincidence. The third time it's enemy action.*

This was an admittedly odd time for a James Bond reference to resurface in my brain, but my mind had no boundaries.

Over the past decade, I had purchased three bridesmaid dresses for three separate weddings. While all three empire waist gowns participated in making me look like I was entering my last trimester, exactly zero of them participated in a recessional. I was three times a bridesmaid, yet there was never a bride.

Zero for three.

I was the enemy of love.

I was Bad Luck Bridesmaid.

I did not come to this conclusion alone.

# Two

My zero for one occurred a decade before this third non-union. I was twenty-two and proudly living in a mold-infested shoebox with a flex wall disguised as a "charming two-bedroom" West Village apartment. For the first time in my life, I was unhinged—living up to my own potential, without my parents telling me how high to set the bar.

I was barely making forty thousand dollars a year as an assistant planner at a boutique New York City ad agency, the Wheelhouse, where employees coasted on four hours of sleep, Adderall, and the vain hope that something better was right around the corner. I had marched through childhood with misplaced fervors, without a worthy outlet for my convictions. It took one strategic marketing course in college for me to recognize that my brain was wired to connect a product to a person. Advertising was *my place*. My counterparts complained daily, yet my only complaint was having to spare hours in my day pretending to empathize with entitled kids who stacked their Cartier Love bracelets—like badges of unearned honor—around their wrists. I truly did not care that I made barely enough to coast. Monotony was the death of my soul, and advertising promised the thrill of an unknown tomorrow. I loved the chaotic ride, the dusks that bled into dawns on the worn couch in the breakroom, the tight deadlines, the shifting clients, and the fire drills. After hours, I would sneak into our executive creative director's office and pore through his creative briefs, believing I could both easily have that corner office and do it better.

I never slowed down enough to worry about my next step. That wasn't my style. Upon my first year in Manhattan, I gleefully discovered that young adults in the Big Apple also didn't lament over their futures—they didn't have the means or the time. There was only one goal: day-to-day survival. This was the way I had always operated.

My early childhood was spent as a middle-class kid in Connecticut—living in the worst ranch-style house on the nicest English Tudor mansion–lined block in the wealthy suburbs of New Canaan. Mostly all the parents were the Joneses, with no need to keep up with themselves. As a result, their efforts were directed toward their children's potentials, toward mapping out boastful futures for their Penn-bound offspring.

I was the only child of two academics. My mother was an adjunct professor of Judaic studies, and my father was a communications professor specializing in classical rhetorical theory. These intellectual peas in a pod should have birthed Aristotle. Instead, they were blessed with me, Zoey Marks, someone whose first word was undoubtedly a curse word.

Before I started the fifth grade, my father decided to leave Yale in favor of aggressively chasing tenure-track positions at neighboring colleges. As a result, from the age of ten onward I moved every couple of years, becoming "that weird new girl" at different private schools around the Northeast. I wasn't academically predictable enough for either of my parents. I excelled in subjects that challenged my soul—literature, art, and exploring shitty white men throughout history. On the other hand, no stimulant was strong enough to help me retain the definition of a protozoan. I was a mystery, even to myself, but I liked it that way. I never fit in. To be fair, I tried really hard not to.

I was Robert Frost, with scuffed Converses, dancing my way down the road less traveled—and yes, it made all the difference. Thus, my first encounter with Chelsea Moore was an embarrassing one.

I met Chelsea at a mutual friend's packed rooftop party during my first summer in New York City. Surrounded by twenty-somethings anxiously chewing on the edges of their Solo cups, I spotted a petite brunette laughing under the canopy, and instantly, my cheeks blanketed in heat. Chelsea and I were wearing the same leopard peplum top with dark-wash skinny jeans, which meant we spent the first portion of the night on opposite corners of the roof, our eyes deliberately pointed away from each other at all times.

I was not the type of girl to embrace the cuteness of casually twinning at a party. I spent the early years of my childhood sporting a collared blouse under a navy jumper, and then my awkward years wearing different school logos atop a white polo neatly tucked into a navy kilt, which was "no less than three inches above the knee!" There were only so many ways to showcase originality at Ivy League starter kits, and this colored the efforts I made as an adult to be anything but your basic bitch. My skin became an extension of my soul, housing delicate minimalist tattoos. My clothes were usually an effortless mix of clashing patterns. Therefore, wearing the same outfit as a stranger at a rooftop party was not unfortunate—it was a threat. It taunted, *"You are not as cool as you think you are, Zoey Marks."*

After hours of dancing around each other's hip-accentuating blouses, Chelsea and I found ourselves reaching for the same bottle of warm seven-dollar chardonnay. We exhaled a shared "well, this is embarrassing" chuckle, and one bottle later, we realized we were both crushing it at entry-level ad sales positions, we were both living with hellions we had met on Craigslist, and we both had apartment leases that were up by the summer's end. Securing a compatible roommate while drunk at a rooftop party was the New York City equivalent of striking gold—minus the awkward fashion situation.

Prior to moving to New York, Chelsea spent four years at Boston University falling madly in love with a nice, agreeable guy named Chris. He wore wire-frame glasses and ironic T-shirts and was the type of guy who would say yes to picking up an acquaintance from the airport. Right out of college, Chelsea and Chris both got jobs in New York City, but Chris's start-up gig quickly rerouted him to San Francisco.

The long distance was wholly devastating for Chelsea, as I could gather from her desperate need to play Death Cab for Cutie's "Transatlanticism" on loop. I had never let my heart find itself even a little bit wounded by a man, so I didn't understand Chelsea's rumination ritual. I used music to rage. During my first year at sleepaway camp, my art counselor, Tamara—an always-in-her-feels twenty-two-year-old—only allowed three artists inside her wax-spattered jukebox: Tracy Chapman, Sarah McLachlan, and Alanis Morissette. I worshiped Tamara's epic coolness—if I could have sketched an adult version of myself, I would have sketched her. She birthed my undying love for angsty female singers of the nineties. They spoke to my soul, even if I had not yet lived most of their lyrics. I was the uninhibited kid jumping on her bed with a Walkman clipped to her pleated skirt, headphones on her ears, the outside world muted. An hour of understanding for a misunderstood child was a reset button. I danced shit out—the more depressing the lyrics, the more aggressive the dance. I surmised that Chelsea's Music and Cry situation was what our species found to be wholly therapeutic, but I couldn't fathom being lonely enough to let an indie rocker boy's lyrics bring me to my knees.

For the second month in a row, I found Chelsea spending her Friday night curled up on her bedsheets, gazing longingly at a photo of Chris on her phone, as if he had gone off to war and died. I had just returned home from happy hour work drinks, and I plopped myself down on the edge of her bed, swinging my legs along to Ben Gibbard's howl. I was two beers past sober, and thus the embodiment of the world's greatest wisdom.

"I'm just saying, wouldn't it be simpler to let Chris go? Let him live his best life in San Fran, while you get to enjoy the hell out of New York. And look, if you're both . . . *much* older and still into each other, you can always revisit the relationship."

Chelsea usually grinned and rolled her eyes at my unsolicited advice, but this time was different. She sat up, her wide brown eyes scanning mine.

"Zoey, he's my compass. How am I supposed to walk around

New York, enjoying my life, knowing that he's out there, living, breathing . . . without me? I want to go wherever he goes."

A mediocre male was now Chelsea's North Star. I sucked in my lips, forcing my opinions to stay in the place they had formed. Chris was hardly the kind of guy worthy of a Carole King song, but where Chris led, Chelsea would blindly follow. Smiling in a straight line, I offered Chelsea a "to each her own" nod.

I knew Chelsea's father was rarely around growing up. Chris was the first stable man in her life, and he filled a specific void for Chelsea. No part of her felt like she was wasting her young-adulthood by latching on to this comfort. My heart broke for her past, but it was difficult for me to understand how clinging to Chris might mend such a large void in her world. To be fair, I had never experienced a void.

One frigid weekend in December, Chris finally put a stop to Death Cab's reign, arriving at our peeling apartment door, dropping down to one knee, and surprising Chelsea with her grandmother's ring. She would follow Chris to San Francisco— with a pear-shaped diamond on her way-too-young finger.

I said yes to being Chelsea's bridesmaid with the naivete of a person who had yet to see the price on the mint chiffon dress she would soon purchase. I said yes to being her bridesmaid, all the while believing Chelsea was making a big mistake. Who gets married at twenty-two? This wasn't the 1950s. This was 2011. This was New York Fucking City. But Chelsea loved furiously and thoughtlessly, desperate to find a safe destination for her fragile heart to land.

We were opposites in every way. For Chelsea, there was trauma in being alone. It meant she was unloved. A voice inside her head would grow louder and louder, questioning, "Are you *worth sticking around for?*" I was fiercely independent. I guarded my heart with the strong belief that it could guide me wherever it pleased, but at the end of the day, it was absolutely more than fine if no person was ever tethered to it. Freedom was *not* having plans next Thursday. Why have an event loom over you? Life could happen. Your parents could move you to Portsmouth before the start of high school, with five days' notice.

Yet here I was, a first-time bridesmaid, which meant that I had to type in a mountain of future events for Chelsea and Chris on my iPhone's calendar. The Miami bachelorette party. The New York shower given by our friends. The *other* New York shower given by her mother-in-law's friends. The Boston shower given by her *mother's* friends. How many unique ways were there to receive All-Clad cookware? The most eye-roll-inducing of all these events was Chelsea's engagement party . . . in Boston . . . *in February*. There should be a law against such crimes.

The only thing that made having to board the packed Megabus to my roommate's engagement party during the "coldest weekend Boston has seen in four years" less horrible was gaining entry to The Country Club at Brookline, one of the oldest country clubs in the United States. *Pretentious* was too small a word for the club that Tom and Gisele had to claw their way into.

I shivered, wrapping my puffy jacket around my tall frame, wind-stung smoky eyes taking in the timeless three-story, yellow colonial mansion. Hunter-green rocking chairs on the porch matched the perfectly groomed golf course right below me, and the color scheme continued as my chattering teeth ventured inside, fully prepared to experience the thrill of jaw-dropping bougieness.

The intimate ballroom and dance floor were enveloped in

muted floral drapes, penguin-suited waiters passed around cold glasses of Dom, and I downed one after another, treating the glasses of champagne like they were finger food. To be fair, they were passed around on a tray.

As the party raged, I danced like a maniac with Chelsea and her friends. The poised grown-adults watched in silent horror from the corners of the room, dissecting both my ability to destroy any dance floor and the tattoos on my arm—as if this combination were a threat to the American flag waving outside. Sweat dripped down my curls, and a buzzing in my ears rang louder and louder as the curtains began to swirl. I sidestepped out of the ballroom in search of a restroom, weaving down a floral hallway, opening each importantly marked door without reading what made it so very important.

Behind mahogany door number five, a cramped supply closet, was a woman who looked like she won prom with her slip-for-a-dress pulled up to her chest, bare legs encircling the naked backside of Chelsea's fiancé. Evidently, Chris was the type of compass that promised to lead you out of the woods but actually directed you to a cave of ravenous bears.

"Get the fuck out," he barked, slamming the door on a visual that made me wish I could reach back into the closet and grab the bleach, so that I might pour it into my eyeballs.

Heart beating out of my chest, I stumbled back toward the party room. I was fuzzy on all the bridesmaid duties—this being my first time—but I assumed that divulging this kind of news to the bride four months before her wedding was a *must*. I looked on as Chelsea danced in a circle with her college friends, throwing her ring finger out while singing along to "Rolling in the Deep." I let Adele finish, and under a banner reading,

CHELSEA AND CHRIS FOREVER, I broke the news to Chelsea that her "Forever" was banging some girl in the janitor's closet down the hall.

Later, after an all-too-easy hack into Chris's email and phone, Chelsea and I discovered that Chris, for lack of a better description, was morally a smidge better than the worst person you know. He hid the horribleness from us all—a charming psychopath next door. He had a fake name, Kris, that's "Chris" with a K, that he used to pick up women in bars, and an e-mail address and Facebook page to match. The engagement went up in flames, literally, with a ceremonial burning of Chris's Phish memorabilia and a vow: I would never let a man become my North Star. Keeping my heart untethered was a goddamn great move.

While I didn't stick out my leg and cause Chelsea's fiancé to trip and fall into his ex-girlfriend's vagina at the engagement party, I did harbor some guilt for discovering them, and even more guilt for having to be the one to break the news to the bride. However, none of this was my fault.

*Once is happenstance.*

# Three

Sticking to my word, I spent the next few years blazing my own path, leaving man after man behind me on the shoulder of the road as my job led the way. I was career obsessed, and it showed. At twenty-six, my fast climb upward to executive creative director was both earned and impressive, yet I sensed I was reaching a dead end.

My specialty was marrying brands with dazzling experiences, and with every proposal, the C-suite above me tilted their heads, wary that my out-of-the-box brain would be too risky for their by-the-book clients. My campaign results should have spoken for themselves, but I was both female and young, so I had to prove myself after having already proven myself. I never doubted my instincts, and I was tired of fighting to be right. The unbreakable ceiling above me was uninspiring, and the banality of going to battle with our CEO and CCO had finally settled in.

Just as I began the soul-crushing task of updating my résumé, our CCO was caught with his pants down, literally, and the board ousted him as fast as the intern threatened to expose him with a tell-all in *Ad Age*. I was the only employee who had solid client relationships and a knowledge of every active campaign. As a result, our CEO gritted his teeth and appointed me the interim CCO. Our numbers during Wheelhouse's first quarter under my reign went up 25 percent. I was so successful in the role that our CEO had no choice but to let me stay there and pay me what I was worth.

Our undervalued associate creative director, Sara Pine, was seven years older than me, and I was now technically above her. She handled my promotion better than every one of the fragile man-children around us. The first move I made was pulling her up into the executive creative director position.

When I nonchalantly stood around dark oval tables in cold glass offices pitching clients branded experiences—such as promoting their new line of hiking boots with a virtual reality mountain climb—Sara was by my side to assure the long faces that the young millennial standing in front of them wouldn't toss their company into a garbage fire. She was my ruthless cheerleader, my pseudo big sister, and my work lifeline.

A handful of months into our well-oiled partnership, Sara and I realized we had enough contacts and more than enough brainpower to start our own experiential agency. We were tired of fighting our older CEO, who was still anchored to traditional advertising methods, which we knew were dying out. Creating meaningful brand experiences that directly engaged with consumers was the wave of the future. We cofounded Illumination, starting small with just four employees in a cramped office space in West Midtown, and then knocking the competition out of the water, expanding our offices to half the floor and hiring a dozen more employees. For the first time in my life, adults who usually looked at me sideways were listening. Our goal was to not rest until every suit in advertising knelt at our scuffed Golden Gooses, and we were well on our way.

It was during Illumination's first year that Sara met Jackson thanks to Bumble. More accurately, Sara met Jackson because a guy she was talking to on Bumble stood her up. Sara was thirty-four years old, sitting alone at a small round table inside the posh Aviary lounge of the Mandarin Oriental hotel, *not* having drinks with her Bumble date, a gregarious pilot from New Jersey. Perched high above Columbus Circle, Sara stared through the floor-to-ceiling windows, watching the cars, just like her life, pass her by. She was close to crying into her third overpriced martini when a big guy, Jackson Zane, strolled in with a briefcase in hand, searching for a place to take a load off.

"Waiting on someone?" he asked, gesturing to the very empty leather seat across from Sara. It was like getting hit by a car, and then dragged down the street for good measure.

"Does it look like I'm waiting for someone?" she hissed. Jackson's eyes widened to the size of saucers, and he backed away from Sara like she was a land mine.

"I'm sorry," she said, realizing what an asshole she was, but only reluctantly sorry, because at that moment she wanted all men to suffer. "You can sit here if you want, I guess."

Jackson tiptoed back to Sara, sitting down across from her and loosening his tie.

"Can I buy you another?"

Sara turned toward Jackson. She got a good look at him, and her body slowly rose from the slump of rejection. He was unassumingly cute, a bigger guy with soft dimpled cheeks and a full head of messy brown hair.

"I mean, if you really want to," Sara said with a shrug, not wanting to give in so easily.

"Hmm. Well, I think against all better judgment, I really want to."

Jackson was thoughtful and unapologetically nerdy, which paired well with Sara's eccentric boldness. He let her be The Unhinged Person in their relationship, as there can only be one. He nodded along passionately when she needed to vent—not daring to give her a piece of unwanted advice. Jackson was impossible to fight with, which Sara found infuriating. Her traits that most people found offensive, he found wildly charming.

A year after they met, when a client decided our branded Super Bowl experience was too edgy and needed "heavy reworking" seven days before the actual fucking Super Bowl, Sara and I Postmated Shun Lee, and braced ourselves for an all-nighter that would include writing a new voice-over script for the commercial, rewriting ad copy, and making our editor want to switch careers as he re-cut a once-locked commercial. We took over an empty industrial conference room, shoving the dozen swivel chairs out of the way and littering the oval desk with piles of creative. I was ready to dive in and make this spot my home for the next ten hours, when I got a text from Jackson.

Hey, can you talk privately for a sec. Without Sara knowing.

I pretended I needed some air, and I took my starving-for-Chinese-food body down the elevators, through the marble lobby, and outside the heavy revolving door as the sun set on Fifty-Seventh and Eighth—creating a Manhattanhenge so beautiful that not an iPhone in sight wasn't drooling in its direction.

"Everything okay?" I asked, after dialing Jackson's number on the crowded street corner. I put him on speaker as I elongated my body using the tips of my sneakers, snapping an excessive number of Instagram-worthy photos.

"So, I was going to do this thing tonight. I was going to propose to Sara, and then . . ."

I took Jackson off speakerphone immediately. "And then my Coke client really fucked you," I finished.

"Sure did. So . . . I need to ask you for a favor," he said.

I stepped back into our offices, mazing my body through the empty industrial bullpen, past the colorfully decorated cubicles. I watched Sara through the glass door of the conference room as she furiously erased throwaway slogans on the whiteboard. I knew this woman's life was about to change in a matter of hours, and I had to pretend I knew nothing. Thankfully, years of getting into trouble had armed me with an epic poker face. I entered the room, telling Sara that we had to pivot and get into an Uber—something about our luxury fashion client having a meltdown.

Inside the dark SUV, I kept Sara glued to her phone, forcing her to take notes as I spitballed one idea after another for a less-edgy soft drink Super Bowl experience. A handful of minutes later, we screeched to a halt at the river on West Thirtieth Street. Sara kept her nose buried in her phone as I pushed her up a few stairs and inside a nondescript small black building.

The door to Blade Lounge opened. Before she could wonder why the fuck our client wanted to meet *here*, the Blade concierge led Sara outside to a helipad sitting on the water. In front of her stood Jackson, windblown and nervously stammering at the foot of a buzzing helicopter. I watched from the window of the lounge as Jackson handed Sara a glass of champagne. She stared at him, wind beating locks of her dark hair into her eyes, her head tilted sideways, completely not registering that she was about to step into a helicopter, where Jackson would propose over Lady Liberty, and Sara would screech "of fucking course!" instead of "yes."

It was six years after Chelsea and Chris's bitter ending. I was twenty-eight, and the curious marriage critic inside me, who was alive and well during Chelsea's engagement, was still thriving. However, unlike Chelsea, Sara was self-sufficient, emotionally stable, and *not* twenty-two. Sara was now thirty-five, and she wanted babies yesterday. A week before she met Jackson, Sara decided to grab life by the balls, making an appointment to meet with a fertility specialist to discuss the path to parenthood as a single mother. I loved the badass image of Sara strutting down the uncommon road in Valentino Rockstuds while pushing a stroller. However, Sara canceled that appointment after her fifth date with Jackson. She decided to take the path of walking hand in hand with a partner to help realize her dreams. This was a road foreign to my soul.

Sara "just knew" that Jackson would be the father of her future children. While I was optimistic that this much would come true, I refused to cave to most societal pressures—the need for a legally binding event to precede parenthood being one of them. Marriage was never a part of life that I spent time hoping for or dreaming about. Yet, I said yes to being Sara's bridesmaid with the hope that at the very least, this union might produce some cute curly-haired children. I said yes with a sigh of relief, trusting that Sara had found happiness with Jackson, a grin having barely left her face since the moment she met him.

Three months later, Sara and I arrived at the busy New Orleans airport—her wearing a cheesy light-up veiled tiara on her head, and me wearing an airbrushed BRIDESMAID trucker hat and a matching SARA'S SQUAD T-shirt. Waiting to pick us up at baggage claim with glasses full of vodka soda was a cardigan-wearing woman named Pam, Sara's best friend since high school and proud classroom mom to five-year-old twins.

I flung my exhausted body into Pam's Cheerios-littered minivan, finding myself face-to-face with rows of sticky car seats. While Pam threw our luggage in the trunk, I spent a good thirty seconds attempting to figure out how a car seat unbecomes one with a car. After concluding that straddling the car seat would be much less stressful than uncovering the nuclear codes I apparently needed to remove it, I buckled in with my head hitting the ceiling. I began to down my first cocktail, ready for a relaxing weekend of drinking and chatting until ten at night with Sara's friends, who I assumed would all go to bed early, given the fact they had small children at home. Pam plopped into the driver's seat and looked back at me.

"Do you have any MDMA?" she asked.

I almost choked on the dick straw around my lips. Yes, Sara's three other bridesmaids were also in their mid-thirties with small children, but *fuck no*, they did not want to relax. To say these women wanted to let loose would be an injustice. They wanted to rip the town to shreds.

The morning after surviving a night of jazz, bedazzled vape pens, and mixing too many drinks on Bourbon Street with PTA Gone Wild, I fought off the swampy elements as I boarded the shaky docked airboat, each of Sara's Squad with a freshly poured hurricane in her hands, and me cursing whoever thought exploring the vast Louisiana waterways was an acceptable way to nurse a raging hangover.

I sat down on the wet plastic seat and looked at the bride, whose eyes were fixated on our swamp tour guide, Captain Mitzi. Mitzi had a shaved blond head, Lara Croft–toned arms, and a thick New Orleans drawl. Sara downed her first hurricane, eyes not leaving our captain. When Sara reached for *my* hurricane— her gaze still fixated on Mitzi—I knew we had a problem. These weren't the eyes of someone eager to learn about alligators.

As it turned out, Mitzi was a doppelgänger for Sara's collegiate "toe dip" into lesbianism. Sara's "toe dip" at Tulane was more of a perfect sunset swim that she had desperately tried to forget. The daughter of a conservative family isn't "maaaybe a lesbian." But she was, minus the "maybe." A vitriolic combination: the bride-to-be, her consumption of cheap hurricanes, and a wistful reminder of her sexual past. Our innocent search for baby alligators resulted in the bride's reflection that she did *not* want to have or to hold a penis from that day forward.

As Sara tearfully unloaded her truth to me that night in our shared double-bed hotel room at the Ritz-Carlton, I nodded along, fully supportive of my friend no matter whom she decided to love. Yet behind the scenes, a question danced in my mind, creeping into my thoughts for the first time.

*Am I Bad Luck Bridesmaid?*

First Chelsea. Now Sara. I tried to shake off the thought, hoping the ridiculous theory would die with Jackson and Sara's mediocre unused wedding hashtag, #JackSar.

*Twice is coincidence.*

But the weight lingered, and then morphed into something heavier. It wasn't merely the idea that I might be bad luck. It wasn't just the fact that I, approaching age twenty-nine, had never fully embraced an adult relationship. It was both of those things, coupled with a mounting anxiety about the construct of Forever. As the years flew by, I had a difficult time wrapping my head around the idea of weddings and marriage, the celebration of something that could so easily fall apart. Why do we take this fragile thing and work tirelessly to make it permanent?

I knew I was capable of love. I had known it ever since I was eight years old. The claustrophobic and oddly comforting scent of popcorn, electronics, and industrial carpet swelled in the air—the smell of my Friday nights, the smell of Blockbuster. I felt my heart flutter with excitement. I was only in the second grade, and the thought of committing a crime made my body light up like the Fourth of July.

The cashier—a teenage girl with a nose ring and choppy blue hair—glanced down at the PG-13 rating on my VHS. Her cold eyes took me in: the young-looking-for-her-age girl in a school uniform with a blouse messily untucked, safety pins recklessly hemming the bottom of her plaid skirt, untamed curly black hair, a fake tiny hoop ring in her nose, and a stretchy plastic choker around her little neck. The cashier either didn't give a shit, or she recognized that I was trapped in a life of conformity and needed *this*. She snatched my worn plastic membership card from my hand and threw my crime into a white-and-blue plastic bag.

I flew into my tiny floral-wallpapered bedroom—which I had rebelliously covered head to toe with Absolut Vodka ads and melancholic posters of various angry lady singers. My shaking hands shoved *Romeo + Juliet* into the tape player below my tiny TV, and I plopped onto my quilted bedspread, dragging my stomach to the edge of the bed so that my big brown eyes were as close to the heat of the TV screen as possible.

It was the moment Leonardo DiCaprio locked eyes with Claire Danes through the fish tank. My entire body lit up like wildfire, and I was in love with him. Almost every night for the next two years involved me fantasizing about Leo showing up on my redbrick doorstep wearing a knight-in-shining-armor costume. Yes, both the moment and the man were plucked out of fiction, complete with a Des'ree soundtrack, but the feeling it inspired was real, and it didn't scare me.

I was capable of experiencing love, but I was wholly stifled by the concept of an everlasting kind. I was stifled by love's ultimate goal.

If only I had been a child of divorce. If only my parents had failed so spectacularly that their only child had nothing to live up to but shattered dreams and empty promises. *That* I could do, but that was not the case. My parents had an enviable marriage. My dad opened a frat house door for my mother on her first day of college at the University of Tennessee. It was that simple. They were the rarest of soul mates, and by all accounts, I had a road map for Forever working out pretty damn well. Yet, that map seemed impossible to follow. It included relying on another person to walk with me, Forever. What if the pace changed? What if I found myself pulled toward another person at a rest stop? I liked maps that didn't lead to destinations. I was all about the journey, refusing to give intense thought as to where it would trap me.

I spent the ages of ten to eighteen yanked from one city to the next. Any feelings of stability were bundled with the threat of *"Don't get too comfortable,"* and so, I didn't. I learned to embrace the unknown—a space where the majority faced apprehension. Expecting the unexpected was a seed planted in my childhood. That seed grew into a tree, upon which I built a sturdy tree house to take refuge in. As an adult, standing still twisted up my insides, as if I were peering down the edge of a mountain, gripping a zip line handle, and begging for the green light to jump. My wanderlust heart beat for a kaleidoscopic journey toward a mystery, and marriage was an eternal destination—a clear picture of who would be standing next to me once I made it to the other side. Forever was someone else's fairy tale.

My relationships were moments of wildfire, each ending the moment a man started to have the hopeful "where are we going?" conversation. I was explicit from the start, delivering the warning of "just to be up front, I don't want a relationship right now." The words lived in my back pocket like a Get Out of Jail Free card, and somehow each man thought I was bluffing. No part of me enjoyed hurting these edgy, hipster creatives who had found themselves tangled up with the wrong woman for one month, two months, and the longest—three months. A feeling of terror caused my heart to beat out of my chest the second someone opened a map and asked me to illustrate what the next year looked like. They started The Conversation, eager to go all in, and the pages inside my rule book screamed, *"Run, Zoey. Fucking run."* Like clockwork, I watched their hopeful eyes turn pained and ultimately cold as I reminded them of the time I showed my hand on our first date, folding with, "I want to keep my options open."

My aversion to Forever grew as I bore witness to Chelsea's and Sara's broken engagements. Here lay proof, exhibits A and

B, that there was nothing flawed with Zoey Marks's rule book. There was nothing wrong with me—except for the possibility that I was engagements' bad-luck charm, which was circumstantial at best. I believed from the depths of my fiery soul that I did not need fixing, and that there was nothing wrong with a badass woman who didn't believe in mapping out her future.

That was then.

# Four

My best friend, Hannah Green, and I met in the womb, according to our mothers who were next-door neighbors in Connecticut, both pregnant and due within months of each other. I had the worst house on the best block, while Hannah had the best of the best. We clutched the same penguin stuffed animal when we got our ears pierced at Claire's. We had our first French kisses the same summer on the same log at sleep-away camp—with the same boy. We attempted vegetarianism for the same thirteen days in fourth grade. We cracked my family room television's parental control, discovering the absurd delight of Skinemax.

We were home to each other—even after my parents moved me from New Canaan to Albany before the start of fifth grade. Our goodbye rivaled the melodrama of *Casablanca*'s tarmac scene. Thankfully, for the remainder of our young adolescence, Hannah and I never lived more than a four-hour drive from each other. We spent summers together at sleepaway camp and long weekends at each other's houses. Hannah Green's friendship was one of the few constants of my childhood.

I was always the more unhinged one. The first one to smoke a clove under the bleachers. The first one to lose her virginity. The first one to call her mother a bitch, steal her father's station wagon, drive three hours, and end up at the other's front porch in a fit of angry tears. Only Hannah knew how to calm me down, to pull back from a moment and put it into perspective so that I didn't set fire to my childhood bedroom. Conversely, I added a burst of flames to Hannah's patiently simmering life. Without me, Hannah would have grown up believing that Saturday swims at her country club were as good as it got. I pulled her away from sleepy comforts, bathing us in life's real thrills, like skinny-dipping in Lake Wampanoag after curfew.

Hannah was a perfect child, a trait not lost in adulthood. Even more frustrating than perfection was how easily it came to her. Every "t" was crossed without effort. I was less perfect, but purposefully, which took effort. There was comfort in knowing that by coloring outside the lines, I was in control of where I wanted my pen, and it was not where someone else told me to put it. It was a practice that had gotten me in trouble, a practice that had made me a young CEO. After college, Hannah moved to Colorado for law school and never left. We were thousands of miles apart, but we remained closer than ever.

While I skirted long-term relationships, Hannah embraced them with open arms, skipping merrily down paved roads hand-in-hand with one nice guy after another. She convinced herself she was happy with Mr. Good on Paper and Mr. Lovely in Person, and she held on, waiting to feel a spark. This was what her parents had: perfect without the fireworks. It was the only model she knew, and I was the first person in her life to demand that she aspire for more.

Hannah always looked to me to tell her it was okay to

embrace a difficult truth deep inside her. The moment I recognized that Hannah was merely convincing herself she loved someone, I would tell her what she already knew, yet needed to hear. "Yes, he's great, and yes, he adores you, but Hannah, you do not love him the way *you deserve* to love someone. I can see it in your eyes."

It was exactly one month after Sara's failed engagement when Hannah decided to give me a taste of my own truth medicine. Hannah had just broken up with her boyfriend of two years, Daniel, and I flew her from Colorado to New York for a weekend of heavy drinking and apartment dance parties—the latter of which were an extension of our childhood.

Anytime life felt like it was punching back, Hannah and I had a ritual: turn the music up as loudly as possible, and dance it out. In third grade, when Hannah received her first and only B, she stormed her blond locks into my house, her tiny fists balled up in anger. I set *Jagged Little Pill* in the boom box and pulled Hannah on to my bed. I showed her how to properly tell the world to go fuck itself. Rage. Do not ruminate.

Two decades later, with Alanis living and learning in the background, Hannah and I collapsed, sweaty and breathless, on the floor of my self-proclaimed "last shitty" West Village one bedroom—furniture shoved to the corners of the room, our legs spread out in our finest athleisure, and my big mouth running.

"I'm just saying, I think you should take some time for yourself. You move from one long relationship to the next, and you'd learn a lot about yourself by being alone for a little while—you haven't been single since you were eighteen, Hannah."

Both Hannah and I were only children, a circumstance that

bonded us to each other in huge ways. However, we both inherited very different traits from our lack of siblings. I was wildly independent. In the moments where some would have enjoyed having a little brother or sister to play with, I built sandcastles in my mind—I created imaginary characters to talk to and play with, and I got to know myself in the process. I was enough for myself, always. For Hannah, in the quiet moments where I wasn't around to fill the silence, she was epically lonely. As a result, Hannah craved and coveted intimate relationships. Gaps in having a partner reminded her of the loneliness of her childhood. I wanted Hannah to embrace herself in that exhale—to appreciate the person she had become—a badass divorce lawyer who just bought a fancy townhome all by herself. I wanted Hannah to discover how amazing she was without someone else telling her. She looked at me with a hardened expression that said she wanted me to shut the fuck up. For Hannah, self-discovery was best found with a partner by her side. Loneliness was not an agony she wanted time to fix, but rather a space she wanted a partner to occupy.

"If we're on this subject, I think you've gotten too comfortable being alone, Zo. You invite surface guys into your life and miss out on all the opportunities that real love comes with," Hannah said, wiping away a tear, making a horrible point about the opportunity that love had in store for me—which by the looks of it involved the prize of crying into one's fourth glass of Pinot.

"Hannah, I love my life. I'm not missing anything."

"You can't miss what you don't know."

Hannah sat up straighter, taking my olive hands into her pale fingers and staring wide-eyed at my face. I arched my neck back, fearful of the owlish, tipsy, heartbroken version of my shy best friend. I had taught her too well.

"I want you to feel all the big feels. You're the most passionate person I've ever met, and you've never given yourself a chance to have that with another person. Seriously, how are you the woman who loves rom-coms, yet isn't curious about a happy ending?"

"I have happy endings all the time. Way above the national average. My mother would be alarmed, I promise."

Hannah exhaled, shaking her head. "You tell guys you don't want a relationship right from the start, and it's a cop-out."

"No, it's the truth."

"No, you wave a white flag before you even try. I understand you're afraid of giving someone else the power to hurt you, but Zoey, it's time for you to let your guard down."

In almost twenty-nine years, this was the first time Hannah had read me wrong. In her defense, even I didn't know how to explain it. I wasn't *afraid* of getting hurt. I wasn't afraid of love. I feared the implied next step. Panic lay in the "then comes" part of that nursery rhyme. Killing two birds with one stone was a percipient choice—if "first comes love" never comes, then I didn't have to confront the marriage part. I wanted to say this aloud, but instead, I stared at Hannah with a thin-lipped expression. I usually let my hard truths run wild, but I had learned as a toddler that there was no reason to yuck someone else's yum. What good could come of telling my hopeless romantic best friend that I believed marriage was an unrealistic goal?

"Hannah, let's just pretend I never brought any of this up, okay?"

"Why? Because this conversation makes you uncomfortable?"

*Yes.*

"No, I just think we have different views on romance."

"Zoey, I love how you see the world. This is me telling you that you're slamming the door on seeing a really important part of it. You can't go around telling people what they need to hear, and then not listen to them when they open their mouths."

"But it's more fun that way."

Hannah glared at me. I threw my hands up in the air, giving her the floor.

"Okay, say what you want to say."

"If you let someone in, you'd be surprised what you might find and what you might learn about yourself."

There she was, using my initial words against me—such a lawyer. The only love "surprises" I was aware of involved the prize of a serial cheater and a sexual awakening. I liked the unknown, but not when it was in someone else's hands. I had spent eight years being a casualty of my parents' realized dreams, and I had no intention of repeating that pattern. I would not be pulled down someone else's goal-oriented road.

"Mark my words, the only reason you're weird about love and marriage is because you haven't fallen yet," Hannah said, as if winking into a crystal ball.

Any eagerness to test out the theory was drowned out by the memory of Jackson's guttural sobs when Sara handed him the engagement ring back in her office. I opened my mouth to say just that—

"And don't even try to use those Chelsea and Sara broken engagements as an excuse."

*Goddamnit.*

"Look . . . I'm single, and I fucking love it. I'm happy, Hannah.

I'm alone, not lonely, and you don't have to worry about me, *ever*, okay? Now, what can we do to get *you* happy?" I asked, rubbing her back, and then offering to take sexy-but-tasteful photos for her Hinge profile.

It was the first time in my life when I didn't long for anything. I had a job I loved with no one above me to tell me how to do it. I was living in the most bustling city in the world. I felt energized by the mere act of walking outside my door.

I, Zoey Marks, was enough.

Then came Rylan Harper the Third.

# Five

A handful of months after Sara didn't make it down the aisle, Hannah phoned me with marching orders to meet her "new to New York, and I promise you, absurdly hot" cousin for drinks.

"Ignoring the fact that you just called your first cousin 'absurdly hot,' which part of me looks like I date bros who have Roman numerals tacked on to their names?" I said with an eye roll.

I stood barefoot in my living room, applying dark red lipstick as I studied my reflection in the gold wall mirror. I had recently moved into a roomy one-bedroom West Village loft, finally tiring of the "charming" apartment rentals that included air-conditioning units dripping in the middle of the night and roaches making themselves comfortable in my bathroom sink. The exposed brick walls and the gray wood floors became the perfect blank slate to paint with a bohemian vibe—gold Moroccan poufs at the foot of a purple sunken couch in my living room, colorful concert posters on the walls, and my parents' old record collection occupying a hand-carved bookshelf. The ability to spend this much on furniture that didn't come from an IKEA catalogue was proof that I was doing a damn great job at faking adulthood. *And I was.*

Sara and I were crushing it, and my nights were spent exceeding our clients' expectations: wowing them over drinks, wooing them over three-hundred-dollar aromatherapy massages at the Peninsula, Giants games, Nobu dinners—whatever on God's green Earth they wanted, I gave them on a gold platter. I reeled them in with a pitch they could get nowhere else, and I kept them by my side with impactful brand engagement. This night, I was rushing to make it across the bridge in time to have a round of drinks at the Dumbo House with my Nike clients.

"I don't have my nights free for your 'new to New York' charity case, Hannah."

"He's hardly a charity case. My cousin is marriage material, Zo. He's only single because he's put his job first for so long—which I think you of all people can appreciate."

"'Marriage material'? I'd rather just find someone to go down on me."

"I *knew* you'd have this reaction," Hannah said.

"Reverse psychology won't work on me."

*She knows it will.*

"Yes, it will," she sang back.

My face scrunched up into a ball as I pictured Hannah's ballet dancer body floating around her Denver townhome, a Cheshire cat smile upon her perfectly oval face, shaking her head at her stubborn best friend seventeen hundred miles away. She knew I'd rather be dead than be predictable.

The downside of someone who finished my sentences before I knew how to speak was that she understood the messed-up way my brain moved. She knew exactly which button to push to turn the wheel in the other direction.

"You're googling him now, aren't you?" she asked.

"No," I said, as I bitterly typed "Rylan Harper III" into Google. *Holy fucking fuck.*

I gaped at his photo: a mud-soaked, shirtless Adonis, hoisting a lacrosse stick over his rock-hard stomach. I sat down on the couch as my red lips found themselves slightly ajar.

"I told you," Hannah said.

"You know, I've always wanted to explore the vapid insides of the Privileged White Male," I said, casually counting all his abdominal muscles.

"Have an open mind, Zoey."

"I'll maybe have an open *vagina*," I joked, not joking.

"That's my cousin," Hannah whined, disgusted.

"Then don't describe him as 'absurdly hot.'"

But he was.

Rylan was absurdly hot, and while taking in his photo, I surmised that at the very *least*, I deserved to watch this man go down on me. I put my unofficial online PI degree to use with one hand on Google, while my other hand pulled Spanx over my neglected winter body.

Rylan Harper the Third lived up to his name. He was all-star lacrosse in both high school and Stanford turned overworked, probably overpaid hedge funder in New York City. I was the opposite (except I was excessively-yet-properly paid). I was more of the type who could *almost* pull off whatever was happening inside a Free People catalogue.

Rylan Harper the Third and Zoey Marks would never make any sense, which was perfect. This edgy, creative woman would never fall for the preppy guy who wore boat shoes like he owned a marina (his grandfather actually *did* own a marina). My first fuckup: I underestimated him right out of the gate. Rylan was, to my shock, so much more than a replacement for my aging vibrator.

Rylan waited two days to text me. Just enough time to not appear too eager, but also enough time to not let me forget about the photo of his naked torso.

My cousin says your the greatest person she knows, and that I would be lucky to buy you a drink. How's next week?— Rylan

"Your" howled at me. I shoved my phone into my back jean pocket as I stood jammed between winter coats in a claustrophobic line at Eataly—my tired brain in desperate need of a double flat white and my stomach now turning. I learned at a young age that bad behavior should go unrewarded, and thus, if this grown man didn't understand the difference between "your" and "you're," he would never have the gift of seeing me naked. Before I wrote him off completely, my phone pinged with another text.

*You're. I promise, I aced middle school grammar.

Fine. *Maybe* I would let him see me naked.

It was the following week, a random Wednesday night in mid-December, when the weather gods blessed my surprisingly good hair day with unforeseen frigid rain, just three degrees too warm to turn the city into a winter wonderland. I unzipped my puffy jacket and bravely threw it atop my head, sprinting down a quiet West Village street in my Rag & Bone suede booties, which, of course, I had failed to weatherproof. I reached the steps of my favorite little West Village Spanish tapas spot, Alta, exhaling as I descended below street level and inside the dry, warm haven.

I had stumbled upon Alta by accident a year prior. Clients had just canceled drinks, and so out of boredom, I swiped right on a tech guy with a tattoo sleeve, intrigued to find a *Walden* quote across his rib cage. I agreed to meet up with him for dinner after only a six-line text exchange, wrongly assuming that if a man wore Thoreau like a badge of honor, he could carry on an adult conversation. I fell victim to false advertising, bested at my own game by a bro who used the word "gucci" as an adverb. I left dinner as quickly as the check changed hands, trekking down West Tenth Street in search of All the Drinks with the immediacy of someone lost in the Sahara. I curiously walked into Alta, taking in the candlelit atmosphere, the exposed brick, and the wood beams. Alta became a safe place where I spent nights unwinding with two glasses of Pinot Noir, answering work emails in a dark corner, and shifting my stool in different directions to ignore any male who crept up behind me.

When Rylan suggested Alta for our first date, I almost said no. This was my Cheers, the place I went to after a bad first date, not the place where I *had* a bad first date. This was the place where the bartenders knew my name. But Rylan's texts were witty and charming. He had the ability to banter with the Queen of Banter, going line for line with me about nothing and everything. And so, a little voice inside my head kept me from asking him to move our date, unwittingly allowing Rylan to infiltrate a place no man had gone before: my Safety Zone.

I arrived thirty minutes early for our first date, with just enough time to warn the southern bartender, Luke, about my impending setup. After convincing him *not* to take Instagram stories detailing "Zoey on a Date," I made myself comfortable at the far corner of the bar, burying my nose in work emails.

You know that moment you lose your footing, and you're one second away from face-planting down a flight of stairs? That mere second when your heart drops below your chest and everything moves in slow motion? I looked up from my phone toward the door as Rylan stepped inside, and it was the slow fall, the moment when I had to take in every part of this man, because what if I never set eyes on someone this beautiful again? Also, I hadn't yet heard him speak, which I believed would take away most of his appeal.

Rylan Harper the Third breezed in through the doors of Alta with the confidence one would expect from a man who looked the way he did. He stood tall at six two and ran one large hand through a thick head of wet dirty-blond hair. He effortlessly swept his hair to the side, the rain somehow having made him even more attractive. I withheld the urge to high-five myself.

I grabbed my glass of Pinot as if it were the banister and took a much-needed gulp, letting the earthy liquid roll down my dry throat. Rylan unbuttoned his wool jacket, revealing himself in a fitted suit, a crisp blue business shirt hugging his arms in all the right ways. Heat rushed through my chest as he navigated past a crowd of people surrounding the bar, walking toward me with a distinctive jawline that seemed too perfect to be natural.

"Zoey?" he asked.

I nodded, hoping my mouth would rediscover the ability to form sentences.

"Rylan. Nice to meet you."

We did that awkward dance where I went in for the handshake, and he went in for the hug. I relinquished my businesslike approach and hugged him back, thrown by the warmth of his embrace—as if his arms had been around me a thousand times. He smelled like soft cedar—a woodsy musk. Le Labo, but not your basic bitch's Santal 33—something else. A city scent, possibly. One you could only buy the month of September. *Maybe Tokyo.*

He sidled up next to me, and my suddenly light-headed body somehow sat back down on the leather stool. He grinned at me a moment too long with a smile that doubled as a Crest Whitestrips ad.

"What?" I chuckled, both hating and loving the way his green eyes seemed to smile right through me. It was disarming and unfair.

"Nothing," he said, with a devilish grin that hinted *"not nothing."*

Rylan nodded across the bar, getting Luke's attention. Luke raised his eyebrows at me, a silent *"not fucking bad."*

He was not my type at all. The pages of my rule book were singing, *"Nothing edgy here. Move along, Zoey. There's no way Rylan has ever worn a beanie to the beach."* But this man, he somehow sat upright without being told he was slouching, and it was sexier than any dude I'd ever seen in ripped jeans and All Stars. His confidence was alarming, and most shockingly, it was not a turnoff.

One round later, we found ourselves graduating up the three

stairs to Alta's dining room, extending our date to include food, which meant it was going well.

*Way too well.*

I leaned my top knot against the wall, ambient lighting and wooden beams surrounding me, my chin resting on the back of my hand, trying not to laugh out loud as I swallowed a forkful of saffron rice. I watched with wide eyes as the amber candlelight danced on Rylan's impassioned face while he discussed New York politics. He used his hands when he spoke. He didn't say things lightly. Yes, he was privileged, but no, he wasn't vapid. The boat shoes were a cover for the guy who spent his free time feeding homeless families, who spoke openly about his disdain for his entitled coworkers—a hatred that turned me on more than his chest beating under his shirt buttons. When I spoke, he did this little thing—he leaned in as if he wasn't just trying to hear me, he was trying to *understand* me.

It was there among the flickering candlelight, the authentic paella, the bottle of Malbec, it was right fucking there that I was overcome with a humming in my body, a glow I had never felt before. I wanted to bottle it up, and at the same time, I wanted to push it far away. I felt it right there on our first date: this man had the power to utterly unhinge me. I had to save myself.

I shifted in my seat, the Get Out of Jail Free card burning a hole in my back pocket. On the tip of my tongue was the warning, *"Just to be up front, I'm not looking for a relationship."*

"Wait, so back to your work friend." He paused, searching for her name. "Sara, right?" I nodded. Of course he remembered her name, I'd only said it once. *This guy.* "She really moved in with her first girlfriend *ever* . . . after only three dates?"

*Speaking of, there is an expiration date here—*

"Sure did. They met at a bar three weeks ago, and now Sara

is moving to Gramercy with someone whose middle name she probably doesn't even know. I've never seen her like this."

"What do you mean?"

"She looks like she's been hit over the head, all the time. Like at any moment, she could break out into song."

"So, she's happy."

"Yes, it's wildly disturbing." I smiled.

A grin hit his lips, matching mine.

"I guess you get to a certain age, and when you know, you just know."

He said it in a gentle voice, but it punched like a challenge. Was he the kind of guy who would "just know," and then I would have no choice but to also just know, because who doesn't just know when a guy like this smiles at you and knows?

*I had to run.*

I found my body leaning forward, Rylan's eyes pulling me in like a magnet. I felt the corners of my mouth dance upward to match his. I couldn't run.

I couldn't even look away.

I had sauntered into Alta with harmless intentions: to treat this first date like an experiment—a giddy exercise in exploring the vapid insides of the Privileged White Male. The joke was on me.

I, Zoey Marks, was screwed.

We vacated Alta, walking up to street level with the buzz of two people who'd shared a bottle of red and shut down a restaurant. Rylan typed our second date into his phone's calendar while we both shivered, letting the frigid rain beat down on us on a sleepy West Tenth Street.

"I'm a five-minute walk up that way." I pointed behind him, warming my hands with my breath.

"I'm going to subway it uptown," he said, nodding to the street behind me.

He wrapped his arms around me in a hug, with one-day-old scruff meeting my damp, flushed cheek. He pulled back slowly, taking me in. For the second time that night, life moved in slow motion, and I wanted to fall into his lips. He grinned, pulling a windblown piece of hair away from my eyes.

And then, Rylan Harper had the fucking nerve to disappear into the night.

*He did not kiss me.*

Rylan lit my body on fire and left me standing outside in the freezing cold rain. It was monstrous.

Four days later, we had our second date, where we shut down Cafe Fiorello with matching smiles and bellies full of mozzarella, pomodoro, and basil. We vacated the busy Upper West Side restaurant, standing on the street across from a lit-up Lincoln Center. Rylan waited with me for my Uber—a three-minute wait, plenty of time for his lips to find mine, but instead, he continued to ask me questions about the Spotify jukebox pitch I had the next morning—as if putting engaging Spotify digital jukeboxes in big city bars was more important than our bodies colliding. In this moment, it was *not*.

"So, are you nervous for tomorrow?" he finished.

I shook my head. "I don't get nervous."

"Really?"

"Nope."

He peered down at me and grinned, taking a step toward me.

"Don't worry, I won't tell anyone," he whispered in my ear, looking down at my shaking hands—my stupid traitorous shaking hands.

"I'm not nervous." I quivered, barely able to get the words out. His fingers knotted in mine, and I felt my chest pound, *nervously*.

I was rarely nervous when speaking to a roomful of men in seven-thousand-dollar suits. I was, however, nervous standing in front of this man, his body incredibly close to mine. Even worse, he knew it. Normally I'd have pulled his stammering lips into a kiss by now, but here I was, the stammering fool, the one who was waiting to be kissed.

"Well, you make me a little nervous," he said.

"I can't tell."

He put my hand on his chest. I could feel his heart banging against my palm as he stared at me. His eyes were unwavering, and his wild confidence was undermining my ability to get ahead of myself. I was about to fall behind, I could feel it. The tides were turning.

I, Zoey Marks, was no longer in control.

He took a step closer to me, and just as I felt the cold night disappear between us, just as our lips moved toward each other, a loud honk broke our bodies apart, revealing my Uber on the pavement.

We stared at each other, flushed faces an inch apart, our romantic moment now ruined in the presence of an impatient hipster in a Prius. Rylan exhaled a frustrated chuckle. He kissed my cheek softly and opened the car door like a gentleman.

I bitterly slid into the leather seat as I glared at the Uber driver—the future recipient of my first one-star rating.

Rylan went out of town the next day on business, and he was gone for a week. I had a whole week to think about our almost kiss. I had an entire seven days to think about how much I hated that this man was occupying space in my mind.

I was better than this.

*I was apparently not better than this.*

An infuriating eight days later, we shut down our third restaurant, this one my pick, The Dutch, one of my go-to spots in SoHo. Why SoHo? I had to get Rylan to walk me home.

"Want me to walk you home?" he asked like clockwork, as we grabbed our coats and exited onto Sullivan Street.

"Sure," I said casually, while dancing victoriously on the inside. What I really wanted out of this walk home was for this human to press me hard against a wall.

We navigated our way past the bustling streets of SoHo, finally making it to the quiet side of the West Village, Perry Street. A soft snowfall had begun, lit by the glow of the streetlamps. I watched the snowflakes dance in the air as if it were my first time seeing water turn to ice, and then I inhaled the smell of snow with childlike wonder. The first snowfall of the year had a magical ability to wholly dismantle the cynical adult inside me.

"Well, this doesn't happen in San Francisco," Rylan said, shivering and zipping his gray wool jacket up to his neck. He admired the sky with a boyish grin. The first snowfall: it did it to everyone.

For two people who had turned a dinner date into four hours of nonstop banter, we were oddly quiet as we roamed down the silent street. We took in the neighboring brownstones, eyes somehow not daring to meet each other. I hated silence, but something about this moment, walking on the snowy street next to Rylan—it silenced me. Rylan stared up at a glowing window, taking in a middle-aged couple laughing in their living room.

"New York City is really strange."

I stared up at his curious expression.

"What do you mean?"

He stopped walking, beaming wistfully at the couple a few floors above us.

"I've only been here for a few months, but this city feels . . . untouchable. Like it's moving at lightning speed. But then I walk down a random street and somehow, behind closed doors, people have figured out how to slow it down. How to make it feel like home."

"New York feels like home to me," I said quietly. "I think . . . I think I was born to take comfort in its chaos. Does that make any sense?"

He looked at me. No, he didn't just look at me. He studied my face the way one stumbles upon his favorite line of his favorite novel. There was a knowing smile on his lips that I didn't quite understand, at least not in that moment.

"Wh–what?" I stammered, both amused and unraveled, my heart fluttering.

"Absolutely nothing," he replied.

It was not nothing.

I suddenly wondered if this perfect man was lonely. I regarded loneliness as a construct, a feeling foreign to my soul. The time I spent alone with myself was an exhale that refueled me. Any pang of what someone else might call "loneliness," I deemed "boredom."

I studied Rylan, our bodies pointed toward each other as he looked over my shoulder and took in the not-so-lonely strangers in the window, his eyes longing for what they had. It was in that moment that a very real fear crept into my psyche: What if this man possessed the power to hand me my first taste of loneliness? It was a horrifying possibility, and before I could build a wall of steel around my heart and make damn sure he could never commit such a crime, Rylan placed his hand on my lower back and pulled me into him, closing the gap between us.

He peered down at me, and despite the layers of coats and shirts, I could feel my chest beating against his. He put his hand on my chin, pulling me up to him and kissing me softly. He kissed me like he cared about me. He led my body to the wall of a brownstone, his hand sweetly cupping the back of my head before it could hit the brick. He knotted his fingers in my hair and pulled hard. He kissed me like I was a woman, unbreakable. He kissed me like he wanted to tear me apart. Rylan Harper kissed me like he knew we would talk about our first kiss for a lifetime to come.

Months and months later, he recounted that moment prior to our first kiss. That moment in front of a strangers' brownstone, snowflakes dancing between us in the night sky. It was the moment Rylan realized that being with me felt like home.

# Six

After our first kiss, I stepped into my loft with a stupid smile plastered on my face. My feet were killing me, and I pulled off my booties and ankle socks, my swollen toes finding solace on the cold wood floor. The smell of cedar and soft wood lingered on my curls, overpowering my usual jasmine scent.

I smelled like him, and I liked it.

I longed for Rylan already.

It had been three whole minutes.

Two days later, a purple haze spread across Central Park on a Saturday afternoon in late December. I stood on the steps of a beautiful Upper West Side brownstone, checking the address for the twelfth time, certain I was mistaken. The second floor of this pristine white brownstone with a glossy black door on Seventy-Eighth Street could not be occupied by a thirty-five-year-old man. Rylan was only six years older than me, and yet, he was an actual adult. I had a hoverboard in my loft that I had drunkenly Amazon Primed, and here he was, owning the second floor of a brownstone with a stoop and little burnt orange flowers out front.

I cautiously pressed the buzzer, causing a dog to bark inside. I peered up at the window, eyeing the large yellow Lab as she jumped excitedly into view. This was Sunshine, Rylan's five-year-old rescue pup who I had heard too much about, and I was not as excited to meet her as she was to meet me. I didn't grow up with pets, so the larger the dog, the larger my apprehension toward said dog.

Rylan didn't buzz me in. Instead, he hopped down the wooden stairs and opened the front door for me—a total gentleman. He was fresh out of the shower, face still flushed post-run, wearing sweatpants and a vintage Henley. Casual Rylan was even more breathtaking than Business Rylan, and I worried that despite the frigid temperature around us, I might melt there on the steps.

I found it hugely unfair that the male species could stumble out of their showers, blindly rummage through their drawers, and exit their front doors looking this perfect. My "I didn't try" hair and makeup alone took me an hour. An hour that did not include frantically emptying the continents of my closet to decide which of my six oversized sweaters looked the most unassumingly hot with ripped jeans.

I stared sheepishly up at Rylan, my throat closing at the sight of him.

"Hi," I cracked, with a lame wave.

He grinned at me mischievously.

"Get in here," he said, pulling my jacket toward him and kissing me hard. He twirled me inside the first floor of the walk-up, my sneakers dancing on the black-and-white penny tiles in the sunlit entrance as the front door slammed shut behind us.

We were supposed to cook dinner together.

Our hands did not leave each other as he spun me into his sweeping two-bedroom apartment. The generous square footage was a result of the pre-war brownstone it occupied, but nothing inside was pre-anything. It had been gutted, but beautifully, and the room was airy and minimalistic with bright white walls and chevron wood floors. Carrara marble on the kitchen island matched the marble fireplace in the living room. It was a Room & Board catalogue come to life, and while the bohemian girl inside me felt the need to toss my colorful Missoni throw pillow in the midst, there was something about his place that felt homey. That was, until the dog, Sunshine, came hurtling toward me like I was her long-lost mother. Panic rising, I clutched Rylan's shirt as Sunshine flung her fluffy paws onto me, eager for attention.

"Sunshine, down," Rylan commanded. "Sit, girl."

Sunshine immediately sat, wagging her tail up at me with a smile that no one else would be able to resist. I petted Sunshine's soft head with a "there, there" hesitancy. Her big brown eyes blinked rapidly at mine, and before I had time to wonder what this dog saw in me, my eyes were closed.

Rylan's peppermint tongue found mine as he backed me against the cold steel of the refrigerator. His mouth made its way from my lips, to my earlobe, to softly kissing my clavicle as my legs weakened, and I held on to the damp nape of his neck, gripping at the base of his hairline. I felt his lips back on mine as his fingers unzipped my jacket, sending it to the floor. His hands finally settled an inch below my waist, and I could feel him hardening against me as I pulled my face back to look at him, both of us breathless. His green eyes were ablaze with the setting sun, lightening into twin pools of lime green. He deepened his fingers around my hip bone, as if asking permission to go further.

"Are you hungry?" he asked, politely reminding us both that I came here under the guise of cooking pasta.

*"No, but I would like you inside me"* was probably not a polite response to the polite question.

"No. Not hungry . . ." I managed.

He fastened his fingers into the belt loops of my jeans, tugging me against him. I stood on my tiptoes and wrapped my hands back around his neck, taking in that cedar woodsy scent as our kiss deepened. I felt his teeth tug at my bottom lip, and I pulled back, stunned. What men with boat shoes and Roman numerals attached to their names bit lips?

*This guy.*

Rylan kept shattering my expectations, and it was terrifying.

"What?" he wondered aloud, taking in my expression.

"I really wish I didn't like you so much."

The words fell out of my mouth, and I couldn't shove them back in. In that moment, I spilled two truths to Rylan. The first: I really liked him. The second: there might be something wrong with the woman who wished she didn't like someone so wonderful. Thankfully, Rylan was a straight white male. Meaning, Rylan was hardwired to hear what he wanted to hear, and all he heard in that moment was, *"Zoey Marks likes me."*

Rylan grinned, effortlessly lifting me up with one strong arm as I locked my legs around his back. I felt his cool hand glide under my sweater—grazing the side of my ribs, tracing the curve of my neck, pulling the sweater off my body. Suddenly, I was floating down the hallway in his arms, his mouth on my mouth, my fingers knotted in his hair, our bodies spinning into his bedroom. My college hookup Jonny Umansky once tried to carry me to a second location, and it took him twenty seconds to lift me, which were some of the most cringeworthy seconds of my life. This was the opposite. Being held by Rylan Harper made me feel weightless.

He unhooked my bra with one hand, gripping his fingers around my thigh with his other as we slammed against the bedroom mirror, his lips barely leaving mine. Rylan let go of me on his platform king bed as I kicked the sneakers off my feet.

He grinned, hovering over me. "Hi."

"Hi back atcha."

His hand moved to unbutton my jeans, and I felt a chill up my spine as his fingers tugged my pants down, taking my lacy black underwear with them, his head moving downward and kissing my inner thighs until my pants were on the floor and his tongue was inside me.

The guy who goes down on you before you even see his penis? God bless *that* guy.

I stared up at the ceiling, about to lose my mind, as his tongue danced inside me, his finger pressed hard right above. A million light-years later, my body naked and bathed in sweat, breathlessly exhaling pleasure, I watched as Rylan came back up toward me, his sandy-blond hair perfectly messy. I sat up and tugged his shirt off, and his lips met mine as his torso thumped naked upon my burning chest, with a hand cupping my ass and sending my body back down to the pillow. He was hard against me, and I slid my hand under the elastic of his running pants, gripping his dick in my hand, sliding back and forth as he stared upward, his hands tightening around the pillow under me. He felt great in my hands, but that wasn't exactly where I wanted him.

"I have a condom in my purse," I said.

He exhaled a smirk down at me and reached to his night-stand for a condom of his own, rolling off the bed and taking his pants off as he ripped the gold foil with his teeth. I took him in, his naturally tan skin bathed in the glow of the sunset. He was not just beautiful—he was perfect, as if sculpted by the gods without one flaw.

Naked, he leaned down and kissed me, and I ran my shaking fingers over his skin, over the dark freckles on his chiseled chest, upward until I twisted the cold gold chain around his neck and hungrily pulled the rest of him into me. It was as if my body had discovered a missing piece—a piece it now had no idea how to live without—and this was troubling for someone who was enough for herself. I was fucked. *Really fucked.*

An hour into sex with Rylan, sixty minutes into completing every position possible—and even positions I thought not possible—I rolled off him, gasping for air, with sweat dripping down the curls on my forehead. I rested my flushed cheek on his damp, pounding chest.

"I think I'm hungry now," I barely managed, as my body lay on top of his.

Suddenly, he tugged my hair up toward him in a rough way that I enjoyed entirely too much, and electricity jolted through me as he devilishly brought my face up toward his lips. He stared at me for a moment, and then he clenched his other hand around my waist, flipping us both over—him now on top of me and my head nearly hanging off the side of the bed.

"I'm not done with you yet," he whispered, as the warmth of his mouth against my ear sent heat waves pulsing throughout my entire body.

*Well . . . fuck.*

I arched my damp neck back as his finger slowly traced a sweaty line from my lips, to my throbbing throat, all the way to the side of my breast. His hand kept moving downward as his body trembled over mine. My hand clutched onto his back, and I lost my breath as his fingers entered my shaking and writhing body. It was as if, all at once, I had both found and lost solid ground.

An hour later, we ordered in.

# Seven

Rylan was going to run for office one day. His goal was to make so much money that he could leave the hedge fund world, shift his efforts toward advocating for alternative energy, and then casually become a congressman or senator—as one does. He unloaded this to me two months into dating, as we were walking down Columbus Avenue. It was the night I found myself powerless in the face of both tequila and Aperol, the night I forgot that this combination could only end one way: with my face using his cold marble bathroom floor as a pillow. This is not how Michelle Obama spent her thirties. But he liked me anyway.

Rylan crossed his arms and shook his head at me, watching from the bathroom doorway as I washed down half a loaf of challah bread with orange Pedialyte, two things he now kept in his townhome at all times. I was a hot mess, mascara down my cheeks, wearing only a pink thong and one of his white T-shirts over my body.

"That's better," I sighed with my last mouthful, my eyes closed and the back of my head resting against the wall.

I opened my eyes, seeing his tighten onto me.

I sat up straighter, thankful to discover the room was no longer spinning. He plopped down next to me, studying his fingers. His green eyes met mine, then darted back to his hands, and suddenly, I realized this always confident man was uncomfortable.

"I can't do this anymore," he said.

I felt my heart drop, and instinctively, one hand actually went over my chest, as if to keep it from falling. I tucked my knees under the shirt, pulling my arms around my body as I swallowed hard, surprised by my own emotions, ones I wasn't sure I had experienced before.

I was not the First Lady type and this was not an Aaron Sorkin rom-com. I was naturally creative, which my overly educated parents found troubling. I was always outside-the-box. I cursed without reservation. I could be wildly shallow. I had Lilith Fair poster art tattooed on my ankle—an illustration of the mythological woman who said, *"You're cute, but not THAT cute,"* to Adam and abandoned the Garden of Eden in favor of her independence. There were a thousand too many selfies on my iPhone. I didn't know how to mix drinks without ending up on the bathroom floor. All of these obstacles were low hurdles I thought Rylan had embraced, but I guess he had reached his threshold. At some point, the Cool Girl became nothing more than a liability.

"Okay," I said quietly.

I felt tears welling, and I told them to un-well. *There's no crying in casual dating!*

"I know your weird hangover cure. I can't unknow that," he said as my brow furrowed, wondering where that sentence was going. He pulled my scrunched-up face toward him.

"Zoey, I can't do the gray area with you."

I stared at him, puzzled.

"I have to either go all in, or walk away. I know too much about you, and I like everything I know," he said softly.

The Cool Girl was still cool. He liked all my little weird pieces so much that it would break his heart if I shared them with someone else. I felt my heart climb back into my chest, but then it beat faster, as if reminding me that this was the chapter of the story where *I* walked away. I turned to look into his eyes, and just like the first time I set my irises on his, I couldn't run.

"I'm all in," I said. And I was.

Slow smiles beamed across both of our faces as I soared over my first relationship hurdle: actually having one.

I kept waiting for the pages in my rule book to shout, *"Run, Zoey,"* for the high hurdle to knock me out. Four months into our relationship, Rylan brought me along to meet his parents at their vacation home in Lake Tahoe, and I was sure it would be the catalyst for our ending. It was the first time I was faced with meeting a significant other's makers, and I could not escape the feeling that I wouldn't measure up. I lived a rebellious childhood surrounded by too many conservative adults, which left me on the defense when face-to-face with Baby Boomers.

Not helping were the horror stories I'd heard in mounting numbers over the last couple of years. The big, mustache-twirly narrative of "my dad owns a gun" implied that men had the most to fear when meeting their girlfriends' parents. *No.* The genuine terror belonged to the females, peering up at their boyfriends' mothers. While the mothers didn't stand on the porch holding a shotgun, they were armed with something much worse: emotional manipulation. It was impossible to go for drinks with a large group of my friends without hearing the words "You won't believe what my mother-in-law did." By and large, the majority of these stories painted mothers-in-law with a unifying brush: a woman waging an unwinnable battle to keep the umbilical cord attached to her adult son, scattering passive-aggressive bread crumbs that would hopefully lead to the final destination of I Matter the Most to My Son. This is why daughters-in-law often wish they had married orphans.

Rylan and I arrived a handful of hours before his parents, and as I anxiously exited the rental car, my jaw dropped. I took in the front of this Incline Village waterfront home as if it were an extension of my soul. The four-bedroom modern mountain home was surrounded by endless panoramic views of bright blue water and towering green pines dusted in snow. The way I felt about the West Village was the way I felt toward this little corner of the universe. Rylan put his arm around me, kissing my cold cheek, and I felt the nerves melt away.

A few hours later, Rylan and I were giggling like toddlers as I chased him around the kitchen with a spatula full of brownie batter. I bent the spatula back to sling chocolate onto his face, when the front door opened. We froze between laughs, and a stunning woman sauntered into the room, her fur midcalf boots making a purposely loud entrance on the limestone floor. Rylan's mother took me in, horrified.

On the plane flight, Rylan had quietly warned that his mother could be "a little cold at first." This proved to be an exceptional understatement. I quickly discovered that close proximity to Gemma Harper required a thick Moncler parka, not a windbreaker. I also discovered that Rylan had failed to tell his conservative and WASPy mother that he was dating a woman who had Hebrew letters tattooed on her forearm.

While Rylan excelled in most arenas of life, he was completely average when it came to dealing with his mother. Growing up, I hardly ever witnessed a fight between my parents. They worshiped each other in an annoying way—and their version of sparring was engaging in intellectual disagreements. The rare juicy throw down was a gift from my loving (yet at times overbearing) paternal grandmother, Rose, my father's inability to create boundaries, and my mother having to do the dirty work for him. It took meeting my boyfriend's mother to understand my own mother's valid frustrations. Grown men, by and large, are wired in such a way that they are incapable of having an uncomfortable conversation with their female makers. Martin Luther King Jr. confronted insurmountable injustice, but do you think he ever had the courage to tell his mother she couldn't stay with him and Coretta for three weeks in the summer? Definitely *not*.

I tolerated an afternoon of glares and curt answers from Gemma, which I responded to in the most adult way possible, with pursed smiles. I tried my best to not leap across the table and slap the judgment out of her, yet with each hour, my pain and anger mounted.

That night, I stood by the fireplace in our bedroom, twisting the cords of my hoodie as flames ran through my veins and beat down upon my back. Through echoes against the wall, I heard Gemma ask her husband if he believed Rylan had "thought this through." "This" being me. Rylan couldn't jump-start a political career with a "bra-less, tattooed woman" on his arm. What if he "winds up having *Jewish* children?" I was not the kind of woman she wished for her son. Not on paper. Not in person.

Rylan walked into the bedroom from the shower with a towel wrapped around his waist. He froze, seeing my eyes welling with tears. He stepped toward me, his brow crossed in confusion as he placed his hand on my chin, forcing my eyes onto his.

"Hey, are you okay?"

Anger boiling over, I shook my head, forcing his palm off my face as I tossed my arms in the air.

"Seriously? Am I *okay?*" I said back, seething. He stared at me, at a loss.

"I'm not a mind reader, Zoey. What's going on?"

"You don't have to be a mind reader to read the room, Rylan. You do it every damn day when you sit at the head of a conference table, so I know it can't be that impossible a task for you."

"Hey, calm down—"

"No. *Get angry,*" I said, fire in my chest, tears stinging my eyes. "You don't have the right to tell me to 'calm down' when you're not paying attention to what's going on around you. It's not your fault your mother is a judgmental bitch, but it sure as hell is your fault for not preparing me for it, and at the very *least*, sticking up for me."

Rylan's shoulders fell. He stood still for a few moments, shifting his jaw. His hand reached to pull me toward him, and I edged my body away, turning my back to his face.

"I'm sorry," he cracked. "Hey, can you look at me?"

I didn't want to look at him. I didn't want him to see me cry. The only tears Rylan had witnessed were those of a drunk girl lying on the floor delivering false promises to never drink again. These were tears full of real anguish, the deep-down kind of hurt. He turned my shoulders around to meet his, and like the mature woman I was, I refused to meet his eyes.

"Zoey, nothing about my mom surprises me anymore. I expect the worst, and I didn't prepare you for it. I didn't stick up for you, and I should have. *I'm sorry*," he reiterated. "My mom's opinion doesn't hold any weight with me. Nothing she could say or do would change how I feel about you."

Rylan lifted my clenched jaw upward. I reluctantly let my eyes meet his, surprised to find his face blanketed in an expression I didn't know he was capable of. While Rylan had never seen me cry before, I had never seen him register pain before. Rylan was hurting, simply because I was hurting.

"Can you please say something?" he asked, tucking a strand of my curls back from my forehead.

My insecurities were in my throat. I grew up feeling like an alien roaming Earth. I was dragged from one wealthy cookie-cutter suburb to another, searching for a place to fit in and never finding one. Most of the time, I only felt like myself when I was dancing behind my bedroom door. I only felt seen when my best friend looked at me. I shared the discomforts of my childhood with Hannah, who had a first-class seat to it. My teenage angst didn't feel safe in anyone else's arms. I wasn't a fragile, bleeding wound. I was an authentically confident woman. Yet no matter how tall I stood inside my own skin, a tiny voice had a way of shrinking me back to my misunderstood youth. Despite being enough for myself, "Are you *good* enough?" was a question that lingered—a monster I had yet to vanquish.

"Rylan, I'm used to being looked at like I don't belong. I'm an expert at pretending it doesn't hurt, but it always hurts."

His thumb wiped a hot tear from my cheek, and he put both his hands on either side of my face. The fire's reflection glittered in his irises as he studied me.

"Zoey, I wouldn't change a thing about you."

He grinned down at me, and I lost my breath. Suddenly, there was a ball of heat in my chest, shooting across every point on my body. I'd felt the fall, but this fall was different. This wasn't the slow fall. This was an emotion that gripped my body like an epiphany. It was the first time I felt it for a real, live man.

I loved him.

I knew I loved him, and all at once, I did not know what to do with this feeling. If he hadn't been holding me, my love for Rylan Harper would have sent me to my knees. It scared me how much I cared about the way he looked at me, about the way he saw me—all of me. It scared me that one moment I was ready to fall apart, and the next moment he held the pieces in place. It scared me how much I could get used to this.

It was right there that I watched helplessly as my rule book flew out the window. Ideals I had clung to, beliefs I had about the opposite sex, were replaced with him. Yet, I held on to some pages. Pages that, unfortunately, couldn't be destroyed by the devilish corners of his smile.

# Eight

Six months into my relationship with Rylan, I turned thirty. Rylan and I decided to get out of the heat of the city for a laid-back weekend at the Baker House 1650, a bed-and-breakfast in East Hampton. We lay side by side on wooden lawn chairs by the pool, which was sunken into a green lawn and surrounded by sweeping leafy trees and lilacs.

Rylan reached over and gripped the bottom of my lawn chair, pulling it closer to his. My eyes followed the solid turquoise trunks tightly hugging his waist, up to his hair lightening with the sun's rays. His cunning smile nodded that I join him on his chair, and my body followed.

I adjusted my white scalloped bikini as I folded into his warm open arms. I rested my cheek on his chest and snuggled into him, listening to his heart flutter and taking in the smell of sunblock on his darkening summer skin, salt and vanilla mixed with a hint of his usual cedar. We basked in the summer air for a while, the sound of the rustling trees, the smell of the nearby ocean, and the heat of the sun baking our bodies. It was an unusual moment for me—perfect silence as I traced my finger along the freckles on his torso, then to the white scar on his rib, a badge of honor from a lacrosse game in college. I let my eyes get heavier upon the rhythm of his chest. I felt his arm pull me tighter against his body, his lips kissing the top of my wild dark curls.

"I'm really happy to be here with you," I whispered.

I turned my face up so I could see him. He took off his sunglasses and met my gaze, staring at me for a long moment. He playfully pulled my body upward, my half-naked frame now dangerously on top of his.

"Careful," he said, a sly warning. I loved how easily I could turn him on. I grinned with my chest pounding on his. He ran his finger on the top of my scalloped bikini, my breasts nearly pouring out of it and onto him.

His eyes deepened onto mine as he put his hand behind my neck and traced a line down my spine, sending a shiver through me.

"Wanna do it in the pool?" I casually asked.

He smirked with a shaking head. Six months in, and I had come to discover that while Rylan was the best sex of my entire life, with no one even a close second, he was not the type of guy who enjoyed sex in public places. Public displays of affection were no problem for him, he enjoyed them more than most, but the thrill of getting caught naked did not do a thing for Rylan. It did everything for me. The fantasy of having sex in a public place with the man I loved—that would be reaching my zenith. Rylan knew this, and he had unapologetically turned me down multiple times.

"You are the strangest woman," he said.

"Would you like me if I were a normal woman?"

"Define 'normal woman.'"

"A woman who wants to have sex in the hotel room, instead of, say, in the backyard of a bed-and-breakfast."

He shook his head at me, taking me in.

"I love you the way you are."

"No one is around . . ." I trailed off, letting my hand slowly move up his leg.

"Zoey." He grabbed my wrist, removing my hand from his crotch, and staring at me with wide eyes.

I put my hands in the air and pouted as I spun off him and onto my own lawn chair with a plop.

"I'll just read my book and keep my hands to myself and let you sit over there like a basic bitch."

I pulled a book in front of my face, a sly smile on my lips.

"A basic bitch?" his voice challenged.

I looked up from the corner of my book to see his face looming over mine, freckles swimming in his light green eyes, and one arm on the other side of my body. His eyes searched the vacant pool area, making sure it stayed that way, and then I felt the heat of his fingers move from my knee all the way up the inside of my leg. I tilted my head at him with raised eyebrows as goose bumps enveloped my body. His fingers stopped right under my bikini line. He traced the seam with purposeful hesitation. I felt my breath become shallow as his fingers went under my bikini, and I exhaled a moan as they dipped inside me. My chest rose and my legs trembled as he pressed down.

He raised his eyebrows as if to say, *Who's your basic bitch now?* He pulled his fingers out of me, rolling over onto his chair like nothing had just happened and going back to a finance article on his iPad.

I readjusted the bottom of my suit and crossed my brow in his direction, my body humming and aching as my heart pounded. I did not appreciate being fingered and left for dead. A blue vagina was nobody's friend.

"That was a little mean."

"Almost-birthday girl, I'll make it up to you later," he said in a husky voice that made me want to tear his bathing suit off.

"Can later be now?" I begged.

He set his iPad down and leaned over me with a boyish grin.

"You want to go upstairs?"

"Uh-huh."

"Me too," he said hungrily.

Rylan stood up, pulling my arms with him. He wrapped his arms around me, swaying my body in a hug.

"I love the shit out of you," he whispered into my ear.

"I'm aware."

"You're *aware*?"

He put his thumb on the dimple of my chin and pulled me in for a tender kiss. I breathed him in, cedar swirling in ocean air.

"I love you," I said, basking in his face.

"You better," he challenged, kissing the top of my nose.

Suddenly, my jaw hit the floor, my eyes blinking rapidly. I removed myself from Rylan's arms and ran toward the inn's lobby doors. Wearing a breezy floral dress, Hannah shrieked, running toward me and wrapping her freckled arms around me as I squealed in the doorway. Well-dressed strangers looked on from the quaint lobby as we jumped up and down. We hadn't seen each other in person in ten months, one of our longest stints apart. I turned around to find a silly grin on Rylan's face. The fact that he'd surprised me on my birthday with my favorite human reaffirmed that this man was solid gold.

Rylan, Hannah, and I spent the rest of the day at the pool. Hannah couldn't get enough of watching her "I don't need love" best friend in love for the very first time. She studied Rylan and me as if she were watching her two favorite TV characters finally get together. Her hazel eyes widened as Rylan and I finished each other's sentences, beaming about the little Hamptons house we were going to rent in Wainscott for the month of July.

She tilted her head, leaning in as if watching a thriller as we argued over my upcoming presence at his mother's sixtieth birthday party in November in Santa Barbara. A pragmatic planner, Rylan was itching to book flights for us both. I wanted to wait, refusing to commit to the idea of being in a room with Gemma Harper and her friends staring at me like I was a modern painting in a room full of frescoes, the anxiety too large. I would decide a few weeks prior, based on my workload. Rylan tried to get Hannah on his side, but best friendship was thicker than blood, and she stayed tight-lipped. He ended the argument by booking the flights on his phone and telling me I could cancel my ticket a week prior if I really didn't want to go with him.

"What?" he asked, seeing my face tighten.

I was knocked off-center by the idea that a man might have a hold on my future.

"Nothing," I replied, quickly shaking it off with a smile, and assuring myself I could get out of these plans if I wanted to.

Rylan excused himself to take a quick work call, leaving Hannah and me to have our first taste of alone time. Her bright eyes beamed at me for too long. I knew she was going to have a field day with this. I sat up closer to her, rolling my eyes with a grin.

"Go ahead and say whatever mushy thing you've been dying to say."

"I had a strange feeling you two would be drawn to each other—that my setup could be more than just 'fun' for you, so I want to take some credit here. But, I didn't expect . . ." She searched for the right words, her eyes widening. "I don't know if I've ever looked at a guy the way you look at him. *Ever.*"

I arched my neck back, my cheeks burning, surprised by her comment. I was a love novice, and somehow, I was more in love than Hannah had *ever* been? I knew what Rylan and I had was special, but Hannah's comment jolted it into a different perspective.

"And the way he looks at you . . . Zoey, I think . . ." She paused, peering straight into my brown eyes.

"Zoey, I think this is it for you."

I couldn't breathe. Hannah's words were supposed to be a glowing declaration about The One. I internalized them differently. It felt like I was done for.

"What?" asked Hannah, perplexed by my face.

I opened my mouth to tell my best friend about the strange feeling twisting my insides, when Rylan walked back toward our chairs, tucking his phone in his back pocket.

"What did I miss?" he asked, leaning down to kiss me.

"Nothing," Hannah and I said in unison.

It was not nothing, but I didn't know exactly what it was, either. And so, I buried away the first hint of a warning sign, choosing instead to enjoy the fact that my two favorite people in the world were sitting on either side of me.

We hadn't reached the high hurdle yet, not even when nine months into our relationship, Rylan asked me to move in with him. My lease was coming up, and as Rylan pointed out, I spent almost every night over at his place—I may as well have lived there. The ease with which I declared "Let's do it" surprised even me. I had grown accustomed to using Sunshine's head as a warm pillow at night. I loved waking up to find Rylan's scruff on my neck, his naked body against mine. Plus, he had an irresistibly large walk-in closet.

I was soaring down a clear path, until all of a sudden, the high hurdle came into play.

# Nine

I t was a year into my relationship with Rylan. Sunshine and I stood under a bright red awning on the sidewalk of a packed Fifth Avenue, our breaths huffing in the December air as we waited for Rylan to get the band replaced on his late grandfather's watch. Rylan stepped out past the glass doors of Cartier, adjusting the new leather band around his wrist. He knotted his gloved fingers in mine, and as I stepped forward to walk home, I felt a tug at my arm. Grinning, Rylan pulled me back toward his chest. His arched eyebrows shifted from the engagement ring beaming in the window to my eyes beaming with terror.

My throat closed, and my heart did somersaults. I swallowed hard and pulled Rylan down the street before he could say one word. We walked silently all the way home, Rylan's brows squinted in thought, my eyes refusing to meet his—both of us afraid to address the elephant between us: our future.

The moment we got home, Rylan tossed his keys on the console and looked up at me with a twitching jaw. His mouth opened—

"I'm going to reorganize my side of the closet," I announced in a high-pitched tone, fast-walking toward our bedroom and cursing my deflection, which I would now have to make a reality.

Rylan found solace in structure and order, color-coding every article of clothing, down to his socks. Conversely, I was born with an inability to put a bra back where it belonged, or part with that one tank top I wore when I lost my virginity in college. My clothes housed memories, and parting with them felt like someone was ripping away the parts that built me, so the chaos mounted. I tucked my AirPods into my ears, blasting Lorde's "The Louvre" and lamenting over which underwear I would throw away. Their usefulness shifted with age. Sexy Underwear became Workout Underwear, and Workout Underwear became Period Underwear. I danced my shoulders up to the sky with a proud grin, deciding that today would be the day Period Underwear would meet its death.

I looked up to see Rylan at the closet doorway, his biceps folded across his chest as he took me in. I grinned proudly up at him and gestured to my underwear, but his green eyes narrowed on my face, quickly sobering my purge pile pride. He took a seat across from me on the floor, pointing to the AirPods in my ears. I swallowed hard as I set the AirPods to my side. Rylan was ready to have The Conversation that had the ability to crush the Very Good Thing we had going on.

"Do you want to talk about it?" he asked.

"Not really."

"Well, I do."

I twisted my fingers around my sneaker's cords, afraid to meet his hardened eyes. I could feel the panic rise in my chest, seizing every inch of my body. Here it was. We had reached the chapter in the Book of Zoey that shouted, *"Run!"* I searched for words to divulge something that was overwhelmingly heart-wrenching. I couldn't even open my mouth.

"Zoey . . . ?"

He lifted my chin up, his eyes scanning every inch of my befuddled face. We stared at each other for a long moment, until my jaw found an open door amid a maze of anxiety.

"I don't think I'm ready for this conversation," I cracked.

And I was not. I felt like one day I could be, with him, but in this moment, a certain future was suffocating. My breathing turned shallow, and he put his hands on both sides of my arms.

"Hey, what's going on?"

My body was tightening as if Rylan were pulling a chain around it.

"Rylan, I love what we are. . . ." I trailed off as he took my hand into his. I studied our fingers locked together. His calloused grip was a comfort, and I felt my pounding heart calm at his touch.

"I love what we are, and I don't want it to go away," I said, surprising even myself.

*I couldn't run.* I didn't want to go anywhere, at least not without him.

He studied my wide eyes, perplexed by my statement.

"Neither do I, clearly," he said, taking me in, his brow furrowed. "I'm not asking you to marry me *today*, but . . . We haven't had a conversation about where this is going, and I want to make sure that marriage is on the table. I want to make sure that we're on the same page."

*The same page.*

My rule book may have gone out the window, but I had clung to a few pages—the "Just Say No to Forever" chapters. Zoey Marks would soar through adulthood on a destination-free road, with no one complicating her ability to pave her own path. As I studied Rylan's eyes, I was gutted with a sinking feeling. For the first time, these celebratory chapters in my rule book had evolved into warring pages, and they were now floating inside me, making tiny paper cuts on my heart.

"You *do* want to get married one day, don't you?"

He may have posed a question, but his expression suggested, *"There is only one acceptable answer here."*

"We live together. We've been doing this dance for a year. I'm thirty-six," he continued, as if I wasn't aware of these facts.

"Well, it's not my fault you're old as fuck," I said, trying to lighten the mood.

"Hey." He placed his thumb in the dimple of my chin and dialed the mood back to serious. "Do you see a future with me?"

I chewed the inside of my cheeks, trying to find the right words. Idealizing any part of my future was akin to holding my life captive in a snow globe. I had faith in Us, but I distrusted certainty more. I peered up into his patient eyes, unable to imagine not staring into them tomorrow. Fifty years from today? That was another story. But, something about Rylan Harper told me I could try to get there.

His eyes widened, waiting for what should have been an easy answer.

"I see a tomorrow with you," I admitted, hoping that the statement would be enough for now, and knowing I was inching toward a white lie—a total betrayal of my authenticity.

"I don't want just a tomorrow with you," he countered.

He wanted all of my tomorrows. I inhaled a sharp breath, my tongue twisting.

"I fucking love you. You know I love you, can we table this for a later day? I'm happy. *We're* happy. It's only been a year, Rylan."

He nodded slowly, clearly not wanting to table this. I took in his pained eyes, and my guilt started to mount. I hadn't run, but I had hurt him. And in wounding him, my insides ached. It was a new feeling, and I didn't much care for it.

I moved across my piles of underwear and folded my body onto his lap, wrapping my arms around his neck. His fingers twisted at the waist of my leggings, and I turned his two-day scruff toward me, running my fingers up his jawline and brushing the hair out of his face. His green eyes shone back, trying to see through me. I leaned down and gently kissed one corner of his firm mouth. I slowly kissed the other side of his lips and crinkled my nose onto his. Our foreheads touching, I inhaled the scent of home, the warmth of his body under mine.

"You know what I hate about you?" I whispered.

"Please, spare no details."

"You make we want to throw out all the pages."

And he did. I loved him and loathed him for it. My once unapologetic freedom-loving spirit was at war with herself for the first time, and it was entirely Rylan's fault. I lowered my mouth onto his, but he put his hands on my wrists, arching back from my lips.

"What do you mean?" he asked. There were flickers of hurt and hope in his eyes as he waited for my answer.

"It's a good thing," I assured him.

I kissed him gently, ignoring the sinking feeling that told me it wasn't *all* good. He exhaled beneath me and stitched together a reluctant smile, shaking his head while his fingers moved up the side of my rib cage and tore the tank top off my body with ease. Rylan ran his teeth across my breasts, like he hadn't just opened a can of worms one minute prior. Breathless, I pulled his lips onto mine, kissing him deeply so that his pounding body would quiet the voices in my head.

And just like that, I buried a warning sign under a fluttering heart. I could only pray that with enough time, my white lie would land somewhere closer to the truth.

Here's the thing about putting the big stuff away for later: later always comes.

We were running smoothly—until I went and fucked it up. Until I gave Rylan the confidence to sprint toward the high hurdle. Marriage was my Voldemort, my He Who Must Not Be Named. I thought this was understood by both parties—seeing as how a diamond ring was never explicitly brought up again. Yet, as I mentioned, I went and fucked it up.

It was a year and a half into our relationship. Rylan had come to discover that my ADD brain required a few hours of alone time on Sunday to prep for the upcoming workweek, so he usually spent that time running in the park, followed by little errands. I paced the entire length of our apartment, arms flailing about as I practiced my pitch for the launch of Bose's new wireless headphones—a silent disco in the middle of Times Square. After nailing the pitch three times in a row, I plopped down onto our tufted sofa and toggled through countless streaming services, skipping over every new release and settling on *The Proposal*, a movie I had seen at least twenty times. My brain had spent enough of the weekend extending itself, and classic rom-coms always helped shift my mind back to neutral. *The Proposal* was a warm hug, historically leaving a smile on my face. I watched the final scene begin, fully expecting my warm hug, but in its place was an emotional assault. Sandra Bullock—once ice cold to love—kissed Ryan Reynolds, gleefully agreeing to marry him. I looked on, powerless, clutching a pillow while tears blanketed my eyes. I, Zoey Marks, let the end of a fucking rom-com unravel me.

As I stared in shock at the flat-screen, a fuzzy feeling bubbled from inside my chest, floating up to my mind and pressing Play on a traitorous dream sequence. I pictured myself in Sandra Bullock's place, exclaiming "yes" as if I were living inside a cotton-candy-colored fever dream. In Mr. Reynolds's place was Rylan, pulling me in for a sweeping kiss as a gaggle of strangers cheered us on. The idea of myself as a bride had previously entered my mind only as a nightmare. I wasn't the middle schooler who scribbled "Zoey + Ben Forever" inside a heart on my Trapper Keeper. I didn't fantasize about what my wedding would look like one day, or keep a secret Pinterest folder for my hypothetical Big Day. Yet for the first time in my life, I could picture myself at the end of a rom-com, wrapping my arms around a happily ever after.

"You didn't even cry during *Marley and Me*," an amused voice interrupted.

I turned my head toward the door, mortified to discover that at some point during my Happily Ever After Awakening, Rylan had returned home. He stepped forward and loomed tall over me, sweaty and flushed as Sunshine twirled around his sneakers. He raised his eyebrows, waiting for an explanation. I cleared my throat, swallowing hard and averting my eyes from his.

"How long have you been standing there?" I asked sheepishly.

Rylan sat down next to me on the couch, keeping his eyes locked onto my wide-eyed expression. He stared at me for a moment too long. He grinned too widely. He knew.

"She's been through *a lot*," I said, defending Sandra Bullock as if my happiness hinged upon her happiness.

Who was this impostor? Who was this sudden defender of happy endings? I searched myself internally, finding only the foundation remained. The walls, the defenses, those pages— they had left quietly and without my permission. His eyes were glued to my face.

"What?" I asked, my cheeks growing hot with confusion.

"Nothing," he replied, his smile widening.

It was not nothing.

I pressed my palm on Rylan's sweaty cheek, turning him away so he could no longer peer into my changing soul. He whipped his face back toward me, continuing to stare me down as I edged a pillow in between our two faces, making a barrier and blocking his hopeful eyes from my line of sight.

I studied the end credits, my mind racing, trying to unravel how I got *here*. How I, Zoey Marks, the defender of open roads, was considering a path commonly taken with a certain romantic future as a destination. Hannah had told me that a first taste of love would change everything. Had it? Had a man softened me? Had I become every protagonist in every rom-com? Was I Sandra Bullock, Julia Roberts, Katherine Heigl . . . but with a rib cage tattoo?

My internal confusion settled down, resting more comfortably on a fathomable reality: the thought of losing Rylan was far worse than the idea of promising him Forever. Either my marriage fears were gone, or alternatively, they had simply been one-upped. I dreaded that eventually, Rylan would make me choose: Forever or bust. I just hadn't realized that somehow during the last year and a half of our relationship, the scale had tipped in his favor.

Rylan tossed my emotional pillow barrier off the couch and placed his hand on my chin, forcing my wide-eyed expression onto him. His body was still, and his green eyes stayed strong on my face, searching for all the right signs, fully prepared for me to open my mouth and burst his bubble.

I couldn't say a damn thing.

After a minute of silence, a smile broke across his face—the crinkles in the corners of his eyes exploded against my warring chest. I felt my heart bursting at the possibility of being the person who could make all his dreams come true, even if they weren't *my* dreams.

*The way he looked at me.*

He looked at me with so much hope that I believed he had enough of it for us both. And so, I bought in. Instead of delivering a warning sign, I twisted my fingers around Rylan's sweaty hair, tugging his salty lips onto mine. Rylan believed my Forever fears had left the building, and I did nothing to stop him from thinking otherwise.

I would soon pay for this moment.

# Ten

Two months later, I leapt out of an Uber and hustled toward a nail salon in Atlanta—my delayed flight from New York making me embarrassingly late for my college roommate Rebecca's very punctual southern-bridal-party kickoff. Rylan was in Tokyo—having to extend his trip at the last minute to land a tricky investor, and so while he was supposed to be my plus-one, I was heading to this wedding solo.

I swung open the door to the nail salon, grinning, thinking of the first day I met Rebecca, which was my very first day at USC.

Eighteen-year-old me took in the large redbrick facade of New North Residence Hall as if I, Zoey Marks, boho chic badass, had sailed the Pacific to find refuge in its hallways. I squeezed my way through the dorm's narrow corridor, inhaling the comforting scent of cleaning solution and cheap vanilla body spray. I reached the door to my room, cringing as the gut-wrenching whines of Nickelback's "Photograph" assaulted my eardrums from the room across from mine—where a gorgeous, curly-haired, blond water-polo player sang along to his chosen anthem. After making a mental note not to lose my virginity to this beautiful Division One athlete, I opened the door to my room, the room where I would later lose my virginity to that beautiful Division One athlete.

A plainly pretty and fragile-looking girl stood smack-dab in between the two empty twin beds, as if dipping a toe onto one side would set her Tory Burch flats on fire. Sweet, quiet, freckled-faced Rebecca James. The moment I crossed the tiny threshold, her body relaxed, as if she had been holding her breath while awaiting my arrival.

"You must be Zoey, I'm Rebecca," she said excitedly, with a soft southern accent that made her impossible to hate. "Which bed do you want? I couldn't choose. I really don't care."

Rebecca meant it. She really *couldn't* choose, and she really *didn't* care. Bile rose to her throat when forced with making a decision when there wasn't a clear answer. I, on the other hand? I loved choosing. I cared too impulsively and too often and with too much fervor. Right from the start, Rebecca was my room-mate soulmate, and we lived together our entire four years of college. I shared two hundred square feet with this woman for four years, and I never saw this coming. Not from a mile away.

Rebecca, the girl who went with the flow. Rebecca, the kind of TV viewer who couldn't decide if Felicity should choose Ben or Noel. Rebecca, the girl who would beg you to pick her nail color at the salon so she didn't have to. *Rebecca.* If you ever want to see the dark side of an indecisive woman, the side that Quentin Tarantino would call his "muse," just shove three carats on her finger.

After we graduated, I spoke to Rebecca once every few

months, smiling and nodding as she gushed about her uncomplicated life in the South. Rebecca's now-fiancé, Charles, was a CPA whom she had met the moment she moved back to Georgia to get her MBA at Emory. After stalking his Instagram, all I could gather from Charles was that he seemed to enjoy golf, SEC football, his Big Green Egg, and Rebecca. No part of Charles was a surprise, except for the disturbing fact that he wore Croakies around his neck—Oakley sunglasses dangling over his chest like a medal. He was exactly who I predicted Rebecca would end up with—a kind smile atop a wardrobe of pastel polos, ill-fitting cargo shorts, and leather Rainbow Sandals. Charles was the guy who would wax poetic about his golf game while engaging in paint-drying missionary sex and ignoring your clitoris completely. They were the kind of couple who would name their first daughter Paisleigh and undoubtedly give all their towheaded children the same initials. Yet according to my last conversation with Rebecca, she was over the moon for this man, and so I was happy for her, because I just assumed she'd never experienced an orgasm before and wouldn't miss that which she'd never had.

I smiled, spotting Rebecca looming over the manicurist station in a simple lilac tea-length dress. I had not seen her in person in three years, yet she looked the same: pearls, tasteful bright dress, and stick-straight auburn hair. I went in for a hug, expecting Rebecca to squeeze me tight, hold on for a few seconds too long, and pull back with a radiant smile—her usual effusive greeting. Instead, Rebecca hugged me quickly without making eye contact. She may have looked the same, but another person had taken over her body. The Bride was in a hurry. The Bride was frazzled. The Bride was . . . a dictator.

The girl who couldn't pick a corner of a WB love triangle (it's Ben, you sadist) demanded I get my nails painted in Ballet Slippers, "only two coats!"

Rebecca loomed tall over my manicurist station, vomiting the details of tomorrow's Big Day as if she were preparing her bridesmaids to storm the beach at Normandy.

There would be a flower crown on top of my head.

*There's a 0 percent chance I can pull off the vibe of Kate Moss's wedding in the Cotswolds.*

My hair would be worn "down and flowy, no exceptions."

*"Flowy"? In this humidity? My Jewish ancestors beg to differ.*

The following afternoon, I crouched in the small, windowless library of the Gothic church, adjusting a butchered bouquet atop my flowy mane and fanning my body with the mauve empire waist dress engulfing my frame.

Rebecca stood in the opposite corner of the muggy room, arms frozen to the sides of her Vera Wang gown. My eyes widened, taking in the bride as she stared achingly at the glowing green EXIT sign atop the door. Gone was yesterday's bride-turned-Stalin, and in her place was a mannequin. Concerned, I shuffled toward Rebecca, trying not to trip over the unnecessary yards of chiffon around me.

"Hey, is everything okay?" I whispered, tucking a strand of Rebecca's hair under her silk veil.

"It's just about go time," I heard a voice say.

I glanced over my bare shoulder, eyeballing the wedding coordinator as she forcefully arranged ten gray-suited groomsmen in a line from tallest to shortest. Suddenly, Rebecca clutched my wrist, yanking me into a far corner of the room behind stacks of Jesus books.

She stared at me with eyes like saucers, her body shaking with anxiety.

"Rebecca, what's wrong?" I asked, gently stroking the sides of her arms. "Can I get you some water? Have you eaten? So many brides faint, I don't want that to happen to you."

"It's overwhelming, Zoey. So many decisions. You know I hate decisions," she said as she trembled.

For someone who couldn't make up her mind, planning a wedding was probably a specific kind of human torture. I relaxed. Rebecca was Rebecca. The bride was fine—she was just living out her own personal hell. It all made sense.

"Rebecca, look at me. All you have to do is walk down the aisle, and then you get to exhale. You get to drink and dance and enjoy the night. No more decisions," I assured her with a smile. "Now just go out there and marry the love of your life."

She stared at me with panicked eyes, her head shaking. My stomach dropped. Rebecca was not fine. It did not all make sense.

"I love him. I love Charles, I really do. I really do."

It was the second "I really do" that alarmed me. The first "really," she was convincing me, but the second "really," she was barely convincing herself.

"Have I told you about Harrison from work?" she asked, knowing full well that she hadn't.

I could hear the distant swells of a violinist performing Ben Folds's "The Luckiest." I craned my neck to peer into the sanctuary where one by one the groomsmen were disappearing into Rebecca's wedding ceremony. This didn't feel like an advantageous moment to have a heart-to-heart about Harrison From Work.

Rebecca divulged that Harrison was her "work husband," a

term I hated, but one I let her elaborate on. She and Harrison flirted, never crossing a line, because she "wouldn't do that to Charles," plus she was "already engaged to Charles," and what was she "supposed to do now?" Not a great excuse for burying away one's feelings, but a very Rebecca excuse. Her life had already been decided, so how could she shift gears to adjust to the unwanted appearance of raw, surprising feelings?

Harrison From Work was a smart-ass, and Rebecca was a stickler for rules. When he started at her accounting firm a year ago, he pushed all of her buttons—even ones she didn't know she had. She loathed him, until one day, they took a work argument to the stairwell. During their escalating shouting match, Rebecca realized she wanted to pull Harrison onto her mouth more than anything she'd ever wanted in her entire life.

"I didn't, though," she said, as she anxiously adjusted her wedding dress. For her *wedding*.

"I would never. I love Charles. I really do."

A third "really." Charles was *really* fucked. I went to open my mouth in an attempt to salvage this—an attempt to assure Rebecca that her feelings for Harrison were probably just a reaction to cold feet. But then, the firm grip of the overenthusiastic wedding planner found my arm, yanking me in the direction of the church doors.

I whipped my head back toward the bride. Rebecca blinked rapidly at me through her veil—her wide eyes asking, *"What do I do?"* With the non-gentle nudge of the wedding planner's bony knuckles, my head snapped forward, and I was suddenly walking down the aisle in Rebecca's wedding.

Cocktail-attired bodies leaned toward me, smiling and nodding as I moved at the pace of a dying turtle, itching to turn around, wondering *how* to turn around. This wasn't the "oh, I left my phone in the car, be right back" kind of entrance I could un-make. I couldn't turn around to talk to the bride about her feelings. Could I?

I should have turned around.

# Eleven

The beaming guests stood from the pews. "The Luckiest" swelled. The orchid-arched church doors opened. Rays of light poured in.

I got my nails painted in Ballet Slippers "only two coats!" and Rebecca never made it down the aisle. Somehow over the course of the processional, Rebecca had grown the confidence and decisiveness of three white men, and she had concluded that she was in fact Team Ben. Her Ben? Harrison From Work. Charles meanwhile was confusedly waiting for his Felicity to walk down the aisle. On the sixth loop of "The Luckiest," tears began to rim the devastated non-groom's eyes. If only Charles had accessorized his tux with those trusted Croakies.

*Once is happenstance. Twice is coincidence. The third time it's enemy action.*

The lines echoed over and over as Rebecca fled the wedding to profess her love to the one that almost got away.

Rylan was somewhere thirty-five thousand feet over Alaska, returning home from a business trip, when Rebecca didn't walk down the aisle. He was blissfully unaware that the woman he loved had stolen a handle of Jack Daniel's from the non-reception. Unaware that she was wasted on the musty deep red carpet of the now-empty church, swollen and sweaty fingers clumsily untangling her "flowy" hair from the flower crown's thorns. Rylan was unaware that I, Zoey Marks, was zero for three.

Maybe if I were a less complicated thirty-one-year-old, I wouldn't have taken the moment Rebecca failed to walk down the aisle so personally. I would have shrugged off the facts: Chelsea, Sara, and Rebecca's collective failures to make it down their respective aisles were no fault of one lowly bridesmaid.

However, guilt was a prize gifted to me via eighteen years of cohabitation with my Jewish mother. The belief that everything bad surrounding me was a little bit my fault was something years of therapy had brought to my attention, but it was clear it would take decades of therapy to actually change the narrative.

I stared up at the crucifix in the dim, deserted church, taking in Jesus's crown of thorns.

"Looks like I'll die with mine too."

Jesus glared back, not engaging with the drunk, cursed bridesmaid. I didn't blame him.

I lay down on the floor, my arms and legs folded about in a way that closely resembled the chalk outline of a body at a murder scene. The flower girl's wasted white rose petals floated all around me. All I could do was watch the church's wooden fans creak around and around.

*The third time it's enemy action.*

I was Bad Luck Bridesmaid.

My fear of Forever was wholly vindicated.

Sandra Bullock and Ryan Reynolds were doomed.

# Twelve

The morning after Rebecca's non-wedding, I plopped down into my Comfort Plus window seat on the packed Delta plane. A wretched hangover pulsed behind my oversized sunglasses, and newfound guilt weighed heavily upon my shoulders. The past eight hours, unfortunately, had not washed away the undeniable truth that I was bad luck.

I looked down at my vibrating phone, seeing a text from Rylan.

Landed and heading home now. Driver is picking you up @ LGA. I know you're going to say it's a waste of $—I'll waste my money on you however I please.

On our first date, I asked Rylan "what exactly" a hedge fund manager did, and the moment "collateralized debt obligations" came out of his mouth, my brain built a wall around the portion that computes information. I was spectacular and hyper-focused when it came to things that excited me, and I was a slight disaster when it came to subjects that bored me. By virtue of this ADD trait, I held a limited understanding of Rylan's job, but I surmised that it resembled a real-life version of Monopoly. Rylan was the kind of player who bought the railroads before the utilities. Meaning, his moves were calculated—he played the fruitful long game, and thus, he did *very* well. I too earned a disproportionate amount of money given my age, but not fuck-you money. Rylan would casually drop two hundred dollars on a car and driver, as if there were no cheaper alternative. My modest childhood, mixed with the constant fear that my mother would one day see exactly what I was spending my money on, meant I was more of a saver than I *had* to be. At this moment, my throbbing head was thankful for my boyfriend's joy in burning cash for comfort.

A few painful hours later, I lugged my suitcase up the creaky wooden stairs of our brownstone, breaking a sweat as I reached the second floor. I clumsily struggled with the old lock and unreliable key, finally getting both to work in unison.

I could hear Bruce Springsteen humming from beyond the door—the one artist we could both agree on. Rylan's type of music was best suited for a drug-filled rave, which meant Rylan's music was not allowed in our apartment. He said my music made him want to "drink heavily in dark corners." Apparently, female singer-songwriters who use intimate storytelling as a means of eviscerating their ex-lovers in a sometimes-histrionic manner were not everyone's cup of tea. Not everyone was born with phenomenal taste. So, we wore out our "Best of Bruce" Spotify playlist, a much better alternative than pinching our noses up at each other's melodious lifelines.

I pitifully edged my shoulder into the door of our apartment, aimlessly throwing my keys onto the console as I made it inside.

I pulled my sweat-soaked white T-shirt off my chest—now only in a black bralette and high-waisted leggings—letting the AC cool my damp body. I exhaled with my eyes closed, setting my back against the kitchen's cold wall. I breathed in the comforting smell of home: cedar and jasmine. It was a scent I could only notice when I had been out of town for a couple of days. I once read that our brains adapt to familiar smells, so when something is actually wrong—such as a fire—our noses can identify a threat. Olfactory adaptation. While my nose didn't detect a *threat*, I opened my eyes to DEFCON Level 1.

My now-shaking hand moved to pull the sunglasses off my face, praying that my darkened shades had deceived my vision.

They had not.

In the harsh light of day, there was a maze of rose petals scattered below my feet, running all the way from our living room to the bedroom door. All I could manage was, "Oh God."

I followed the rose petals with the embodied terror of Jennifer Love Hewitt in a nineties slasher movie. My chest pounded with each small step. I knew it was going to be bad—dead-body-in-a-trunk bad—but nothing could have prepared me for what I found.

I cautiously pushed the bedroom door open, my heart pounding, and there he was, down on one knee. Candles and roses everywhere.

*Maybe Rylan wants me to knight him?*

Instead of a sword, Rylan held a black velvet ring box out toward me with the beaming face of a small child. Sunshine sat wagging her tail next to him. He nudged her, and she bent down to match his stance, now also bending on one knee. This was a trick Rylan had probably spent hours teaching her.

"Marry me."

*If only his smile were less hopeful.*

"Rylan, what are you doing?"

It would be clear to a fucking toddler what Rylan was doing. I was an intelligent person. I *knew* what was happening, but my mind couldn't let it be real.

"I'm kind of proposing to you right now."

I studied Rylan, the man whose grin disarmed me. The man who leaned in closer so he could understand me when I spoke. The man who cared enough to cup my head with his hand before he pressed me against a wall with a kiss that made me want to die. The man who felt like home.

I went to say the obvious words. But instead of words, I found walls. The pages. They had returned, and they were suffocating me.

"You, me, Forever. What do you say?" he asked, eyes flickering with nervousness.

My heart felt heavier inside my chest, as if it were now holding the weight of his world. Here I was: the girl who lives in the moment, faced with The Moment.

*Rise to the occasion, Zoey. Just like every other girl. Just say it—*

"I don't know how. . . ." I quietly cracked, the words leaving my lips ajar in confusion and bringing Rylan slowly to his feet.

Rylan's eyes stayed glued to mine as he repeated my words back to me. "You 'don't know how' to marry me?"

For the first time in my life, I hated myself. Over the course of twenty months, my love for Rylan Harper had successfully triumphed over the curious fears deep inside me. Two months ago, I'd found myself daydreaming about a ring on my finger. Rylan made me want to believe in Forever, even though I worried it was an unreachable goal. Rylan made me want to believe in Forever, even though the common road and a foreseeable future had always stifled me. He made me want to be like every other woman, and a part of me had liked it.

Yet, I was unable to rise to the occasion, unable to be like every other woman. I didn't know how to spend a lifetime with the man I loved to the ends of the earth. I didn't know how to believe in Forever, because all around me, Forever had fallen to pieces. I was a fucked-up maverick who never longed to get engaged, and my unorthodox marriage fears manifested themselves in the worst ways—taking three brides down with me. I was cursed.

My stomach turned, my body thickening with guilt—as if I had just burned down my own house. A sinking feeling twisted into my soul: I was seriously fucked up, and there was nothing worth celebrating about *this* road less taken. If only Rylan were the type of guy to ask for my ring size before getting down on one knee. If only he liked surprises a little less. If only I had gotten Rebecca down the aisle. If only I had been more honest about my fears during our marriage conversation. If only *The Proposal* had ended in an unhappily ever after. *If only* . . .

"I . . . I thought we were going to talk about this one day— you know, before you just . . ." I trailed off, realizing his eyes had now left mine.

He looked down at his loafers and the ring in his hand, eyebrows pressed in confusion, as if trying to play back how the fuck we got here. Nausea took over my body. I set my shaking hand on the dresser for support, but instead of finding solid ground, my eyes were met with framed pictures of us throughout our relationship. I studied our first-ever photo, grainy and sweet, the memory filling me up and tearing me apart. The sun was plummeting as we strolled through Central Park in early spring, warming our bodies against each other. I remembered gazing up at him, taking in the way the collar of his quilted jacket sat on his clean-shaven neck, so precisely. The way the sun turned his green irises a shade lighter with every step. The way a coy grin spread across his sharp jawline the second he noticed my eyes on him. The way he tugged me backward into his strong chest, wrapped his arms around me, and kissed my cheek as the flash of his phone lit up our smiles. I remembered thinking, *I could walk the entire island just to feel this man by my side.*

My eyes scanned photo after photo, each taunting, *"How could you?"* How could I roam the earth with memories this idyllic and not want to make a lifetime of them? What was wrong with me? I swallowed hard, slowly rediscovering the ability to form a sentence.

"Rylan, I love you. . . ."

It was all I could say as my body moved toward him. My fingers reached his, but he let them go, walking out of the room in quiet shock.

I followed after him, tears prickling, body shaking, and my mind in hyperdrive. Rylan planted himself in the center of the living room, arms limp at his sides. He studied the ring box as if he were helplessly watching someone he loved die right there in his fucking palm. I tried to get in his eyeline, but his wounded eyes darted away.

"I just watched my third friend *not* make it down the aisle. Three of my closest friends haven't gotten married. . . ."

"Rebecca . . . ?"

I shook my head.

Rylan knew about my first two bridesmaid failures. It was

something he joked about with a big eye roll—how my presence "ruined" two engagements. No one was laughing now.

He digested the information with squinted eyes, and then quickly shook his head, pinching his forehead in frustration.

"I'm sorry, but what does that have to do with us? If one of those brides had made it down the aisle, you'd suddenly be ready?" he scoffed. "That's not a reason not to want to be with me."

"I *want* to be with you," I cracked through tears. "I just . . . I need more time. I'm not ready for this. Not now."

"Not now, or not ever?"

"I don't know."

"I think you do know."

I didn't know, and it killed me.

I never saw Rylan coming. He knocked down wall after wall. He broke every rule in my book—all but one. I was desperate for more time to see if that wall could come down. This was how much I loved Rylan Harper: He was my New York City. Un-equivocally, without a shadow of a doubt, if I could not make Forever work with him, I could not make it work with any-one. I needed to see marriage as a fever dream, rather than a nightmare. If only I had a time machine and could tug Rebecca down the aisle.

Rylan's pained face floated upward, locking onto mine. He scanned my wet eyes like he had stumbled upon the most gut-wrenching sentence of his favorite novel. "Wilbur never forgot Charlotte" kind of devastation.

"We've been together long enough, Zoey. There's nothing you don't know about me. If you're not ready now . . . you'll never be ready."

His grandmother's stone disappeared inside the velvet ring

box as he slammed it shut, making a sound so massive for a box so tiny, a sound that jolted my entire body. A sound I wouldn't soon forget. It was the sound of The End.

"When I come back tomorrow, please don't be here," he whispered, his chin quivering. I watched as he steadied his emotions with one swallow, a trait I found baffling. My emotions streamed down effortlessly, hot tears falling along with my aching heart.

Rylan started to walk toward the door, and all I could think to do was grab on to him. My hand desperately latched on to his arm like one would cling to a life raft. An attempt to not let him go, to hold on to Us. He shook his head as he unhinged my fingers from his shirt. I stood in heaving shock, watching as he fastened Sunshine's collar to her leash.

"Rylan . . ."

He turned back around, waiting. He was giving me one last chance to save us.

*Say it, you coward. Just say yes.*

I was drowning, and there stood the life raft, reachable. And I couldn't bring myself to take the steps necessary to hold on to it. I couldn't bring myself to say the one word that would save us. Rylan's eyes went ice-cold as my lips stood ajar.

He turned to go, but not without a leave-behind. It's always the parting words that destroy a person.

*Sticks and stones*, what a lie.

"There's something wrong with you. Why do you have to make the easiest things so goddamn difficult?" He shook his head at me in mounting disbelief, a fury darkening his wounded eyes. "Since you're so scared of having something to lose, then here you go." His arms spread out, as if to show me. "You now have nothing. You're empty."

It was the "empty" that tore me apart, blistering through my veins like poison as Rylan and Sunshine walked out the door. I listened helplessly, frozen in the middle of our living room, as their footsteps disappeared out of my life. I could hear the hushed ballad of Bruce Springsteen's "If I Should Fall Behind" humming in the background. What was once Our Song was now an emotional assault. I had fallen behind, yet I was not worth waiting on.

Suddenly, an overwhelming feeling buckled my knees to the hardwood floor.

I was alone.

But I was not okay.

This was loneliness.

# Thirteen

It was like trying to breathe, surrounded by flames.

*Empty . . .*

Rylan and I died. We died, and I didn't call one person, not even my best friend. I spent two nights inside a dark, bare Midtown hotel room staring at the ceiling with wet eyes, letting the existential dread of Fiona Apple's "Criminal" splinter through my motionless shell. My mind played ping-pong with itself, trying to decide if I had sealed my own fate, or if I was a fatalist. The former made me a martyr, the latter meant I was cursed. I tallied up the points and concluded that I was both. I alone was responsible for ruining my romantic future—answering "I don't know how" when faced with the question of happily ever after. Conversely, it was predetermined by some higher power that I would ruin the engagements of the most important women in my life—I had no control over a hex.

Zoey Marks, a cursed martyr.

When my Grandma Anne died, we sat shiva—a seven-day period of Jewish mourning following the funeral. Sitting shiva did not sit well with me. I learned that Jews do the absolute *most* as grievers. We help bury our loved ones at a graveside service—shoveling earth on top of their casket. We sit in our homes for seven days while accepting a rotation of visitors. We cover each mirror in our home so we cannot even look at ourselves. I was eleven and had just discovered eyeliner, so the lack of mirrors felt especially unfair. My mother, a rule follower, explained that covering the mirrors forced us to focus on our grief rather than our vanity. My grandmother went to sleep wearing a fresh coat of movie-star-red lipstick every night—she absolutely would have wanted me to honor my own vanity. She would have understood my *need* for a smoky eye. I was slow to embrace why harrowing rituals went hand in hand with the already painful death of a loved one.

Two decades later, lying alone in a shitty hotel room after Rylan and I died, I finally understood why my people structuralized grief. I pulled my limbs apart from one another, curling out of fetal position as each bone ached, inching toward the edge of the bed as pain throbbed inside my temples—a reminder that I had not eaten in forty-eight hours. I was met with my reflection in the sliding mirror: swollen red eyes, tear-stained ivory tank top, matted wild curls, a strikingly thinning frame. Sitting shiva was akin to pouring hydrogen peroxide on an open wound. The pain was immediate and all-consuming, yet proper healing would follow. In doing the hard things—leaning in to epic grief with a sympathetic audience—you were forced to fight all aspects of the newly born grief monster before it could grow. It was not easier to mourn alone, and it was definitely not safe to look in a mirror.

I tugged my malnourished body over to the nightstand, my arms aching as they reached for my cell phone.

"Hello," beamed Hannah's voice on the other end of the line.

I tried to form a sentence, but instead, my body caved in, and sobs escaped from the depths of my lungs.

Eight hours later, Hannah stood outside my hotel room. She pulled my breaking body into her blue linen dress, and I breathed in her signature Jo Malone scent of lime and basil. Heartbreak had rendered me homesick, spiraling without a safety net, and I didn't realize how much I needed Hannah until I inhaled the scent of my first home. Comfort broke me, and I couldn't stop crying.

This was the first wound that a dance party couldn't heal.

After twenty minutes of watching me sob in her arms, unable to get past the entryway of my hotel room, Hannah undressed me and helped me into the shower, believing that soap and hot water would help me feel human.

Instead of reclaiming humanity, I found my shoulder blades sliding against the white subway tiles and my knees buckling into my heaving chest. I rocked back and forth for what felt like hours, until the only liquid that poured down my face was my tears. I looked up, seeing that the shower was off. Hannah wrapped a warm towel around my shivering naked body and sat next to me on the wet floor. I let my sudsy curls rest on her nice linen dress as her arms folded around me.

She held me as the golden sun plummeted against the tall buildings outside—the world moving and twisting while we sat still.

This was sitting shiva.

We sat there for what felt like hours, until my whisper of "what's wrong with me?" echoed against the shower tiles. It was the only question I could think to ask. Hannah pulled me in tighter, as if shielding my body from incoming battle fire.

"There's nothing wrong with you. You're perfect," she said, squeezing my hand twice.

A perfect woman wouldn't break something that worked. Even a near-perfect woman would know how to fix something she broke. I was nowhere near perfect. All I needed to do was show up at Rylan's door with one word, but I couldn't undo my own heartbreak.

"Zoey, I know you haven't been able to talk about the breakup, and you don't have to if you don't want to. All I know is what Rylan told me. . . ."

My chest tightened. Evidence he was existing without me tore me apart. The mere idea of my name escaping his lips was unbearable. We had died, yet he lived on. I was frozen inside our grave—unable to pull myself out of our ending.

*Romeo and Juliet had the right idea.*

"What—what did he say?" I barely managed.

"That you didn't want to marry him. You didn't want to be with him."

Only one of those sentences was true, and they were not synonymous. Not for me, anyway. I was unable to voice my heartbreak to anyone, because I couldn't quite untangle it myself. Peeling back the layers would involve an admission that I was a self-sabotaging failure at love, and to top it off, I was the bridesmaid who watched unions crumble at her feet.

"You want to be with him though, don't you?" Hannah asked, even though it was not a question. She knew, the way best friends just know.

Tears streamed down in place of a "yes."

"Hey, you know what I think?" Her voice was gentle, and cautiously bright. I pulled my eyes from between my bony legs.

"You both still love each other so much, and that's not nothing. If it's meant to be, it'll be."

I watched as Hannah smiled at no one. Hannah's penchant for optimism was always the yin to my realistic yang. However, this wasn't the Love Optimist caught up in hope for her best friend. She was gazing wistfully at *shower tiles*. This was the face of someone in stupid love.

About three months ago, Hannah had found herself seated next to a beautiful man on a flight from Dublin to Denver, both of them headed home after separate holidays in Ireland. He had been visiting extended family off the coast, while Hannah had been celebrating with a couple partners from her law firm after winning a huge divorce case. Plane Guy and Hannah had The Law in common—him a business attorney, and her a family law attorney.

"Plane Guy is really doing a number on you, huh?" I asked, using what felt like an exceptional amount of energy to form a sentence, but relieved to focus on something other than my own treachery.

"Graham," she corrected.

"We're calling him by his name now? This is serious."

"It is."

Hannah's face curled into a wild sparkle of energy. In thirty-one years, I had never seen this face before on Hannah. She quickly sucked in her cheeks, an attempt at disguising that she was madly in love while a lovesick person sat bare-assed next to her on the shower floor.

"Want me to go pack up your stuff from his place?" she whispered, pivoting the conversation away from her happiness and back to my heartache.

Hannah was aware that I was fully unable to walk back inside Rylan's doors—unable to smell cedar without jasmine. The thought of my things leaving his space brought my head back between my knees. All I could do was nod between tears.

Hannah stayed with me for an entire week, helping me scour apartment rentals while force-feeding me saltines to combat my aggressive consumption of wine. She stayed with me for an entire week and did not ask me one question about why I turned down Rylan's proposal, because she knew—the way best friends just *know*—that I did not have all the answers. Hannah also never asked about Rebecca's wedding, and so I never told her that Rebecca did not make it down the aisle. No part of me wanted to relive the worst weekend of my life, or share the shame of being Forever's curse. I also never told my best friend that two months ago, if Rylan had proposed, I might have said yes. I was *almost* Sandra Bullock, but instead, I was naked and crying over a shower drain.

A few days after Hannah left, I moved into a loveless, modern, white-on-white one-bedroom apartment next to the Hearst Tower in West Midtown—the part of New York that felt the least like home. I hoped the proximity to very few ghosts would make it possible for me to shuffle out the heavy front door without crying into my Hydro Flask.

I roamed the streets like a masochist—searching for the memories and letting them tear me apart, one by one. I saw Rylan's ghost every-fucking-where. I saw us at MOMA, the back of my head resting against his warm chest as we took in van Gogh's *Starry Night*. I saw us through the window of a stranger's aging brownstone, him throwing me across his broad shoulder and carrying me to the bedroom. I saw us in the Sheep Meadow

at dusk, curled in each other's arms on the sprawling grass—
him counting every freckle on my back with his lips. Over the
course of twenty months, our footprints had stretched onto every block as we marked our emotional territory all over Manhattan. Every corner of New York City came alive—a screaming
reminder of what we were, and what we would never become.

I became That Girl on the subway, tears streaming down
her face on the cold bucket seat, peering down at photos of the
first man she let in, armed with Taylor Swift's "All Too Well"
as a battle cry. Going Through Hell's silver lining involved a
reliving of every sad song I had once loved, but never had the
opportunity to sob to.

While I had never experienced heartache before, I had also
never let raw emotion get in the way of my job, and my waning ability to compartmentalize threatened the latter. Amid my
heartache, I had ideated the perfect pitch for an UberPool push
on Valentine's Day. In select big cities, single passengers would
take a quiz on the app—answering multiple choice questions
such as their go-to drink order, ideal date night activity, and
favorite vacation spot. They would follow this up with their
age preferences, and then wait to take a ride with a perfectly
matched stranger. The ride would theoretically be a ten-minute
first date in traffic, with each passenger having a different drop-
off point at neighboring, participating bars. Once the ride was
finished, instead of rating their driver, the passengers would
each rate their date. Five-star matches would receive each other's contact information and could stumble on over to the bar
next door to find their match. It was Uber meets speed dating
meets a Valentine's Day pub crawl—it was genius.

I stood in our conference room pitching Uber, watching

three of the four men in suits lean back in their chairs with surprised grins on their faces, with Sara standing next to me. My eyes zeroed in on the male, stodgy client in front of me, twirling his pen and showing much less enthusiasm. I recognized this expression, and I knew it meant we would have to work in overdrive to convince him that we knew what we were talking about—most likely because Sara and I had vaginas, which somehow implied that our frontal lobes were not fully developed.

"Look, this is cute and all, but 'doing it for the gram' marketing—I just don't know. Experiential still seems like a shallow way to connect with consumers."

It was one thing to attack my pitch; it was another thing to attack what I did.

"Then why are you sitting here?" I asked, with a *fuck you* inflection.

"Because I read that *Ad Age* profile on you."

My insides tightened. I felt dirty. The article was a shiny gold star, highlighting my "inability to embrace the traditional," which had made me a "winner" in business, yet dealt me a shitty hand in the game of love. It was incredible how an ideal I had hung my hat on could so quickly become the very thing that made me feel like I was losing my mind. I could sense Sara's eyes on me, her head tilting, wondering what had happened to her shark.

Sara leaned across the table, into the client's cocky face.

"You can cling to some elitist bullshit, or you can put your money toward impactful brand engagement. Which is it? Because we can pitch this to Lyft in an hour."

I exhaled, thankful that my ruthless coworker could grab men by the balls, when I had been reduced to Jell-O.

Sara pulled me from work that night, refusing to let me subway it home in a wallow-and-repeat pattern. Her partner, Jane, was working late, and Sara—three months pregnant—was finally not puking on the sidewalk during trash day. She wanted to celebrate her lack of nausea by forcing my sad sack of beans out into the world again and get me to open up about my heartache rather than bottling it inside.

"C'mon, Zoey, let's take back one of your favorite places. You can't let a *fucking man* take New York City from you, a *fucking goddess.*"

I smiled in my colorful, glass corner office, giving in to the ruthless cheerleader side of Sara.

A wiser person would have started small. I boldly sauntered into Alta with Sara by my side. Alta was my happy place before Rylan put a dent in it with our magical first date, and I refused to let him take it from me. So what if this was the scene of our first date? *So fucking what?*

I sidled up to the wooden bar, and my false confidence devolved into a weight on my chest. It took everything in my body to keep my eyes from drifting to the two empty leather stools at the far corner of the bar. The place his body first touched mine. The place I first heard him laugh—*I wish I could forget his laugh.*

"How's the boyfriend?" Luke asked, interrupting my lack of self-control.

Sara gripped my arm in support, her wide eyes begging Luke to abort this line of questioning. I went to answer, to say calmly, "There is no boyfriend," but instead, I tasted my own salty tears, which had spilled out without warning. I pushed myself off the stool and barreled out the door, knowing full well I would never be back.

*Empty.*

I missed him in a way that took hold of my body, in a voice so loud it screamed. At least five times a day my chipped nails hovered over Rylan's name, which was still sitting at the very top of my Favorites on my iPhone. I tried to text him. I tried to call him. I tried to delete his name from atop that list. Instead, I tossed my phone across my bed multiple times a day, not having the nerve to pull any of these triggers and hating myself for it.

Six weeks into Hell, the anger came storming in.

*Empty?!*

If I was empty, then where was all this rage coming from? I cut through the claustrophobic Midtown streets using the chip on my shoulder to part the crowd. I marched my anger directly inside the sleek walls of an overpriced hair salon and got a long bob from a stranger. Ten inches fell to the floor as Ani DiFranco's "Untouchable Face" blasted in my AirPods, comforting the scar on my heart.

*"Fuck you, and your untouchable face. Fuck you, for existing in the first place."*

I regretted the haircut immediately and paid two hundred dollars for extensions.

Fuck me.

Seven weeks into Hell, I FaceTimed Chelsea Moore, my zero for one. Chelsea was now living her best life in London, single and running a successful textile company—a far cry from grieving that douchenozzle, Chris. Upon the image of my red and puffy face sniffling on the other end of her phone, Chelsea shut her office door and settled in. I sat under the covers in my undecorated, white-on-white bedroom.

"Who died?" she asked slowly, preparing for the worst.

*Love died. Love died here.*

I opened my mouth, and a mixture of sobs and words fell out. "I'm sorry I made fun of you when you played Death Cab for Cutie on repeat all those times you were lonely," I cried.

"You never made fun of me," she countered, confused.

"I did in my head," I confessed through sobs.

I divulged that Rylan had shattered my heart, and I was now a member of the lonely-hearts club. I *got* pain—pain and I were best friends Forever.

"Zoey, what happened? I thought you two were so solid."

"We drifted apart," I spectacularly lied.

The part about Rylan proposing and my inability to say yes? *Omitted from the narrative.* The part about Chelsea's failed wedding nearly a decade ago being a contributing factor? *Also omitted.* Chelsea and I had remained friendly, but it was a kind of friendship that had drifted to check-ins, not the kind of friendship where we spilled more to each other than we did our respective therapists. "I'm terrified of spending a lifetime with someone" was a little too much information for an acquaintance. Breaking it down inside my own head was a whole other story.

FDR was full of shit. There was *way* more to fear than fear itself. I should have done the emotional work to prepare my marriage-averse mind for an engagement. Instead, I selfishly buried my anxieties beneath a fluttering heart, just to relish in a carefree present. I could have meditated on it, seen a hypnotherapist, or binged every rom-com until my brain was rewired. I did nothing, and now I had nothing.

*Empty.*

Fear itself was the monster that ruined me.

In trying so hard to Robert Frost my way through life, I had failed to peel back a possibility: the road less traveled was less traveled for a good fucking reason. It was paved with confusion, heartache, and loneliness, and even littered with a surprise curse. I was clueless as to which piece inside me was broken, or how to fix it.

# Fourteen

During my third month of abusing Taylor Swift's *Red* album, Pinot Noir, and Ambien as a shallow means of emotional survival, I received a small package from the only person who knew how to cheer me up in a crisis: Hannah.

I sent you something. FaceTime me when it arrives, she had cryptically texted a week earlier. I was drowning in a pitch, and I had forgotten to retrieve the package from my apartment building's front desk, until Hannah finally texted a gentle reminder.

Hannah lived in Denver, so naturally I was praying for the good weed. I FaceTimed her in my white-on-gray kitchen, a room that was open to my white-on-gray living room, stacked with dirty moving boxes containing my colorful life—boxes that, for the most part, I refused to open. It felt disingenuous to decorate my space when I was empty inside. Shouldn't a person match her surroundings?

I unwrapped the package using my teeth, and scooted back in shock. I knew what it was instantly. It was not a care package. It was a bomb.

Wide-eyed, I slowly pieced together the puzzle: a photo of our seven-year-old selves. The question "Will You Be My Bridesmaid?" appeared over our matching leotards.

Hannah flashed a blinding ring into my screen: "I'M GETTING MAAAAARRIED!"

Silence.

"Say something."

I searched for "something" that wouldn't reveal the thoughts running through my head. Hannah and Graham had only been together six months. Hannah was practical and thoughtful. This was irrational and impulsive. What had happened to my best friend?

"I'm—I'm shocked," I finally managed.

"It's nuts, right?"

I exhaled. Hannah was waiting for me to tell her that this was too soon. She was too sweet to say no to Graham, clearly.

"It is nuts. I mean . . . six months. Has he even passed the IKEA test?"

Swedish shelving units had helped bring an end to a couple of Hannah's relationships. There was no way she would commit to a lifetime partnership with Graham before erecting a BILLY bookcase.

"I don't need you to do your Zoey Thing," she said with a gentle smile.

I pulled my head back. Hannah didn't want me to talk her out of this. Hannah didn't need me to tell her how soon this was, because she didn't care what I thought. Her cheeks were glowing. She was too far gone for rationality.

"Zoey, they're right."

"Who? Who is right about what?"

"When you know, you know."

I took a sharp inhale, betrayed by the simplicity of the phrase.

"I can't imagine a day of my life without him."

Hannah's euphoric expression turned me right-side up. My best friend was in love, and it was a love so big that she didn't need me to come out swinging with a practical hammer to save the day. This was a good thing—a *great* thing. My shoulders dropped, and I beamed back at Hannah's starry eyes with a wide grin.

"You're getting married. . . ." I marveled.

"I know," she said with a smile.

We stared in awe at each other for a full minute, Hannah turning giddy.

"So, it's happening kind of quickly," she said.

"No shit."

"No, the wedding. We're getting married in three weeks."

My jaw found itself back on the "are you fucking kidding me?" floor.

"How about I just come and take you to Planned Parenthood instead?"

Hannah's face scrunched up into a ball. Heat enveloped my cheeks, realizing what an absolute shithead I was. Before she could open her mouth, I opened mine.

"I'm sorry. I was just joking. I'm an asshole. I'm an asshole, who is wildly happy for her best friend. Show me the ring again."

Hannah narrowed her eyes and flipped me her middle finger. I had never seen her do this before, and it brought me an incredible amount of glee. Anytime Hannah Green strayed from perfection, I reacted like a proud parent whose child had inherited something wonderful from her.

"It's beautiful. What shape is that?" I asked with a grin, her middle finger still pointed at me.

"It's the shape of 'F You.'"

Hannah couldn't even say "fuck." My influence needed some work.

"Ah, that must be the Ed Sheeran B-side."

Hannah grinned from ear to ear, and I knew I was forgiven.

"What do you need from me? I can plan a fast bachelorette party. Oh God, do you need me to play interference with your mom—"

"I don't need you to do a thing. You're my only bridesmaid, and Graham's brother is the only groomsman. We want it to be easy, and you know how miserable my mother would make a year-long engagement. It's November sixth, in Ireland—where Graham and I met. We're going to make a big, romantic, fun few days out of it. Only our closest friends and—"

Hannah awkwardly shifted her jaw. The end of the sentence was stuck in her throat.

"Family," I said quietly, the realization bringing me down to the couch with a thud.

Hannah's eyes were raked in guilt. I stared back blankly, but my insides were tightening in waves of nausea. He was coming. I didn't even have to ask.

When Hannah set me up with her "absurdly hot" cousin nearly two years ago, I didn't foresee us taking a machete to each other's hearts. I didn't foresee myself broken and sharing the same air as the man who did the breaking. I was barely able to keep it together walking past the bodega on Fifty-Seventh Street where Rylan bought gum this one time; so surely, I would crush it in a faraway romantic countryside with my ex-almost-fiancé.

No better place to contemplate one's vapid existence than Ireland, with its sprawling green hills and prose-inspiring rocky coastlines. Yeats would never write poems about Orlando. *Why wasn't this wedding in Orlando?*

It was sometime around my brain's hatred of Europe when Hannah dropped the second bomb.

"Zoey . . . he's bringing somebody."

What remained of my heart shattered at my feet. Hannah took in my falling face—which I could no longer hide through our unfortunately decent connection. My legs went numb, but somehow my feet wanted me to stand, and so I paced back and forth with panicked energy, as if blood flow might make its way to my brain and undo Hannah's words. Hannah spent the last month reassuring me that whoever Rylan dated next would merely be some "random rebound." Turns out, Random Cunty Rebound had evolved into Plus One to a European Wedding. All my nightmares were coming true.

"Zoey? Are you okay?"

I took in Hannah's cringing eyes and her sympathetic head tilt. No matter how badly I was hurting, this moment was not about me. I swallowed hard and shook off the urge to hold myself in the fetal position, dug down deep, and found a selfless smile.

"I'll be fine. The last thing you need is to worry about me. What can I do? Seriously, you can't tell me 'nothing.' Bridesmaid extraordinaire at your service."

The second the words "Bridesmaid extraordinaire" left my lips, heat rushed to my cheeks. What an absolute lie.

*Fuck.*

It occurred to me that I was going to destroy Hannah's wedding. My Hannah, my next victim. My curse had been sealed, and while I was an innocent participant, I now knew better than to participate. Zero for three. Myself as a bridesmaid did not put the odds in Hannah's favor. I needed to give Hannah her best chance at a happily ever after. As I searched for the least horrible way to tell my best friend that I couldn't be in her wedding, Rylan's parting words found their way back to me.

*"If one of those brides had made it down the aisle, you'd suddenly be ready?"*

I had clung to his "empty" dig for so long, because it was the easiest to defend—it was the most untrue. I was a whole person, and no man could take all of me with him. A person could leave me lonely, but no person could leave me empty.

*If one of those brides . . . ?*

It was a question I deserved the right to answer. What would have happened if Rebecca had walked down that aisle? Chelsea? Sara? Was my inability to embrace Forever nature, or nurture? If I could celebrate marriage rather than watch it erupt into flames, wouldn't that alter my fucked-up Forever fears?

*The third time it's enemy action.*

I was my own worst enemy. I was the enemy of engagements. But, what if I wasn't? What if I could lift both of these weights? I had never actively tried to get one of my brides down the aisle. I was an innocent participant, but what if I could be marriage's champion? Something rushed through my veins—an adrenaline that I couldn't quite place.

Later that night, I sat cross-legged on my bed, my laptop beaming under my chin, and I booked my round trip to Ireland with something new inside me. I had been so consumed by heartache that I had almost forgotten what anything else felt like. I felt hope. I would get my best friend married as if my life depended on it. *Maybe it did.* I would witness wedded bliss rather than destroy it, and I would feel differently about marrying the man I loved. I would get back to being able to picture myself at the end of a rom-com. I would be able to say, with all my mended soul, "YES." I would reverse the fate of the doomed Bad Luck Bridesmaid with the force of James Bond going after a nuclear space weapon, armed with the *Red* album, moderate amounts of wine, and newfound courage.

# Fifteen

Three of the longest weeks later, I dragged my body out the doors of Ireland's Shannon Airport with bags both in my hands and under my eyes. The curb of airport arrivals looks the same no matter where you are, but being in Europe felt different. It forced me to close my eyes and let my lungs take in the crisp Irish air. My eyes widened to the sound of squeals as two tiny, toned arms squeezed the remaining life out of me.

*Hannah.* I squeezed back. I had forgotten what it was like to be hugged, and I needed it. I hadn't hugged her in three months, and her usually pale face was sun-kissed; her long blond hair was somehow even lighter. I took in this beautiful aftermath of a summer of love.

We jumped up and down in public, a gentle reminder that I took my bra off somewhere over the Atlantic. An obnoxious shared squeal, which I would chastise anyone else for doing, made the corners of my mouth turn upward as I dared my first real smile in months. Hannah was getting married.

*Hopefully.*

NO. There were no questions. HANNAH WAS GETTING
MARRIED. I shook the uncertainty out of my mind, choosing
instead to study the massive pear-shaped ring on her finger,
which astronauts could probably see from space.

My eyes drifted upward upon the realization that we were
not alone. Lurking at the curb behind Hannah stood a man so
unconventionally handsome that I almost choked on my own
tongue. This was Graham Hays, in the flesh. I had only seen a
close-up photo, and it did not do him justice. It also hid the fact
that perfect Hannah's Graham was entirely outside the lines.
Minimalist tattoos spilled out of his tight V-neck, of which underneath, abs undoubtedly occupied real estate. A warm smile
and three-day scruff sat upon his face, with a thick head of dark
brown hair on top. Hannah's perfect parents could only be one
thing: devastated. I pictured her mother, Celeste, clutching her
pearls as she sobbed, "Tattoos for *our* Hannah? Where did we
fail her, Richard?"

After Graham sweetly introduced himself and grabbed my
luggage, he threw an arm around my best friend and brought
her close to him.

*The way they looked at each other.*

It was a Google Image result for "what does unbreakable
love look like?" The enemy of love was powerless here. "One
and four" had a nice ring to it.

My cockiness was interrupted by a honk so loud I gripped my
ears. I bent to see Graham pull my luggage toward a tiny neon
Smart car impatiently waiting on the curb. The honker stood
up out of the vehicle, his CrossFit arms crossed over his broad
chest. He shared the absurdly good looks of Graham, but without
oozing any of the charm. A wavy mop of wild strawberry-blond

hair sat atop a face with a stubble beard and chiseled square jaw. Wearing a pale pink button-up—buttoned one button too high—this guy was somehow both messy and inside the lines, and he was *grumpy.*

I squinted, tilting my body as I took him in. He lifted his impatient expression up from his watch, meeting my eyes. Caught, I went to look away—the normal reaction when a stranger catches you gawking—but his eyes stayed on mine, as if daring me back to him. He had the audacity to challenge social norms, scrutinizing me with intensity, as if he were an art critic and I was an abstract painting. I had no excuse but to keep my eyes glued to him, refusing to give this brazen man the satisfaction of winning a staring contest from hell. Finally, his eyes flicked up to the blue sky, as if deciding I wasn't even the kind of art you taped to the fridge.

Hannah leaned in to my ear. "That's Graham's brother, Ezra. He's kind of . . ."

Hannah trailed off, refusing to finish. She loathed throwing insults. Growing up, I usually did that enough for the both of us.

"He's an asshole? He looks like a giant asshole," I finished for her, now openly sneering at him.

Hannah smiled at me with gritted teeth. Her expression jolted me. It was rare of Hannah to even confirm horrible truths about people. Hannah shifted, turning our bodies away from the brothers, who were tasked with Tetris-ing the results of my inability to properly pack for any occasion into a tiny trunk.

"He got divorced a few months ago. Ex-wife was a big-time cheater. He's bitter, and . . . I think he hates me."

"No one could hate you. Hannah, I've known you for thirty-one years, and you've never made an enemy."

Her wide eyes told me Ezra was the exception.

"Ezra keeps telling Graham, if he could get married after being with someone for four years and not really know her, how can Graham know me for six months and think it's going to last? Ezra thinks this wedding is a mistake, and he's not quiet about it."

Sure, Ezra was not entirely wrong. Yet, I assured myself that my friend was blissfully happy, and I reminded myself that my shaky future hinged on getting her down the aisle. This week, Ezra had to be silenced.

I slid into the passenger seat, and I let my eyes move upward into the rearview mirror. Hannah and Graham were nestled together in the tight back seat, her head resting on his shoulder. Their fingers were intertwined, both studying each other's hand as if it were a treasure map.

This picture-perfect image of my best friend in love made me beam, but my happiness was short-lived. I could feel my genuine smile turn wistful, and I couldn't shake the pain trembling behind it. I couldn't shake the feeling that Rylan should be sitting in this car with me.

I willed my brain to not build a fort in Wallow City, but heartache was a fickle force to reckon with, and my Xanax was somewhere in the packed trunk. I closed my eyes and breathed in deeply, trying to shake my newfound inability to be happy for happy people. Instead of solace, all I could find was Jewel strumming her guitar on my flip-flopping heart.

*"It was happy. I was sad. It made me miss you oh so bad."*

Maybe I shouldn't have masochistically listened to a Lilith Fair playlist during the last half of the plane ride.

I felt eyes on me, and I looked up to the driver's seat. Ezra—

the best man, my new worst enemy—stared down at me with piercing blue irises. If those eyes weren't so naturally judgmental, one might lose oneself in them. I swallowed hard, matching his challenging face and chiseled jaw (minus the chiseled jaw) and held his sneer.

"Well, this should be fun," Ezra deadpanned, as he purposefully floored the tiny car over a speed bump. My skull hit the hard roof, resulting in confirmation that Ezra's mad-at-the-world face did in fact know how to turn a dimpled smile.

I was suddenly grateful to find my quiet despair replaced with seething animosity. I would purchase a shovel, dig a pit, and bury the best man under the altar if that's what it took to get Hannah married.

Game.

Fucking.

On.

# Sixteen

Trip Advisor dubbed driving on the regional roads above the coast of Ireland "breathtaking." It was. Teetering on the edge of a cliff in a child-sized car replaced the oxygen inside my lungs with pure hysteria. If I'd wanted to face my own mortality, I would have just sampled my neighbor's homemade ayahuasca again.

"Almost half of Irish drivers haven't passed their driving tests," gloated Ezra as he bent the car around a curve, pouring kerosene on my fear bonfire.

We rounded another tight corner, our car casually two inches away from tumbling off the rocky cliff. I clenched my glutes to keep from shitting myself, which ironically was exactly what happened that one time I drank ayahuasca.

"Graham and Ezra were born in that town *right there*, before moving to Portland when Graham was five," said Hannah. I assumed she was gleefully pointing to a cute village where townsfolk made beer, or cheese, or worshiped leprechauns, but confirmation involved opening my eyes. I was busy imagining my fun-but-devastating funeral. My morbid mind traveled all the way to the eulogy, ripe with Voltaire, when I felt the Vehicle of Death rolling on smooth ground.

I dared my eyes open to find our car passing through tall wrought-iron gates on a paved drawbridge. My jaw followed, reveling in the grandest display of fuck-you money I had ever seen. This was not one's average medieval-castle-turned-hotel. This was King's Landing after a seventy-five-million-dollar renovation.

*Be still, my stabbed Jon Snow heart.*

I took in the magnificent gray stone castle, matching turrets, expansive manicured greenery, autumn colors enveloping each twist and turn, and, not to be outdone, the surrounding lake, or as they called it here, the *lough.* "Lake" was too bland a word for glistening Irish bodies of water. On the lough, Lough Corrib to be precise, several guests were living out their best fairy-tale existence with a mid-afternoon kayak.

"Ashford Castle was built in 1228 and spent nearly eight hundred years occupied by various wealthy families. Now it's a five-star hotel, sitting on three hundred and fifty acres." Hannah was beaming, as if she had discovered the land with her tiny bare hands. "It used to be owned by the Guinness family as their country home—"

"*Oh my God*, you're such an enthusiastic nerd," I interrupted, looking at Hannah with a teasing smirk.

"One of my favorite things about her," Graham said, taking Hannah's smiling face into his hands. I caught Ezra's eye roll, and I one-upped it with a death stare.

Our car rolled to a stop in front of the main entrance where two stone wolfhounds bookended a small set of stairs leading up to a dark steel door—which looked purposely heavy, as if ready to shield us from war. Two valets, older gentlemen dressed in full regalia—black top hats and blazers—opened our doors with warm greetings.

Wide-eyed, I stepped into Ashford Castle, a grand entrance wasted on someone in ripped denim. This place was more appropriate for a lady whose gaggle of corgis followed her every footstep. I took in the opulent lobby, appropriately named Oak Hall, and I inhaled the rich scent of burning woodsy lavender candles. My eyes scanned the deep red and antique oak two-story room, which boasted generous ceiling height and a collection of Victorian paintings showcasing a variety of white dudes looking constipated while wearing wigs.

As I took a sip of the crisp elderflower and gin welcome cocktail from the check-in desk, I felt large jewels dig into my back. The overwhelming scent of Chanel No. 5 filled my lungs, and I spun around to discover Hannah's mother, Celeste. She had her usual blunt, short blond haircut that had not wavered an inch since the nineties. She stood up with perfect posture, posture that made it easier to look down on others from a physical angle, and wore a striking lavender two-piece suit. Celeste was in her early sixties, but she looked to be a decade younger, which was thanks to good genes and even better doctors. Before I could say one word, Celeste clutched my body like it had come to release her from prison.

"Thank God you're here," she said with alarming desperation.

This was the first hug from Hannah's mother that involved full-arm contact. Historically, I was met with a slight bend of one elbow and a distant pat on the back. Celeste had never outwardly disliked me, but she had also never been thrilled by my presence. Hannah was the kind of friend you wanted your daughter to have. I was the kind of friend you worried about your daughter having.

Growing up, Celeste and my mother were close, but as the years ticked on, they drifted into acquaintances, in large part because of my parents' moves, but also in no small thanks to me. My mother and Celeste read the same parenting novels. The results varied. Hannah was a bright and shiny J.Crew catalogue come to life, and I was a walking cautionary tale. Celeste could not help but pass judgment; she'd birthed a perfect daughter who stepped in the lines drawn for her. My mom drew the same lines, yet she realized there was no book for her daughter, no road map. This realization came sometime around when I scribbled "FUCK YOU" in gold Sharpie on the family-room TV—a proportionate reaction to having *Dawson's Creek* turned off in the middle of the pilot. One woman's "this is wildly inappropriate" was another girl's "this is the most important piece of content I will ever witness and if you keep me from it, I will wage a war." I was a humbling force in my mother's well-executed life. Eventually, she grew tired of feeling like she needed to apologize for her unconventional daughter. She reluctantly accepted my differences, because battling me to curb them was unwinnable. It was easier to distance herself from the people in her life who upon meeting me felt compelled to give her the name of a child therapist.

Celeste was one of those people. Celeste never quite understood what Hannah saw in me, and I never quite understood how Celeste birthed someone so non-judgmental and loving. Celeste would crane her neck into Hannah's room and watch me with wide eyes—the loud, hyper third grader jumping on her daughter's pink floral quilt, belting inappropriate song lyrics. Celeste tried to push different "sweet natured" girls Hannah's way—an attempt to replace her daughter's best friend with someone less dangerous—but Hannah didn't bite. I remained a constant threat to Hannah's perfection, yet I never put a dent in it. Yes, I pulled Hannah closer to flames, but Hannah walked away unscathed. Regardless, Celeste never fully relaxed in my presence—she was always on guard, terrified that Hannah might step out of line and wander aimlessly behind her directionless best friend.

Before I could voice my confusion at Celeste's display of affection, she tugged me into a quiet corner of the lobby, settling our bodies across from the fireplace.

"Now look, he's . . . fine. Graham, he's perfectly fine."

*She's already hired a hit man.*

"He holds a decent job—surprising, given the number of tattoos scribbled all over his arms. His family . . . they're not exactly the Kennedys, but they're not serial killers, or rapists or anything."

*Not. Rapists.*

Celeste gripped my arms, as if to deliver the news of a death in my family.

"Zoey, she hardly knows him. This isn't my Hannah. She's not spontaneous like you. She doesn't make decisions blindly, without thought or care."

"What an endearing description of me."

Celeste's face fell—as much as the Botox would allow.

"I fear this is my fault. When Hannah mentioned over Christmas that she was going to freeze her eggs, I told her that was ridiculous. A nearly thirty-one-year-old freezing her eggs? *Absolutely* too soon. I told her to take control of her romantic future instead, and get serious about finding The One."

If only Celeste had known this pep talk would lead her to a son-in-law with bands of leather wrapped around his wrist instead of a proper timepiece. Celeste's eyes narrowed in extreme judgment toward Graham, who stood next to his bride and a few of their friends. She looked back toward me, with eyes that were now pleading.

"You have to talk some sense into her, Zoey. Richard and I have tried, but she keeps insisting to us that that boy is 'the one' and we're being 'uptight.' I'm not uptight, am I, dear?"

I studied Celeste, whose nose was stuck up in the air as if pulled by strings.

"No, you're not uptight."

"So you'll talk to her?"

"Sure, I'll talk to Hannah."

*Surely I won't.*

Celeste exhaled and rubbed my arm, the second affectionate touch I had received from her in thirty-one years. She smiled at me warmly, with blue eyes I'd never seen shine in my direction. I felt my shoulder blades arch back, as if standing up straighter. It was an unearned, yet curious feeling. This was what it felt like to be The Good Daughter. I wondered if this was the reason Hannah so effortlessly navigated the world. Her entire life, she had people look at her as if she could do no wrong. When the world paints you one way, it's hard to throw out that canvas and start over.

Celeste returned to her crowd of similarly well-dressed friends, and I let the warm glow of the fireplace scorch my back. Across the room, Graham and Hannah chatted with the hotel's wedding coordinator, pointing out the window to the lush gardens in the distance and finishing each other's sentences. Yes, my best friend was sprinting toward a quickie marriage with a man bearing a direwolf tattoo. However, I had never seen her smile so widely—a radiant grin that was unmistakably pure and honest. Who was I to stand in the way of her happiness? Celeste was hedging her bets on a wild card: my efforts helping to end this engagement. I was betting all my chips on the opposite. I could only hope that Hannah's bliss was the eternal kind, and as a result, I would embrace my own.

As I strolled toward the check-in desk, it became increasingly obvious that this castle's original owners did not intend for it to be a place where a braless thirty-something would hand off her Platinum Amex and wait for keys to her Corrib lakeview room. I tapped my nails on the antique desk, my eyes impatiently darting from the excessive chandelier above me to the full-scale statue of a knight in shining armor glaring at me. I had never felt so small.

Correction—I had never felt so small, until I heard a low voice from across the lobby, a twist of tongue that ripped through my veins and unscrewed every joint in my body. Heart beating out of my chest, I slowly turned toward the concierge desk.

And just like that, I was undone.

# Seventeen

The Pinterest quotes (that I saved into a folder titled "You're a Loser" during the darkest hours of my breakup) were wrong. The worst thing in the world wasn't loving someone who didn't love you back. The worst thing in the world was loving someone whose tongue was down another person's mouth.

A dizzying wave of heat rushed to my head as my throat tightened. My heart plummeted to the pit of my stomach, revisiting its Summer Home with ease. All I could do was look on helplessly as the man I loved removed his grinning lips from those of a leggy blond creature.

When I was seven, my troubled older cousin spotted an opossum in my backyard and decided it would be hilarious to startle it with the sound of a whoopie cushion. Instead of making a run for it, the sound forced the opossum into instant shock. It curled into the fetal position, playing dead. The freeze response.

Despite begging my body to hide behind one of the many pieces of oversized furniture, or possibly inside the knight's shining armor, I was unmovable. *Frozen.* I was the opossum, floating outside my paralyzed body. Unlike the opossum, playing dead didn't do shit to repel my emotional predator.

Upon spotting me, Rylan managed an apathetic half-wave with an expression so distant it made me eager to meet my death. My eyes shifted back toward him as his strong gait moved forward with *her* clutching his arm.

Before I could catch my breath, Rylan's cedar scent was back in my veins, tightening my throat with a supercut of every emotion I'd experienced since the last time he stood in front of me. His bright green eyes met mine, wrapping my heart up in a rubber band and pulling tight.

"This is Mara," Rylan said, as if in slow motion, as the rubber band snapped on my chest. He appeared unshaken, but I watched with wide eyes as he tapped his fingers against his jeans—a flicker of discomfort amid his usually cool demeanor, as if I were a chore he had to get out of the way before he could engage in free play.

Mara's Disney Princess blue eyes glimmered, matching her perfect peach smile that reached the corners of her mouth effortlessly, probably without the help of medication. I hated every inch of her—there were many inches—and sadly most of Mara was made up of long legs wrapped up in tight red Lululemon pants that did everything for her toned and slim figure. She didn't have a bad angle. She stood a few inches taller than me and looked proportionally perfect next to Rylan. If I were a stranger and saw these two walking the streets of New York, I would physically stop to marvel at their combined beauty. They were a Cartier ad at Christmas.

I thrived off competition in the workplace, but never vain competition with another woman. Nothing was more pathetic than grown women taking measuring sticks to each other's skins. This was a steadfast belief, and yet, I couldn't help but become the woman I loathed. Insecurity invaded my once-confident bones, and I powerlessly handed over my feminist card.

There should be a rule that the man who breaks your heart can supersede you only with someone less attractive. This should be an addition to the Bill of Rights: No Right for a Man to Move on with Someone Hotter. Someone Hotter opened her naturally full lips.

"I've heard so much about you," the perfect body spoke. Correction: she did not speak, she breathed, with an effortlessly husky voice that winked, *"I swallow!"* Mara smiled, bringing my sorrowful eyes up from her legs to her heart-shaped porcelain face.

I forced my lips into a pursed smile, a fictitious acknowledgment of Mara, as if to say, *"I approve of you having sex on the regular with the man I long to pull into a dark corner and slowly undress. Ideally, we'd have sex by the fireplace, for old times' sake."*

Oh, the fireplace . . .

My mind began to wander toward the section that stored memories. I started to open the heaviest door of my frontal lobe, the door marked "Rylan and Zoey"—but I stopped myself. I would not rewind to the moment Rylan and I silently fell in love in front of the roaring fire in Lake Tahoe and then had the most emotional sex of our lives. *I would not.*

With the sound of Rylan clearing his throat, I came back down to Earth. I looked up from the fireplace, locking eyes with his hardened expression. He knew where my mind was daring to go, and I prayed he was overcome with an equally crushing emotional assault.

Mara slipped her dainty hand through his restless fingers, and he tightened a grip around them, grinning quickly at her. Before I could picture the horror movie of Rylan fucking Mara by the fireplace, Hannah heroically sidled up next to me with wide eyes atop a forced smile. She clutched my limp arm, and I took her hand in mine. She squeezed my hand twice, like I was a toddler receiving a shot.

Growing up, Hannah had always sensed my descent into Danger Zone, and she seemed to defuse the overreactions looming inside me with two simple squeezes of my hand. It was a tiny thing she did, but to me, it was everything. My mother effortlessly added fuel to fires waiting to erupt within me, and I longed for someone who could just tell me to take a deep breath without making me feel like my emotions weren't valid. Hannah was that someone. I gripped her hand back.

"What are you two up to?" Hannah asked.

"We just made an appointment for falconry lessons," Mara said, like I should know what "falconry lessons" were.

Since I had lost the will to speak, Hannah stepped in, explaining the Irish "privilege" of learning how to fly a falcon, which consisted of releasing a winged creature into the air and then getting it to land back on your hand. One person's privilege was my personal nightmare.

Mara's eyes lit up with excitement. "You guys should come. I hear it's *exhilarating*," she hummed, raising her thick lashes at Rylan and reinventing the word "exhilarating."

She may as well have grabbed Rylan's shaft right in front of me. I had very recently been on a lease-to-own trial with said penis, of which ownership terrified me. However, each time Rylan touched a new place on Mara's body, I microdosed on embracing ownership, embracing Forever. Hannah squeezed my hand again, taking the reins.

"You can probably get Graham to go with you, I think he's dying to do it. I personally wanted to see the inside of the spa, but then my mom started nagging me for some 'quiet time' this afternoon. She wants to steal me away before the guests arrive later tonight." Hannah sighed. "She doesn't think we'll have one-on-one time until after the wedding."

My head whipped over to Celeste, who was chatting with Ezra in the corner of the lobby by the staircase. She touched Ezra's arm with an exaggerated laugh, which he echoed. Had the two soldiers against this blessed union become unlikely allies? I didn't have the luxury of doing reconnaissance. There was a more immediate threat: under no circumstances could I allow This Marriage Is a Mistake Celeste to have alone time with the bride-to-be. I was bad enough luck on my own. The last thing this engagement needed was a disapproving mother of the bride getting inside Hannah's people-pleasing head, just two days before the wedding.

I had to keep Hannah away from her mother. But first, I had to muster the courage to form words. I pulled Hannah in close, my vocal cords finally deciding to come to my rescue.

"How often do you get to do falcon-y things with your best friend?" I asked.

"Well, never, considering your history—"

"Great. Quiet time with Celeste can wait." I threw my arm around Hannah. "We're in," I declared.

Rylan and Hannah looked at me with matching puzzled expressions, stating in unison, "You don't do birds."

I caught Rylan's sheepish expression. It was as if he was

angry with himself for remembering anything about me. But, he was *not* wrong. I didn't do birds.

When I was eleven years old, while visiting Connecticut's Beardsley Zoo on a school field trip, an ostrich at the zoo attacked me. More accurately, I had wandered away from our class, depressed over the visual evidence of wild animals in cages. I stood with my back against a chain-link fence separating ostriches from humans, humming Sarah McLachlan, when an ostrich barreled up behind me and bit me through my pleated skirt. I had to get a tetanus shot in my ass, at the zoo. Ever since then, close proximity to birds—both big and small—inspired PTSD.

I studied Mara's palm, which lingered on Rylan's chest. I stepped closer to Hannah with gritted teeth, my eyes bathed in Rylan and Mara's display of affection as my stomach tied itself in knots. Fuck my fear of birds. Fuck all my fears. I had to reverse my fortune so I could rest *my* hand on Rylan's goddamn perfect torso for the rest of time.

"We can't leave them alone to enjoy nature," I said under my breath. My eyes darted from Rylan and Mara to Celeste, who looked over at me with a pointed expression.

Hannah glanced at Celeste and gritted her teeth into a pained smile.

"Birds it is," Hannah declared, finding winged creatures less threatening than a conversation with her disapproving mother.

"You talking falcons?" asked a deep voice.

I turned, seeing my enemy, Ezra, looming beside me with a glass of Irish whiskey in his hand and a disdain for life in his heart.

"I'm in," he said, staring down at me with eyes that I wished would bore a hole into a different victim.

"The more the merrier," said Hannah with a smile, trying.

"Not sure that phrase applies here." I smirked, eyes on Ezra.

Hannah turned to me with a pursed smile and wide eyes, tilting her head toward the corner of the room, where Graham was waving her over. Graham stood in between two men in their thirties. They had sweaty bodies and were incredibly fit, both post-run and doing calf stretches and knee bends while they chatted with the groom.

"Graham was a Division One sprinter in college," Hannah apologized through gritted teeth.

"Oh God. Does that mean you have to feign interest in running?"

I had no patience when it came to hearing about anyone else's physical activity. The worst, by far, were the runners and the way they celebrated and shared with the world their ability to put one foot in front of the other. It was possible that my hatred came from a place of both lack of coordination and envy, but you didn't see me Instagramming a map of where I drunkenly stumbled from happy hour drinks on the Upper West Side, to dinner in Hell's Kitchen, to late-night drinks in Battery Park. And let me promise you, that was much more of a victory than the roundabout trail of some guy leaving his apartment at five thirty in the morning and ending up back where he started two hours later. Mazel tov on finding an innovative way to run in a circle, but stop publicly asking me to celebrate it.

"If I'm not back in three minutes, rescue me."

"I will be your Enrique Iglesias," I promised, as Hannah slid away to hear in excruciating detail about resting heart rates.

Ezra started to step away, and I shifted my body toward him, my shoulder cornering his surprisingly hard chest. He stood still in front of me, raising his blond brows at me.

"Getting to know Celeste?" I asked, attempting casual.

"Oh, Celeste? She's just . . . *lovely*."

This was undoubtedly the first time Ezra had used the word "lovely," and I knew with all my broken heart that he didn't mean it. I inched closer to him.

"Can I help you?" he asked, his full lips curling into a coy smirk that I was eager to wipe off his face.

"I understand that you're dying inside over your ex-wife, but if you take it out on my best friend, if you ruin her big day, I will castrate you."

He swirled his drink in his large hand, a tight grin on his mouth as he scanned every freckle on my face.

"I find it strange that you, the bride's 'bestie,' are more concerned with me ruining this wedding, and less concerned with what it means that you think I could."

I narrowed my eyes at him, too exhausted to piece together his twisted words.

"You think they can weather a storm? A light drizzle, and those two are done," he pontificated.

I looked across the lobby, watching Graham lift Hannah's fingers up to his mouth, playfully biting her knuckle in a smile. It lit me up, but a warning twitched in my gut—a little voice whispering, *"Ezra might be right."* Unbreakable unions only succeeded if a couple sheltered each other through life's storms. Hannah and Graham were about to spend the rest of their days together, and they had never even faced the rain.

"From what I hear, you're not exactly the expert on love," I said, covering lingering doubts with vitriol.

"I've heard the same about you, sweetheart."

Before I could wonder who told Ezra what, against my will,

my eyes drifted toward the evidence of my failure, low laughter coming from the concierge desk. Rylan and Mara grinned at each other, sifting through a spa pamphlet. I felt Ezra's eyes narrowing on me as I studied Rylan. I was painting a picture for my enemy: here lies Zoey's emotional kryptonite—do with it what you please. It was reckless. But I couldn't stop myself. I couldn't look away. I was a moth, Rylan was the flame.

The idea of someone else giving Rylan something I could not, the mere idea of Mara giving him Forever—it was a thought so nauseating it made me want to burn down a small town to make it untrue. I didn't understand why jealousy got such a bad rap. Maybe it wasn't a poison, but rather, a cure. Maybe jealousy was the maker of clarity.

I turned back toward Ezra. A shit-eating grin split across his dimpled cheeks. His personality was wholly unappealing, yet he had a jawline that could get away with bloodshed. I preferred when outsides matched insides. Ezra stepped closer, his eyes drifting from Rylan to me. I could feel the heat of his chest against my forearm as he looked me square in the eyes.

"So, are you going to have some sort of meltdown or something?"

It was a good question.

# Eighteen

I lumbered into my lake-view room, refusing to take it in, and instead plopping face-first onto the bed with an exhale. I buried my face into the green sham and dug from deep below my diaphragm to exhale a full-body scream, which I muffled into the pillow. I waited for my heart to return to an acceptable pace, and then I flipped over, kicking off my boots and opening my eyes to find a sweeping cream canopy above my head. I shifted, taking in every corner of this hotel room, finding that the bed, just like the room, was covered in emerald green with hints of gold throughout. The quiet lough glistened outside my window. Swans smiled back at me from yards away. It was heaven.

*I was in hell.*

I grumpily sat up and flipped through the hardbound guest booklet on the bedside in hopes that this castle came equipped with on-site therapists. Instead, I found information for on-site archery. Clay shooting. Zip-lining. I had to hand it to Ireland. Here was a peaceful country with so many ways to take out one's misplaced rage. Luckily, a double knock at the door stopped me before I could make an appointment to hold a gun. I opened the door expecting my bag, and instead, I found my baggage.

There Rylan stood, just inches from me, not a Mara by his side, and appearing unfairly huggable. He stared down at me, biting at his bottom lip, and all I longed to do was step in and help.

As I fought the urge to pet him, Rylan shifted his body, glancing down at his fingers. A rare flicker of discomfort from the most confident man I had ever known gave me hope that I meant something to him, but in a flash, his discomfort was gone. His spine straightened and his green eyes turned cold, looked right past me. It was as if he had changed the channel on his emotions, and I was currently tuning in to the IDGAF network.

"I came by to make sure this won't be awkward, for Hannah's sake. I just . . . I hope we can get along as adults this weekend. As friends, even," he said.

The mouth that I wished would devour my face had just wished me to be its friend.

*Knife, meet heart.*

"I'm here to celebrate Hannah," I somehow managed.

He stared at me with a reluctant expression. Silence lingered between us, and while it would have been an appropriate time to keep my mouth shut, doing so was difficult, seeing as I hated uncomfortable silence. So I kept going.

"They're great together . . . Hannah and Graham. They really seem like they're meant to be"—and I glued my eyes onto his, purposefully trying the word out—"Forever."

Maybe if I said "Forever" aloud enough times, maybe if I said it without swallowing a little bit of vomit, I could convince myself that I wanted it. He looked down at me with a curious expression.

*I would die to press my forehead onto his furrowed brow.*

"'Forever'? Aren't you allergic to that word?"

I was allergic, but I had just started taking Emotional Claritin. Hannah would make it down the aisle, and I would find myself rid of this self-sabotaging allergy.

"People change," I said, shrugging coolly, as if I weren't trying to convince myself (I was).

Rylan pursed his lips together. His iciness stunned me. There were no hints to reassure me that his heart was breaking at the sight of me. His hands were steady, unlike mine, which were shaking, desperate to reach out and take comfort in him. I longed for him to stare at me with force behind his eyes, sadness, fire, anger—anything but the way he was looking at me now, like I was a stranger. Meanwhile, my brain was busy battling the masochistic urge to bring up All Things Mara. All the things I didn't want to know.

*I have to know.*

"So, Mara . . ." I cracked, pretending his girlfriend wasn't the reason I was going to sob into my pillow that night.

"I met her a couple weeks after . . ." Rylan refused to finish the sentence. I guess the elephant standing between us in this tapestried hallway was to be ignored completely.

"I wasn't looking for anything," he continued. "Mara was my point person at Feed the Children, and we just—well, you know."

Oh, *now* I knew. My stomach knotted up with wild insecurity—yet to be fair, I'd asked for it. I now had confirmation that Mara was not only otherworldly beautiful, but also the Feeder of Hungry Babies. Which was cool, because I had just ideated a personal lubricant experience for K-Y, which involved a Slip 'N Slide competition in the Hamptons. Up until three seconds ago, I had actually been proud of my brainchild. However, I did not use my potential to save hungry children, and for the first time in my life, I felt vapid. Only one of our jobs suggested "First Lady Wikipedia material." Even worse, only one of us was insecure enough to keep score.

*Mara, one. Zoey, zero.*

I looked up at Rylan, whose eyes were *now* registering anxiety, as he clenched his palms and stared down the sprawling hallway. I peeked out of my doorway to see what had made him come to life, and I spotted a tall, dark-haired woman sauntering in our direction—her glowing frame dwarfed in an oversized plush robe. She was fresh from a spa treatment, and with each forward step, the air began to thicken with wafts of lavender oil and superiority. *Gemma Harper.* My body tightened and my eyes matched Rylan's. His mother stopped at her door, searching for her room key as she spotted Rylan. She opened her mouth to greet him, but her jaw followed as she noticed me standing across from her son.

Gemma had only ever looked at me sideways, as if I was a mystery unworthy of solving. The worst part? I had proven her right. I weathered an excruciatingly long moment of silence, taking in Gemma's arctic expression with wide eyes. She was openly displeased to see me, and especially horrified to see me in close proximity to her son. Rylan's eyes darted between us both, uncomfortable and searching for a non-existent Eject button.

"Zoey. Well . . . you would be here, wouldn't you?" Gemma said, with a passive-aggressive tone.

I maintained a smile on my face—a smile that doubled as a middle finger. "I am the bridesmaid, after all."

"Bridesmaid . . . I was told that hasn't worked out so well for you in the past," Gemma said, as she glared at me coldly.

My stomach twisted in shame and anger. I slowly turned to Rylan, shocked that he'd divulged any part of our ending to his mother. He looked back at me with blank eyes. He knew that my bridesmaid failures weren't something I shared with the world. They weren't a piece of my history I wanted to arm his disapproving mother with. He knew all of this, yet his expression told me it was no longer his duty to give a shit. Gemma took a baseless and immediate disliking toward me—an animosity that never wavered. Rylan had once cared so deeply about how much his mother hurt me that it drove a wedge between them. That guy and that wedge? *Gone.* I pictured Rylan detailing our breakup to his mother—Gemma pretending to be devastated for her son, while silently throwing a gala.

"Have you met Mara?" Gemma asked, taking my pained eyes away from Rylan. This bitch really wielded an unstoppable verbal sword.

*Has your fist met my face?*

My pageant smile managed to stay in place. "I have," I said.

I looked at Gemma, holding my smile, seething inside. She raised her eyes at Rylan, eyes that begged him to leave my presence, immediately.

Rylan awkwardly spun his brass room key between his fingers, barely meeting my eyes. Any other day, he would have apologized for his mother's rudeness. But not today. Not after I had wounded him. Today, Zoey Marks deserved all the cold fronts in the world.

"Well . . . umm . . . take care," he said, finding his Eject button with cowardly ease as he tucked the key into his pocket.

*"Take care"? TAKE CARE?*

"Take care?" I repeated incredulously, this time aloud.

"What?" he replied, confused as to my tone.

I felt my composure slip away. I could no longer pretend that his apathetic attitude toward me didn't make me want to leave this earth. How do you shrug your shoulders at someone who used to make you weak in the knees?

I stared into his eyes like a storm.

"Your dick was in my mouth, like, ninety days ago, but sure, address me like I'm your banker."

My body trembled right in front of him, forcing him to see the pain stinging all over me. His eyes flickered in discomfort, but returned to neutral just as quickly—giving both nothing and everything away. Rylan was just two steps away from wrapping me into his arms—and yet, he stood there with open palms at his sides. The man who'd once pulled me in close as tears formed had now caused the pain, and even worse, he gave zero fucks. Before I could let his lack of expression shoot me dead in the hallway, I edged my back against my door, disappearing into my room and letting the heavy door shut in his face.

I clasped my hands over my mouth and fought guttural sobs, my back sliding down the door as hot tears made their way down my cheeks. All I could think about for three whole months was how much love I had for this man—love I did not know what to do with. Meanwhile, Rylan had built up a wall, a barrier reserved only for me. Everything that was once tangible about him—his effortless charm, his warmth, his green eyes that searched for the meaning behind my every word—all the qualities that had pulled me toward him, they were now hidden behind a fortress of apathy. Rylan was punishing me in a way that was crueler than physical torture. The Rylan I loved—that man was reserved only for people who knew how to love him the right way.

I got what I deserved.

Indifference.

# Nineteen

A catnap and cry later, I threw on a gray mini sweaterdress and pulled suede boots over my knees. This was one of those incredibly sexy outfits that hinted, *"She didn't try to be sexy, it just happened naturally,"* even though clearly, *she fucking tried.* I caked on some undereye concealer and scurried out the hotel door to meet Hannah outside the castle's back entrance patio.

"You did *not* say that," Hannah snorted with a shocked laugh after I recounted my hallway nightmare to her. Our arms linked as we made our way down the hill of an impossibly perfect green lawn.

"Oh, but I *did,*" I said, my cheeks burning with horror as I relived the moment in which I reminded my ex-boyfriend about the time his dick was in my mouth . . . in front of his mother. I had caught Gemma's face widening in revulsion out of the corner of my eye, which was a small victory amid utter defeat.

"I guess when in doubt, bring up the last time you got down on your knees for the guy who's treating you like you don't matter?" Hannah asked, attempting to make me feel better.

I winced as I took in the sign with a white arrow pointing to the School of Falconry, which was hidden somewhere behind a distant path. Not only was I terrified to come face-to-beak with a large bird, but I was one of two females inching her way toward a narrow trail in dense woods. This appeared to be the beginning of our horror movie. It was a toss-up as to who would die first.

Hannah and I passed a group of energetic twenty-somethings who were laughing and shooting arrows into wooden targets. They looked so carefree. Carefree was how I lived my life, and yet I'd forgotten exactly what it felt like. I hadn't seen that version of myself in months. I was a prisoner in my own body. I stared longingly at the bow and arrow in a young woman's hand.

"I'm sure she'll let you borrow it," joked Hannah, sensing my interest in a violent sport.

I had no appetite for shooting the arrow. I, however, was considering throwing myself in front of the target, taking comfort inside the fantasy of someone else putting me out of this self-inflicted misery.

Suddenly, the wind began to howl, effortlessly undoing my recent attempt at taming my untamable curls. Shivering, I inched my sweaterdress's sleeves over my icy fingers as I inhaled autumn—the crisp, earthy odor of fallen leaves taking their final breaths. As leaves are torn from the trees, they emit gases and compounds into the universe—the smell of change. Autumn is a literal death of the old and a preparation for the new.

My eyes followed the golden leaves rustling over my boots, as they danced into the cloudless blue sky. Watching the wind tear the leaves off the trees was a reminder that I had come to Ireland to rewrite my heartache, to rewrite my luck. Everything around me was evolving and shifting into the next version of itself. Why should I be any different? I came here to get Hannah down the aisle. I came here to find the courage to say yes to the man I loved. But first, I had to actually change. The weight of fear was crippling me, and I had to allow a greater force to strip away the old me—the scared girl who held me captive. I felt the possibility of rising to the occasion tremble through my body.

"You okay?" Hannah asked, as she took in my wistful expression.

*Just contemplating my place in the world. No big deal.*

"Mara?" Hannah guessed, sensing I did not enjoy seeing Rylan give affection to another human.

"She's . . ." I trailed off, stopping myself before I finished with something like "a fucking cunt," because most unfortunately, Mara was not a fucking cunt.

"She's the worst?" offered Hannah, saying it, but clearly not believing it.

"It's her saving of children that's the most unforgivable. And her hair, how it just lies there so . . . correctly. I bet she has a fairy godmother and a slew of little birds just constantly wanding her bouncy hair."

Hannah threw her arm around me.

"Zoey, if you want Rylan back, just tell him. Tell him that you've changed your mind, and that you want to marry him."

*If only my brain will let me.*

"I don't want him back, per se," I said, unconvincingly, as reflected by Hannah's eye roll.

"Then why are we not letting them be alone in nature together?"

*Because I cannot let you have alone time with your disapproving mother.*

"I don't want him back . . . I just—I don't want him to be happy with anyone else. And I want his body, like . . . all over my body."

*Smoooooooth.*

"Zoey Marks, do you really want to succumb to Death by Bird just to try and show a boy that you're better than the woman he's with?"

"Do you think Rylan would cry at my funeral?" I asked, all too hopefully.

"Letting a falcon land on your arm isn't going to get Rylan back. Never in the history of humankind has a man responded to a subtle hint. You have to drop an anvil, and then you have to shove the anvil down his throat. And then, you have to wait a few days for his mind to come around."

Hannah had a point. I could march into these bird-infested woods and show Rylan that I was not the Zoey he'd walked away from. I had planned to partake in falconry as merely an innocent bystander with my hands covering my eyes at all times. I only brought Hannah here to keep her away from her mother, not to engage in some sort of wild fear-torture. Yet, why not kill two falcons with one stone? I *could* allow a horrifying winged creature to throw a party on my hand. I *could* shock the shit out of Rylan with my bravery, and paint him a picture: Zoey's "I don't know how" was not a "no." Zoey *can* face her fears. Zoey *can* change. I needed to show Rylan that there was hope for me yet. I was two days away from getting Hannah down the aisle, and I needed him to have faith in us. I ignored the other parts of Hannah's speech, the parts about this not working.

Hannah slowed her steps, stopping to stare into the distance, her shoulders bowed. I followed the direction of her pained gaze, spotting a mom chasing her young daughter across the greenery. Hannah's freckled skin turned a shade paler as she studied the squealing child.

"Hannah? Are you okay?"

She was frozen in silence. I moved my body in front of her, trying to get her face to meet mine. To my great concern, her hazel eyes were anchored on the child and the mother.

"I went to freeze my eggs this past January," she said slowly, not meeting my eyes, as if doing so would cause her to break. "I knew it might be a little early for a thirty-year-old to freeze her eggs, but you know me. . . ." Her shaking voice trailed off.

I did know Hannah. I knew my best friend like the back of my hand. I could finish most of her sentences, yet I had absolutely no idea how this one would end.

Hannah turned her head toward me, her chin quivering as tears began streaming down her cheeks. I had seen Hannah experience slight heartache before, but I had never seen her look raw. She historically expressed sadness in a controlled manner, as if properly giving herself a moment to wallow, all the while knowing she would be fine. The Hannah in front of me was broken, with no assurance that she could be put back together. Something had caused a seismic crack in Hannah's universe, and my heart beat out of my chest at the mere thought of a perfect woman in pieces. Only Zoey Marks was allowed to be shattered without glue. My eyes widened as she crossed her arms and held on to her own shoulders.

"The doctors went to retrieve the eggs and—" Pain twisted in her throat, making it nearly impossible for her to finish.

I held on to her hand, squeezing it hard, twice, the way Hannah always did for me. I was the one overly sensitive to life, constantly twisting and turning as I navigated the world. While Hannah had spent her adolescence on the shyer side, she had somehow matured into a woman who breezed through young adulthood with confidence. She sometimes needed a forceful nudge in the right direction, but she rarely needed an extra hand. But I sensed that she needed my hand here.

"The doctors, they couldn't retrieve any eggs. There's no chance I can have my own biological children."

I blinked rapidly, internally reeling. Hannah operated with the mindset that leaving her future to chance was irresponsible. She should have been rewarded accordingly, but fate didn't discriminate. Hannah's reproductive destination was a thirty-one-year-old house built very poorly and rotting away: a diminished ovarian reserve.

Hannah slowed her eyes down to her mud-stained boots, as if this cruel reality was somehow her fault. My heart dropped, aching for my best friend, and I squeezed her hand. Her fingers stayed limp in mine. I knew I couldn't make this better. What I didn't know was that it was about to get so much worse.

"Graham doesn't know," she confessed through tears, clutching her chest in shame.

*Enemy. Action.*

My lawyer best friend sure knew how to bury the lede: the groom was unaware that his bride couldn't have children. I nodded slowly, trying my best to keep my jaw in its proper place.

"We had just started dating after I found out. Zoey, I swear I tried to tell him. I swear," she pleaded, her wet hazel eyes fixed on me. It was as if her ethics were on trial.

"I believe you," I assured her, stroking the side of her arm.

Hannah stepped back from my hand, pressing her fingers into her scalp, as if sickened by her own silent betrayal.

"I tried to tell Graham, but every time, something just shoved it back inside me. And then I fell in love with him—I fell so hard—and the idea of this thing that I can't control, this thing that I wish weren't true, this thing I hate about myself—the idea that it could cause him to leave me—I just couldn't tell him. We're getting married in two days, and my fiancé has no idea that we can't have children. I'm a horrible person, right? Tell me I'm a horrible person," she begged, the final words breaking amid tears.

I pulled Hannah into my arms as her chest heaved.

"You're not a horrible person. You're just human, Hannah."

I held pain in the back of my throat. Three months ago, Hannah had been the one by my side when I couldn't stand. It killed me that I wasn't by her side six months ago when she got this news. Why didn't she trust me to help her through this? My gut sank further, realizing the hypocrisy of expecting the truth from someone I was holding back from.

I didn't divulge the full scope of my breakup to Hannah. I didn't tell Hannah about my third bridesmaid failure, which had cemented coincidence into curse. I knew deep down that this wasn't a result of us growing apart. We had simply grown up. Our problems were bigger, harder to fix, and harder to admit aloud. Holding pain, guilt, and shame as close to our chests as possible meant they were ours. Releasing our pain into the world, sharing it with the people who matter the most—that's when pain gets legs. That's when pain becomes a reality, an inescapable truth. When a Truth Monster walks among us, we're forced to face it, to fight it. In conclusion: denial was a beautiful place to live.

My eyes widened as I pulled back from Hannah, seeing Graham and Ezra walking toward us in the distance. I sucked in my cheeks, watching Mara and Rylan following behind them, hand in hand.

"We have company," I whispered.

Hannah quickly cleared her throat, wiping tears from her blotchy cheeks. I bunched the sleeve of my sweaterdress over my fingertips and erased the hints of mascara out from under her eyes as Hannah took deep breaths in and out, calming herself down.

I stepped back from Hannah as Mara came into view. She wore black stilettos, dark jeans, a red trench coat, and a matching wide-brimmed hat.

"Don't worry, Carmen Sandiego is here to save the day," I said through gritted teeth.

Hannah let out a tiny laugh, and I bumped shoulders with her, relieved to find comfort in my ability to spew petty insults amid our personal horrors.

"Am I good?" Hannah whispered, obviously praying there was no evidence of "Graham, I can't have our babies!" on her face.

"As unfairly beautiful as ever," I said softly.

Holding a smile, my eyes drifted to my side, where I could smell the winds of change wafting Le Labo in my direction. Mara's arm was wrapped around the back of Rylan's quilted jacket, her perfectly manicured fingers resting above his hip bone.

*That must be nice.*

On my other side, Graham knotted his fingers into Hannah's

and pulled her toward his denim jacket. He kissed her hard, and her nose scrunched up in the cold air, beaming from ear to ear as she stared up at his grinning, scruffy face.

I was slightly relieved to see genuine happiness splashed on Hannah's face. Yet, my stomach was in knots over the devastating truth grenade she had just tossed in my direction. I clenched my jaw, working in overdrive to keep a smile on the corners of my mouth, refusing to let Bad Luck Ovaries bolster Bad Luck Bridesmaid.

Here Hannah and I stood.

Two smiling faces.

Two best friends.

Two withholders of truths.

*Denial. What a place to live.*

# Twenty

I pulled my sweaterdress down to make certain my vagina wasn't out to the world, feeling the discomfort of a rough, damp log below my ass, and wondering how in the actual hell I let myself get here—both physically and emotionally. How was Zoey Marks, hater of winged creatures, suddenly staring one in the face? How was Zoey Marks, lover of Rylan Harper, watching him sit across from her, with another woman occupying the warmth of his lap? How could Zoey Marks, best friend to Hannah Green, so easily sweep her friend's lack-of-fertility confession under the rug?

Somehow, I was here, and "here" geographically was the School of Falconry, a dilapidated small log cabin located at a clearing in the woodlands of the castle grounds. Amid the acre of greenery enveloped in thick autumn foliage—firs, spruces, redwoods, and pines—my eyes swept past Hannah, Graham, Rylan, Mara, and Ezra, all of us sitting on fallen logs arranged in a semicircle. Our falcon instructor, a sort of sexy aging Robin Hood, held the horrifying brown creature (which I was assured was a falcon, but believed to be a dinosaur) on his arm, pacing with it.

"This is Karen, the pride of Ashford Castle," he boasted, displaying Karen to us as if she were going to lead us to the Promised Land.

I tried my best to mirror the group's awed expressions as the instructor boasted about Karen's temperament. Karen was apparently a bossy bitch—the "dominant one" of her group. I could have gone a lifetime without learning about Karen's attitude and royal lineage, or how to catch and release a large bird—and been better for it. The instructor explained how we were to extend our arms as wide as we could and then sweep the bird across our bodies. We were to hold a dead mouse by our side, and then when we wanted Karen to return to our hand, we would lift the mouse in the air and Karen would come back to us.

As the instructor talked entirely too eagerly about handling birds and decaying rodents, I watched Rylan's Zoey Upgrade brush a layer of mud off her four-inch stilettos. Mara was no Princess Diana in the land mines. There was no way her perfectly oval Big Apple Red nails would touch a feather, let alone a dead mouse.

*Mara one. Zoey—not so fast.*

I sulked on the log as I watched Mara release Karen effortlessly and then hold the dead mouse up in the air like she was waving a fur coat. Karen swooped down from the opposite corner of the woods and landed on Mara's gloved hand to a chorus of cheers. Mara pulled the hideous creature to her face, cooing at it. She looked into Karen's dark eyes, and it was as if they had an epic backstory. Mother and daughter in a past life?

*Possibly.* Whatever their connection was, I would watch that Pixar movie.

My cheeks burned and my chest ached as Rylan looked on grinning, his phone turned in Mara's direction, capturing the moment with pride—and probably imagining Mara cradling their future children.

And then, all eyes went to me.

When I replaced the CCO of Wheelhouse a handful of years ago, I was fired up. I had ascended to the C-suite at age twenty-six. I was a certified badass. All would kneel at Zoey Marks's Converses. However, the day before I began the position, a terrifying anxiety set in. I was an impostor. I was too young. My zero for two, Sara, came over to my apartment with Xanax and a pep talk. Our fired CCO was deeply hated, so the bar for success was low. I would have only had to worry if I'd been following a legend. "You never want to be the person who follows a legend," Sara warned.

Well, here I sat, terrified of birds, following Mara the Legend. The instructor hovered over me, shoving his ratty glove and Karen the falcon into my personal space. My eyes wandered toward Rylan, who stared back at me. All the adoration he had extended toward Mara had vanished, and his expression was simply . . . unconvinced. He leaned back, as if he was waiting for me to disappoint everyone. A need to substantiate my worth boiled through my veins—but it did not, however, do a goddamn thing to etch away at my bird fear.

I closed my eyes with a sharp inhale—a reminder that I wanted to prove to both myself and Rylan that I was capable of change. I opened my eyes on my ex-boyfriend, suddenly emboldened, and I felt myself pull two hardened worker's gloves over my cold fingers. I felt my damp ass ascend from the wet log. I felt one gloved hand grow heavier, and my courageous brown eyes drifted downward to find my hand occupied by a small dinosaur.

A pointy black beak was inches from my face. Two beady eyes blinked back at me. Sharp claws etched themselves onto my gloved fingers, and the rest of the world disappeared. In the expansive green patch of heaven, the forest surrounding us, all that existed was me, Zoey Marks, and Karen, the winged creature who would murder me and then peck away at my decaying body.

The pounding of my own chest sounded in my eardrums as anxious sweat enveloped my body. I clenched my eyes shut.

And I ran.

"GET IT OFF ME, GET IT OFF ME, GET IT OFF ME!" I screamed, as I zigzagged across the lawn with a bloodcurdling yell, an assault upon this peaceful landscape.

I ran for what felt like miles, my feet hardly touching the ground, as if I were weightless, soaring aboveground. The cold wind pounding against my face slowly brought me down to earth, and I opened my eyes to discover that I had barely made it a handful of yards from my original start. I was running through the opening in the woods in a circle, swatting my arms in front of my face, trying to get this winged creature away from me. But Karen was still there, attached to my glove like a new appendage.

"STOP FLAILING YOUR ARMS, YOU'RE GOING TO STRIKE KAREN!" the horrified instructor shrieked, running on my heels.

I clenched my eyes shut again, and suddenly, I felt my arm grow lighter.

"IS IT OFF ME? IS IT OFF ME?"

"It's off you," assured Hannah, from somewhere in the distance.

"*Kaaaaaaaaaaaaren!*" the instructor howled.

I dared my eyes open, only to find Karen swooping down from the sky, barreling toward *me*.

I scrambled, fighting to become one with the wet grass below me, pulling my body into the fetal position and clutching the mouse in my fist, holding dead Ratatouille up in the air. It helped greatly that my ex-boyfriend and his hunger-fighting girlfriend were watching with open mouths as the tiny dinosaur dove onto my innocent hand.

"GET IT OFF ME, GET IT OFF ME, GET IT OFF ME!"

Our wide-eyed instructor saved Karen from my flailing arms as I hyperventilated in the middle of the open field. I rolled my grass-stained face toward the sunny sky, rediscovering how to breathe. I was alarmed that I could move my tingling arms, that I could feel my chest beating . . . that I was alive. I wiped the beads of terror dripping down above my top lip, realizing instantly that I was wiping my mouth with the white fur of a dead mouse. My following scream woke neighboring villages.

Trembling, I slowly sat up and took in my surroundings. Standing a few feet from me, Hannah tried her best to appear sympathetic, but I could tell her clenched jaw was fighting not to crumple into hysterics. Next to her, Graham rested his hands on his knees, his body curled into tears of laughter. Hannah ribbed him in the stomach, trying to get him to pull himself together, but he could not. And I did not blame him. Next to Graham, Ezra held his phone in my direction, filming me with a wide-eyed shaking head and a sarcastic thumbs-up.

Suddenly, I felt a gentle hand rub my back in a circular motion.

"Are you okay?"

Mara's sympathetic big eyes peered down at me as she consoled me with a fucking back rub. Mara, hero to all. My eyes drifted from her up to Rylan's crossed arms in the distance. His expression showcased the reality that he expected nothing less from me. Here lay visual evidence that Zoey Marks was no Fighter of Fears. If men could take hints, this one would have screamed, *You dodged a bullet.*

We made our way back to the castle as I attempted to wipe grass stains and shame off my body. Hannah picked a leaf out of my hair, flicking it to the ground.

"I think I got most of it," she lied.

"Did you see the part when Mara rubbed my back?" I sulked.

"That was a nice moment for her," admitted Hannah.

"Less so for me."

"Much," Hannah reluctantly agreed, sympathetically linking her arm in mine as I watched Mara's bouncy blond curls rest on Rylan's shoulder, their in-sync bodies strolling side-by-side in front of me.

Hannah tried to take my mind off my bird failure, letting me know that she planned to spend the next couple hours with her mother, a plan I quickly thwarted with the announcement of surprise spa appointments. This was a lie I prayed I could blame on the innocent spa reservation desk once we got there.

My fake plans were upended when Graham got a phone call. Apparently, if you plan a wedding in three weeks, you can expect a little poo in your caviar.

"So, we've got a problem," Graham said as he ran toward us, tucking his cell phone into his jeans.

It turned out that the wedding band, which Graham had assured Hannah he would take care of, would not play one tune on Hannah's song list. This band only performed songs by Irish singers, no exceptions. The band's name was Irish Only, which Hannah forcefully said to Graham "should have been a *hint*."

Hannah did not care about flower crowns, or nails, or matching shoes. Hannah (and I) lived for music. We treated our favorite albums like security blankets, like beta-blockers, like time machines. Not having the right music at Hannah's wedding felt more ominous than my future.

"Relax," Graham said, putting his hands on either side of Hannah's trembling body.

I grimaced, sucking in air and preparing for the End of Days. When a man tells a woman to relax, it is the verbal equivalent of extinguishing a brush fire with gasoline. Without question, Adam told Eve to relax after she ate that apple and got all naked, and *that's* why we are eternally fucked.

"*Relax?* U2 is now the soundtrack to our wedding. We're going to have our first dance to 'Beautiful Day.' YOU RELAX," roared Hannah.

"What's wrong with 'Beautiful Day'?" questioned Graham, not realizing he was digging his own grave.

Hannah stared up at Graham as if he didn't know her at all. How did Graham not know her intensely negative feelings regarding U2?

"Wild thought, but shouldn't you know your almost-husband's favorite band?" Ezra interrupted, at the same moment I tried to suppress that very thought echoing in my mind.

The question lingered in the air. Hannah and Graham both scowled at Ezra, and then turned back toward each other. Hannah was not done. Hannah had only gotten started.

Hannah was a divorce lawyer, which shocked most people

who knew her personally. While Hannah went out of her way to please everyone—sometimes at her own expense—at work it was a different story. Hannah granted herself permission to unleash every ounce of unused fury—which she had bottled up from years of smiling and nodding—onto opposing counsel. The first time I witnessed Lawyer Hannah, she was on the phone, pacing in my New York apartment, her usually delightful expression darkened in a furrowed brow, her usually gentle hand clenched into a white-knuckled fist. It was like watching your friend shop at Goodwill for twenty-five years only to discover she lived in a mansion. Lawyer Hannah came out to play when she was challenged or threatened, exposing the shark side that earned her over three hundred dollars an hour. Depending on how you looked at it, Hannah was an excellent fighter. She was also admittedly not a *nice* fighter. Once she got going, she often got so wrapped up in winning an argument that she would say absolutely anything to get there.

"Remember the time that Apple forced a U2 album onto all our iPhones, like that was a gift we asked for? It was an *assault* on my music catalogue, that's what it was. An auditory assault. I had to delete each song. *Manually*."

Hannah seethed, putting a final exclamation mark on her Fuck U2 argument. "I don't even like that song from *Reality Bites*."

This seemed especially petty given that Hannah and I had watched the end montage set to U2's "All I Want Is You" so many times that the Blockbuster tape got jammed in my VHS player. It was like taking a knife to Bono in a dark alley for no reason, after he had just donated money to save innocent children. Again: not a nice fighter.

Graham stared slack-jawed at his spiraling fiancée, most likely weighing his prideful longing to defend Bono with his impending nuptials. I, for one, refused to give Bono the satisfaction of birthing my zero for four. My eyes darted between the bride and groom, the grinning best man, the man I loved, and the woman whose hands were keeping warm in his pocket. I had to do *something.*

"THE CRANBERRIES ARE IRISH," I said, extremely loudly, anticipating that no one could argue over the masterpiece that was No Need *to* Argue, and knowing full well it would make Hannah crack.

Eyes drifted toward me. Graham and Hannah looked back at each other. I could tell Hannah wanted to release her stubborn convictions, but she would never be the first to crumble. To my great relief, Graham did not have much of an ego. He carried himself with confidence, and lucky for him, unlike most people, his outward confidence did not come with a host of hidden inward insecurities. *Fuck him and his probably wonderful childhood.*

Graham placed his hand gently on Hannah's cheek.

"Look, I'm sorry. I should have done more research. Irish Only had all of these great reviews, and I just—"

"Stop," interrupted Hannah, looking up at him apologetically. "I'm sorry. We planned this so fast, *of course* not everything is going to be perfect."

My body exhaled as Hannah wrapped her arms tightly around Graham's jean jacket.

"I'm sorry I overreacted," she whispered with a smile, her lips close to his. He leaned down and kissed her with a sly grin. Hannah then took back her skewering of *Reality Bites,* asking for forgiveness from Ethan Hawke's spirit and promising Graham that U2 could have its moment in the sun at the reception.

"I do like the Cranberries," Hannah muttered softly, looking down at her heavy-footed stride as we approached the castle's entrance.

I took in Hannah's drooping posture, her expression empty as she twirled her engagement ring. I had seen this look before, but not from Hannah. Right before she walked down the aisle, Rebecca had the same faraway look in her eyes, which I had chalked up to a nervous bride.

*Lesson learned.*

After Rylan walked out of my life, guilt snowballed through my body and settled in my chest. It left me moving through life with the weight of regret tugging at my heart. There was another regret that echoed over and over again: Why did I walk down the aisle instead of turning back around and reasoning with Rebecca? If I had really done everything in my power to defrost Rebecca's cold feet, if I had put in the work to get the bride down the aisle, then I probably wouldn't be bathed in loneliness with a cursed soul. If I had seen Rebecca make it down the aisle, I might have said yes to Rylan with the enthusiasm of a Disney princess. Not all bystanders are innocent.

Screw the spa appointments I didn't make. I would march up to the concierge, demanding information on every live band in a fifty-mile radius. I went to do just that, when I heard Graham's voice.

"Hi, can I speak to Max at the concierge desk?" he asked into his phone, winking at Hannah.

"Graham, stop. Our wedding is in forty-eight hours. Just let it be—"

Graham interrupted her, tucking his phone under his ear and holding on to Hannah's arm with wide gray-blue eyes that stared into her soul. "I'd move a mountain if it meant I'd never have to see you look this sad again."

My heart fluttered. I believed his words. I believed this man would move a mountain to put a smile on my best friend's face. Staring back at Hannah, I knew she would move a mountain to hold on to him Forever. Hannah's fertility secret was a looming rain cloud. But the sunshine was strong. So what if this was happening quickly? So what if they didn't know each other's favorite bands? So what if Hannah was hiding a life-altering piece of information from Graham? So fucking what?

*Mountains. They would move mountains.*

Hannah stepped to the side of the trail with Graham as he talked on the phone. Ezra plodded beside me, clenching his jaw at the now happy couple.

"He'd move mountains for her," I said, gloating, enjoying the fact that this quick resolve was probably eating away at Ezra's soul—if he had a soul.

Ezra spun toward me on his heels, and I drew in a breath, stopping short of slamming into his torso. He brushed his wavy hair out of his eyeline, looking down at me with a bitter smile. I kept his gaze and purposefully took a large step backward.

"They don't know a goddamn thing about each other, and they're getting married in two days. But yeah . . . *mountains.*" He paused, his sky-blue eyes squinting at me. "This should bother you more."

"You bother me plenty," I assured him.

"You know what I mean."

"I really don't, nor do I care to."

I lifted my chin to the air and charged past Ezra, sideswiping his solid shoulder as I caught up with Hannah.

"What was that?" she asked, eyeballing Ezra.

"Just casual hatred."

"It looked kind of . . ." She raised her eyebrows.

"Kind of *what?*"

Before Hannah could finish her sentence, Graham hung up the phone and sidled next to her. It turned out, there was one band that was available the night of their wedding, and they were playing at a tiny pub in Cong right that minute. Hannah's face brightened at the good news. She didn't need that fake facial after all.

"Who likes live music?" Graham asked with a sweet smile, pulling Hannah in close to him.

"I love live music," I heard Mara whisper, as if "live music" were a novelty.

*We all love live music, you basic whore.*

My muscles tightened as pain ran down my jawline. I wondered how long I'd been clenching my teeth. I could feel myself slipping. I could feel the green-eyed monster taking over as we piled into the castle's complimentary Range Rover. I wanted to scream, but I had no one to scream to.

Ezra moved to click in the seat belt next to mine. His knuckles aimlessly brushed against my leg, causing a tingle up my spine. I shoved his hard thigh out of my way as I dug for my seat belt under his leg.

"Buy me dinner first, princess."

I shot him a look of disgust, and he cocked a brow back at me as the seat belt finally found its home.

I glanced in the rearview mirror where, to my shock, Rylan's eyes weren't fixated on Mara, whose face was nestled on his broad shoulder. Rather, his green eyes were locked onto mine. But this time, nothing about his expression was indifferent. His eyes burned with anger. Before I could make sense of his fury, Rylan unglued his eyes from me.

Our car rolled down the bridge, leaving the castle in the distance. I turned away from the rearview mirror to find an even more perplexing sight: Ezra was looking out the passenger-side window with a distant smile on his face. It was the first time I had seen his lips curl into anything resembling honest positivity.

It was a smile I had every right not to trust.

# Twenty-one

We stepped into a claustrophobic, dimly lit bar off Abbey Street, one that had been there since 1818 and hadn't changed much since. It was mid-afternoon, mostly empty, except for a handful of plump older gentlemen seated at the worn wooden bar, clutching their Guinness pints and coughing atop their own hearty laughs, as light cascaded inside through the stained-glass windows.

We looked to the stage, where an adorable old man who had roughly five years left in his life span sat hunched over a microphone with his unenthusiastic and aging band behind him. He sounded like an Irish Bob Dylan. Not Bob Dylan at peak Bob Dylan time, present-day Bob Dylan. He was singing Selena Gomez's "Hands to Myself." It was an assault upon both our ears and our imaginations.

I glanced over at Hannah, whose jaw was on the floor as she took this in. I drew my cell phone out of my back pocket, desperate to find another band, to make every part of this wedding perfect, to never see sad-faced Hannah again, but the bride-to-be stopped me. She was clearly confused as to why this meant so much to me.

"This is the part where you're supposed to do your Zoey Thing and tell me we 'can't control life, but we can drink the hell up.'"

Hannah smiled at me, cheeks that assured me they weren't going to be flailing against the wind as they ran away from the wedding. Irish Only was playing her wedding. It was "meant to be."

Three bitter ales later, I was alone at the bar, accidentally sitting next to Ezra. The other two couples had found corners of the room to gawk lovingly at each other, while we sat at the bar in silence, shoulder to shoulder. I hated him. Even more, I hated silence.

"So, have you always been such a killjoy?" I asked, cutting the silence with an attempt at pleasant conversation.

"I don't know how to stop. It just comes so naturally."

Ezra shifted his body toward me on the squeaky stool, setting his drink down. He looked directly into my eyes, studying my face with such intensity that I fought the urge to hide under the ratty barstool.

"W-What?" I stammered.

He picked up his ale and took a purposefully long sip. "I don't buy your act," he finally said.

"My *act*? What act? This isn't a stage play, asshole."

Ezra nodded to Rylan, who was arched back into his chair, laughing with Mara. She grabbed his hands and gazed into his eyes, beaming at him.

"That guy just broke up with you a couple months ago after *years* together, and now you're a shitstorm of smiles in the same room as him and Miss Universe?"

I whipped my head back to Ezra, a heated anger bubbling.

"It's called 'being the bigger person.' You might want to try it."

"You're eager to watch your best friend in an infant relationship get married, when it should be you standing up there?" he questioned. "No one's that selfless."

"Nice to know you've done a thorough background check. My period's coming on the twenty-fourth, if you're keeping a journal."

"There's no way you don't think that is a mistake," he continued, nodding to Hannah and Graham.

I looked below the stage, seeing Hannah sit across from Graham at a small round table, howling in laughter as they studied a picture on her phone. Graham pulled her freckled face toward him, cupping her chin and smirking at her. It filled me up in every way.

I leaned into Ezra, prepared for a battle. I was close enough to smell a hint of the beach on his hair, coconut and orange, likely the result of salt spray taming his bedhead. *Nothing special.* I took in the light freckles swimming in his squinted eyes as he raised his brow with a smirk. It suddenly occurred to me that Ezra and I were inches from each other, and I was choosing to lean in closer. I swallowed hard, looking over my shoulder and arching my neck back coolly. He was *nothing special,* yet I was letting him crawl under my skin. I raised the bottleneck of my glass.

"I can't imagine why your wife left you, you're such a pleasure."

"Princess, there's a reason no one's put a ring on your finger," Ezra hit back, clinking his glass to mine.

I fumed. Ezra didn't know the details. He didn't know that I'd turned down Rylan's proposal. There *could* be a ring on my finger. If I wanted. Which . . . I was working on wanting. I went to tell Ezra how eternally desirable I was, when I realized he had a slow smile spreading across his mouth, and his eyes were no longer pointed in my direction. Ezra winked across the bar at the old singer as if they were drinking buddies, as the band began playing U2's "With or Without You."

If Ezra was hoping for a breakdown from our bride, she did not deliver. Hannah was too busy holding her phone's flashlight out, swaying back and forth and fully embracing Bono.

"You're an actual idiot," I huffed, rolling my eyes.

I dug my elbow into the counter and twirled around on the leather stool. I came back to Ezra and froze, realizing Ezra's eyes weren't fixated on Hannah. All of his attention was on Graham.

Across the bar, Hannah was in her one-ale-past-sober phase of drinking, bopping her straight blond hair along with dramatic enthusiasm to the worst rendition of Bono one might ever encounter. Graham stared up at her with a wistful gaze that appeared thematically closer to despair than happiness. As the singer painfully scratched past the lyrics, I digested an uncomfortable realization: I recognized Graham's expression. Graham was building a fort in my home away from home. He was an emotional time traveler, visiting Wallow City. *The way he looked at her.* It was as if Graham was searching for solid ground. Then, tears began to rim his eyelids.

"What did you do?" I whispered to Ezra, my chest pounding.

Ezra looked me dead in the eyes, horribly only inches apart from me.

"In a couple years, this'll be the story of how my brother *almost* married that girl whose name we all can't remember."

"What did you do?" I was now seething.

"This was Graham and Lindsay's song," Ezra delivered.

Before I could wonder who the fuck Lindsay was, Ezra happily filled in the blanks. Lindsay was Graham's ex-girlfriend, and they were together for five years until she broke up with him, only a year ago. Graham met Hannah roughly six months after the breakup.

"*Their song?* Bullshit. Guys aren't evolved enough to trade stories about their relationship-defining bops. That's just not a thing."

"When your little brother spends months crying himself to sleep, crying in the car, crying on a jog, months and months crying to one song over and over and over again, you talk about it. She broke his heart, by the way. It's interesting, like a week before he met your best friend, he referred to Lindsay as, let's see if I can remember the exact phrase. . . ." He drifted off, feigning a search for *the exact phrase.*

My stomach dropped. I knew how Ezra's sentence would end before he found the words. Lindsay was "the one that got away."

I watched Graham fight back tears, staring up at my best friend whom he was supposed to marry in two fucking days. According to Graham's glossy eyes, Lindsay occupied heavy real estate in his mind, and Hannah was following her.

*"You never want to follow the legend."*

*Fuck.*

Hannah turned her buzzed face to meet Graham's wistful unraveling. She tilted her head, her hazel eyes taking him in with a sideways *"What the hell?"*

This was it.

This was the moment Graham would reveal to Hannah that he was still in love with his ex-girlfriend. This was the birth of my zero for four. This was the crowning of an unforgivable curse. My wide eyes darted away from Graham and toward the man I loved. I watched the corner of Rylan's mouth dance upward, and I ached for nothing more than the possibility of melting into his mouth. Newfound adrenaline shot through my veins. I had to steal the hammer before Graham nailed our coffin shut.

"Are you okay?" Hannah asked Graham.

As Graham opened his mouth, I threw myself off the barstool. The three glasses bubbled to my brain as I elbowed past Rylan and Mara, who were engaged in witty banter. Breathless, I grabbed Hannah's wrist and tugged her away from Graham.

"Ow, what are you doing?" Hannah asked, as my grip led her into a chair yards away from Graham.

"I have a surprise for you," I yelled over the singer. "An early wedding gift."

"Okay . . ." Hannah looked at me sideways, full of skepticism.

I rounded past the elderly drummer, making my way to Irish Bob Dylan. I whispered in his ear and handed him a crumpled-up twenty-euro note. Ezra's Ode to Lindsay quickly faded, ending the best man's attempted assault on Forever. Ezra shifted his strong jaw, perhaps realizing he had underestimated his enemy. I slowly glanced around, seeing all eyes in this bar on me. Thankfully, the band filled the awkward silence, and the opening keys to "It's All Coming Back to Me Now" filled the room. A nostalgic grin spread across my face as Hannah's jaw dropped.

Hannah and I lived just an hour away from each other when

we began the Bat Mitzvah party circuit of our summer camp friends. At thirteen years old, attending these Bat Mitzvahs was the perfect alibi to spend as many weekends as possible with Hannah at her house—since most of the honorees lived close to New Canaan. The flimsy justification of "Mom, God wants me to attend this simcha at Dave & Buster's" somehow delivered. My mother was powerless when faced with the mere possibility of Zoey Marks embracing her Jewishness. Saturday nights were spent at various ballrooms, with different Céline Dion songs marking the first slow dance of the night. Céline echoed through each room like a starter pistol, sending anxious teenagers scrambling for a dance partner before they erupted into flames.

Hannah was shy. She was much more outwardly beautiful than I was, yet her confidence waned when faced with the possibility of failing, of being the girl on the dance floor searching for a partner. As a result, Hannah slipped away to a quiet corner the moment Céline opened her lips. I was the disproportionately confident girl dancing alone, at first searching for a partner, and then deciding it was totally acceptable to just dance by myself. At our third Bat Mitzvah, our third Céline ballad, I looked to my shy friend nursing a Shirley Temple at a table by herself and decided: we must take back these songs. I refused to let "It's All Coming Back to Me Now" hold memories of middle school hell, of not fitting in.

We spent hours in Hannah's basement, choreographing dramatic dance routines to accompany the most epic power ballads of all time. The following Saturday nights, surrounded by a sea of slow dance anxiety, we found pure joy. Hannah and I danced together among the rest of the couples, embracing our friendship, embracing our weirdness, embracing the fact that we did not need a romantic partner to feel bliss.

"Oh my God. You did *not*." Hannah squealed, springing out of her chair and instantly forgetting Graham's teary stare.

Hannah and I stood side-by-side, eyes dramatically closed, our fingers clasped together. We let our hands go, slowly drifting to opposite corners of the bar as we began our choreographed routine. We remembered every step. We were thirteen again, but way hotter and more emotionally damaged.

I danced like no one was watching, even though everyone was watching. I breathed a sigh of relief as I saw Graham's face light up—a far cry from the devastating expression that almost ruined all our futures.

"I had no idea you were an unhinged person!" Graham yelled at Hannah, tugging her down for a passionate kiss, a kiss that said "Lindsay who?"

Hannah grinned, twirling herself off him, and dipping down in sync with me in a dance move that should have gotten our thirteen-year-old selves kicked out of all the ballrooms. I took in Graham's beaming face. Why couldn't I compartmentalize like a man?

Behind Graham, Ezra bore a hole through me, hopefully realizing he was no match for this bridesmaid, but most likely not accepting it. I could see the corners of his mouth curiously twitching, as if he was forcing himself not to find any joy in my half-baked dance skills. I was a goddamn delight, and he knew it. I could see Mara's curious expression out of the corner of my eyes. Her face scrunched up as she studied something across the room. She answered her phone and her toned body peeled out of the pub door.

I tried not to look at him. I tried not to see his tall frame leaning against the wooden archway, his arms crossed across his broad chest. He was staring into my eyes with a clenched jaw. *Staring* was the wrong word. Rylan was seething.

Fucking Céline Dion. Leonardo DiCaprio wouldn't be the only one to suffer at her hands. I had forgotten this song was over seven and a half minutes long. I had forgotten it was gut-wrenching. I had never given the lyrics much reflection at thirteen, because at thirteen I didn't know I would one day live inside them. At thirteen, I couldn't foresee that the man I loved would stare at me with biting hatred while I danced like a fucking idiot to this song in front of him. He used to love my bar-dancing-wanderlust side.

*Love.*

My mind went flying, busting open the heaviest door of my frontal lobe, the door marked "Rylan and Zoey." Inside was a montage of bliss. However, pressing the Play button on any one of our cinematic moments was akin to flying too close to the sun. It felt like a warm hug, until it burned. Yet here I flew, peak Icarus, ascending past the photosphere.

Rylan and I were driving to my parents' house in Connecticut. It was five months into our relationship. He commanded the driver's seat, and I shook my head at him, my eyes darting to the speedometer that read "25 MPH." Rylan was one of those grandpa drivers who actually went the speed limit. My eye roll stopped as I took him in, his impossibly handsome grin and chiseled jaw making my insides swoon. His dark jeans and his mustard V-neck against his olive skin killed me, but they were no match for his eyes, which were nearly yellow, as if they swallowed up the dusty setting sun around us. I had it bad, and my heart was about to explode. I rolled down the windows, the warmth of the sunset wafting into Rylan's BMW.

"Why do I even bother with the AC?" he asked, shaking his head at me.

"C'mon. What's better than feeling the warm air fighting with the air-conditioning? Best of both worlds."

"Why are you like this?" he asked.

Clearly, he was both amused and appreciative that I was *like this*. I pinched his cheek, playfully pushing his face away, when suddenly, I heard Tracy Chapman's "Fast Car" on the radio. I scrambled toward the Volume dial; turning it up so that people could hopefully hear it from inside their homes. To enjoy this song, one must enjoy it in such an over-the-top manner that other people become unwilling participants. It is the rule of "Fast Car." You cannot "Fast Car" alone. You must "Fast Car" with others.

I began to sing Tracy Chapman with unearned conviction, my hands dramatically finding my chest as I tried not to butcher the Pride of Lilith Fair. Rylan slowed the car to the shoulder of the street, taking a long moment to study the wild girl next to him.

Suddenly, he grabbed the dimple of my chin and turned my face toward him. I stared at him open-mouthed.

"I love you."

I could barely hear his words, and a part of me wondered if I had imagined them.

"What?"

"I LOVE YOU," he yelled over Tracy, with the purest smile I had ever seen in my whole life.

My entire body floated above us, as if taking in the moment

so that all of it would be etched into my brain (and come back to skewer me later). I felt his fingers on my chin begin to shake. It was a little thing, but it took my breath away.

For that past month, I had known that I loved Rylan, and yet I was waiting for him to say it first. I didn't have Love Insurance, so I simply pretended I wasn't lovesick, praying the insurance would kick in before the sickness killed me. Praying he would say the words so I could cheerfully yell them back. For thirty days I knew I loved this man, and in the span of thirty days, I had gone from believing undoubtedly that he felt the same way, to convincing myself there was no possible way someone who cursed the way I did could be worthy of someone so perfect.

As I felt his hands shake, I realized something massive. "I love you" were not words that Rylan Harper said lightly. He loved me, but he loved me in a way that really meant something to him.

I opened my mouth, my voice cracking and tears filling my eyes.

"WHAT TOOK YOU SO FUCKING LONG?"

I pulled Rylan's chain necklace toward me, bringing his wide smile onto mine. We sat there kissing in the car as the sun set around us on a quiet street in Connecticut. It was the sweetest moment of my life. It was a love so great Rylan had to pull his car over to declare it in the middle of the fucking street.

*He hates me.*

I stared at Rylan as Hannah twirled me on the sticky floor of the shitty Irish bar. His current expression said, *"If I ran you over with my car, I'd probably keep going."*

Rylan didn't love me anymore. I had created this mess. I

deserved to be looked at like I was a criminal. I kept the dance going, but I could feel the hot tears surfacing. I willed them away, and I wondered if I was doing a better job of hiding my lovesickness than Graham just had.

*Graham.*

It occurred to me how monstrous my dance was—a dance to divert attention away from the fact that my best friend was about to marry a man who still loved his ex-girlfriend. I had always been Hannah's bearer of truths, good or bad, and here I was, actively betraying my best friend so that *my* heart could be whole again. The thing Hannah relied on me for was the thing I was keeping from her.

My tears were seconds away from falling. Through the haze, I could see Ezra taking me in with a puzzled expression. Something about his head tilt told me he was putting a piece together that I didn't want to arm him with. His eyes floated back to Rylan, then to me. Suddenly, Ezra's face softened, as if he was setting down his weapon. He didn't want to fight the weakest person in the room. Ezra realized what Rylan already knew: Zoey Marks was not a worthy competitor. Rylan wouldn't fight for me, Ezra wouldn't fight against me. They had laid down their weapons, because quite simply, I was broken beyond repair.

If I crumpled into a ball on the floor, if I vomited all the truths warring inside me, it would surely not be a great look. It may be "all coming back" to Céline, but there was no coming back from that.

I turned toward Hannah's ear. "I have to pee," I barely managed.

Before Hannah could catch a glimpse of my watery eyes, I

pulled away from her arms. I shoved my body past the row of chairs, holding back the tears, darting toward the sign for the bathroom at the back of the pub. My shoulder slammed into a hard body, springing hot tears from my eyes.

I peered up to find Rylan staring down at me. He searched my face, and I helplessly reached toward the door behind him, slipping into the bar's bathroom: my tried-and-true favorite place to sob when a little drunk.

I leaned against the back of the peeling door, my wet eyes staring into the mirror. I took in my reflection: the monster I had become. Grass stains on my dress from almost killing a falcon, tears down my cheeks for the love I actually killed. I had spent the day watching the man I longed to hold put his arms around someone else. I was replaceable—replaceable with better parts, parts that didn't need fixing. Even worse, I had kept secrets from my best friend, using the nostalgic sounds of our child-hood to make sure she would marry someone who couldn't give her his entire heart because it still belonged to someone else. I'd come to Ireland to reverse my fortune, to get my friend down the aisle and be able to say yes like every other woman—but at what cost?

I was a selfish, broken monster. I had to tell Hannah the truth. All the truths.

I splashed cold water on my face and stepped out of the bathroom, ready to wave a white flag at Forever. A strong hand gripped my elbow, tugging my body behind a dark archway.

I looked up, my throat closing at the sight of Rylan's green eyes on mine. His fingers were dangerously pressed against my pelvic bone, and flames tore through my body at his mere touch, a touch I had longed for. I wanted to hold every part of him, but all I could do was set my palm on his thundering chest—a confirmation that feelings for me lived there, that I meant something to him.

His expression was tortured, soft, and familiar—somehow all at once. He took me in as if he were a cliff diver standing on the edge, weighing the water below. Without a word, his grip tightened around my waist, and his broad shoulders led my back against a wall, the weight of his pounding chest pressing against mine. He was hungry for the free fall—throbbing, hard against me. But the pencil-thin gap between our open mouths told another story—he was wary of the impact.

His eyes hardened onto mine, slow fingers moving over my sweater, drawing a line up the side of my ribs. I arched my throat back, my body crawling toward daybreak as he traced the curve of my neck with the heat of his mouth. His parted lips moved upward, hovering over my ear and setting fire to my skin as I sucked in air. He knotted his hand on the back of my head, bringing my lips up to his. I could feel his exhales grow hot on my mouth—one move away from disappearing onto my tongue. And then Rylan tore every inch of his pulsing body off me like I was wildfire.

I dropped down to reality, gasping for air, my heart trying to remember how to beat without him holding it upright. I steadied my weak body against the wall, taking in his reddened face, just inches from mine. I longed for him to finish what he'd started, and I knew I was woman enough to take one leap forward and tug his every throbbing muscle onto me. But Rylan had to be the one to take that step. He was the one who'd walked away and found someone else.

Rylan held the nape of his neck, pacing in a small circle as if he were searching for solid ground. Clearly, he was thrilled with himself for falling for someone so horrible while someone so perfect was on the other side of this wall.

I brought my hands to my lips slowly, realizing something huge, something that filled up the weakness inside me.

"You still love me."

I didn't mean to say it aloud, but I couldn't not. The indifference Rylan had displayed toward me the entire day, it was body armor—it was a way of emotionally distancing himself from the person who could untether him. The look of hatred that was splashed on his face while he watched me dance, it wasn't hatred toward me. He hated himself for still loving me.

*He loves me.*

Rylan took a step toward me, his tortured face inches from mine, our burning irises glued to each other, my heart living outside my chest. With his jaw clenched in agony, he gripped his fingers onto his hair and spun around, storming away from me.

Rylan knew better than to hand the sword back to the woman who stabbed him in the heart. Rylan loved me, but he wasn't going to touch me until he had confirmation I would love him Forever. He was too rational and forthright to be guided purely by emotion.

Maybe it was the power of Céline, maybe it was the one-too-many drinks, maybe it was the crippling heartbreak, maybe it was a fear that his lips might never quiet the hunger inside me, but for the first time as I watched Rylan walk away from me, I had a feeling that I never wanted to watch him walk away again.

*Never.*

Never, the flip side of Forever.

I forced my trembling legs to regain movement, cautiously stepping back to the bar. Rylan pulled his jacket tight around his torso, as if he needed to cover up the crime—the reason his chest was on fire. He shuffled out the pub's door to find Mara still glued to her phone outside.

I looked back at the bride and groom by the stage. Graham smiled, shaking his head as he leaned back on a wooden chair, adoringly taking in Hannah swaying above him.

I exhaled with a grin, a realization that a childhood run by the World's Greatest Worrier, my mother, may have rewired my brain to look at a snowball and see an avalanche. I spent a lifetime cloaked in defensive layers around my mom—my re-belliously free spirit going to battle with her ability to worst-case-scenario any given situation. The thing about mothers? No matter how much you put up a fight, they eventually win the war to shape your neural pathways. After Rebecca's non-wedding, and for the first time in my life, I began catastrophiz-ing everything that didn't sit right—a practice that threatened my ability to live in the moment. If I was going to fully em-brace the Forever of it all, if I was going to lay down my sword and surrender to marriage, I needed to lean into hope—not worry—for Hannah and Graham.

The optimistic lens was fully on display, right in front of my eyes. Graham loved Hannah, and Hannah loved him back. *Love was enough.* The ex-girlfriend-pining and the fertility issues—they were hurdles, but it wasn't my place to force the happy couple to jump over them two days before their wedding.

There was a difference between being cursed and being an agent of destruction.

I pushed my tingling body outside the pub, letting the November air quiet my flushed cheeks. A few yards down the road, Rylan and Mara slipped into a taxi. Rylan gazed back at me through the rear window, and his eyes refused to leave mine as the car disappeared into the dusk.

For the first time, *Zoey One* had a fighting chance.

# Twenty-two

Istood in the still-steaming gray marbled bathroom, wearing a lacy black bra and matching underwear. I paused to study my body in the mirror. The breakup diet—situational depression—had effectively given me defined abs for the first time in my life, which would have been a victory, except for the fact that no one had seen me without clothes on in three whole months. Thus, my accidental abs were a victory I could share with only myself, which compounded the joys of crippling loneliness. I unhooked the white robe from the back of the door and secured it tight around my body, which I had just lathered from cleavage to toe with rich jasmine body cream. I smelled like flowers blooming in spring, and I felt like a new human.

I stepped barefoot out of the bathroom and let my damp toes dance on the soft green carpet. Grass stains were finally washed from my face, leaves were out of my hair, and my once-swollen feet had returned to a size that didn't imply I ran like a fucking moron through an open field in knee-high boots being chased by a falcon.

I pulled my wet curly hair into a top bun, plopping faceup on the bed's velvet duvet, my arms spread out wide. The sun had set, and the gold nightstand lamps softly lit the emerald room. Thankfully, there were no official plans for dinner. I would order room service and then have a few hours to pull myself together before I went to meet everyone in the billiards room for a night of gambling with Hannah and Graham's closest friends. I was unsure of what steps I would need to take to be in the same room with Rylan and keep my hands from physically tearing his clothes off his body. This was a newly sober alcoholic venturing into a bar. No good could come of tonight, of that I was certain.

I snatched my cell phone from the nightstand and my muscle memory found Taylor Swift's *Red* album on Spotify. I froze, pulling my fingers back before they hit Play. What happened in that pub was not a memory to ruminate over. It was a moment to bring back to life and revel in. It was a moment to get drunk off. My thumbs pivoted, finding Taylor Swift's *Lover* album. I pressed Play out of optimism and rolled over with a gutsy smile on my face, taking in the canopied ceiling above the bed.

My fingers grazed my mouth, which sat ajar in confused disbelief. It had been two hours since Rylan shoved himself off my body, and with each inhale, the longing for him to do the opposite grew stronger. My eyelids closed, and my fingers traveled between the opening in my robe—my entire body was on fire.

I begrudgingly opened my eyes to the harsh sound of a knock at the door and a rush of blood to the head, which threatened to bring me back to reality. I wanted to stay in the memory of Rylan's almost-kiss until it became a fantasy—until all my clothes were off and Rylan was on top of me. A housekeeper wanted to vacuum the fucking carpet.

"Can you come back later?" I called, breathlessly.

When I heard another knock, this one louder than the last, I grumbled and aimlessly pulled my hands off my body, tugging my silky legs off the bed.

I pulled open the door with a furrowed brow and a flushed face, as a gush of wind from the hallway brought the scent of cedar into my lungs. The sight of Rylan standing there in my doorway sent me to another galaxy.

Stunned, I took in his expression. It was soft, but infuriatingly unreadable. My eyes studied him from top to bottom, finding Casual Rylan at his very best. He was also fresh out of the shower, his blond hair wet and tousled. He wore a white T-shirt and navy breathable workout pants, which were perfectly snug in all the places I wanted to touch. Rylan's eyes scanned my face, then the hallway, as if weighing two sides of a coin.

If he took one step inside my room, I knew he would devour me. The thought was an intoxicating drug—it was a high I had never quite experienced before. This was floating, not falling. And so, I floated, taking two slow steps backward into my hotel room. My wide brown eyes simply dared him to follow me inside as his hand stopped the door from closing.

His eyes came back into view, somehow darkening to echo the room's wallpaper. I felt my hands shaking, desperate to touch him as I let myself drown inside his emerald eyes, for what felt like a heart-pounding century, until his unreadable expression tightened into a hunger. He unclasped his palm from the door, swept his body inside, and grabbed the back of my wet hair, pulling my tongue into his open mouth as my trembling hands found familiar ground around the back of his neck. He tasted like peppermint. He smelled like home. Cedar and jasmine swirled around us in a kiss that lit fireworks all over my body.

I tangled my fingers in his wet hair, pulling him tight against my body. I felt him get hard against my leg, a turn-on so immense that it sent a pulse below me. Our mouths not leaving each other, we spun hungrily toward the bed. I heard a lamp crash to the floor, but neither of us cared. This mess was ours, and we would clean it up later—all of it.

I tore myself off Rylan's lips, feverishly pulling his shirt off, the fallen lamp casting a shadow along his pounding torso. I settled my hand on his chest for a moment, taking him in, and he folded my body into him with hands clenched above my hips. I ran the palm of my hand along the torturously thin nylon where his dick throbbed beneath, and then I tightened into a grip, hard, the way he liked.

He spun me around quickly, forcing my hands away from him. He moved behind me, his teeth finding my earlobe, the heat of his mouth and his tongue against my ear sending my throat to the ceiling with a moan. His lips soared downward, raw desire engulfing the curve of my neck as he untied my robe from behind. He peeled the robe off my body, leaving me in my lingerie in front of him. I could feel him throbbing hard against my backside as his cool fingers slowly traced the area below my hip bone, before they dipped inside me, and with increasing pressure they stayed there, lighting a fire inside me until I couldn't take it anymore, my lungs gasping for air. I needed his touch, but more so, I longed to see his face while he was touching me. I had pined for this man, and nothing about this moment seemed fair if I could not look him in the eyes while he burned my body to the ground.

Breathless, I spun around and pulled his mouth onto mine, as I used my other hand to untie his workout pants. He helped finish the job, sending them to the floor. His body was now naked against mine as I wrapped my fingers around his balls, sending his face to the ceiling. My other hand fastened around him, gliding back and forth, the combination forcing him to steady himself against the wall. He moaned, biting his lower lip, and I cautioned myself to not let this moment end before he was inside me. I let my fingers glide up the side of his ribs as he pulled my body onto his, my swelling breasts resting below his racing chest.

I was one moment away from buckling to the floor—every part of my body on fire. He moved down the side of my chest with his warm tongue, and I felt his mouth on the lace of my underwear. I bit my lip, trying to find solid ground with my quaking legs, and I looked down the very moment that his eyes looked up at mine. His hair was an adorable mess, and there was a devilish grin splashed upon his parted lips. My heart grew two sizes. He bit the center of my thong between his teeth, twisting it in his mouth and torturously keeping it between his lips as he ever so slowly slid his warm tongue past my throbbing inner thigh. He brought his jaw back up to my flushed face as my wet underwear fell to the floor. His fingers grazed up the inside of my leg until they glided inside me, and heat enveloped my body as he effortlessly pressed hard while turning his fingers on a point that sent a heat wave through my body. My arm wrapped around him as I arched myself backward, fingernails clutching for gravity along his naked backside.

Suddenly, as I lost my ability to breathe, I felt his fingers leave my shaking body. I went to grab his wrist, to demand he put his fingers back where they belonged, but before I could regain the use of my limbs, Rylan was tightening his hands around my waist, lifting me with strong arms and easing my body onto the bed.

I felt a gust of wind as he appeared on top of me, but I could not catch my breath. His naked body hovered over mine, yet he refused to let himself sink into me. Rylan knew I was horrible at waiting. I was wildly impatient, and while anticipation was one thing—this was human torture. His clenched arms kept him an inch above my body, and I could feel his hard dick tracing a line down my leg while his tongue danced from my lips to my clavicle. He kept going, his teeth lightly biting through my lacy black bra, tugging at my hard nipple as his cool hand traveled between my burning thighs. I tightened a grip around his wet hair, my knees buckling around him, my body absolutely unable to do anything but hold on for dear life, my chest pounding and my insides enveloped in heat.

His fingers still inside me, he moved downward below my shaking legs. He removed his fingers to replace them with his tongue, and just as I was about to melt into another galaxy, just as my uncertain life began to flash before my eyes, he appeared breathlessly at my face, fastening my wrists above my head with his hand, leaving my body writhing and helpless as his emerald eyes took me in. His warm tongue filled my mouth as he sank himself deep inside, his hard body throbbing inside me. I had never wanted anything more.

All I could do was erupt.

Beads of sweat dripping down my forehead, I caught my breath, opening my eyes and learning how to inhale air. Rylan moved effortlessly on top of me, coming down to my mouth and biting my bottom lip. He let go, and I peered up at him with a breathless grin, our naked chests beating against each other, our eyes locked—our glistening sweaty faces inches from each other. His eyes darkened to uncertainty, and I moved to fill the gap between our lips, to wipe away his hesitation—when he arched his face back.

His cold necklace dangled on my chest in the space between us, and my heart fell as I soaked in his wounded expression. His eyes darted away from mine, so I held his chin, forcing them back to me. It was as if he refused to let me have power *here*, in this bed, because I had already done enough damage—I had wielded an emotional pull that led him to this room.

I was fully aware I had hurt Rylan when I turned down his proposal. However, I had been so consumed with my own heartache that I did not stop to think that maybe Rylan, like myself, was still broken. I had made a cut so deep that despite having a Mara Band-Aid, underneath it all, he was bleeding for me—bleeding because of me. The pain in his expression enveloped my eyes with hot tears. Why had I hurt this man? What was wrong with me?

His expression softened against my tears, and he stroked the wet curls away from my face with one hand, letting his palm settle on my cheek and his thumb on the dimple of my chin. I entwined my finger through his chain necklace as an exhale graced his lips, as if surrendering to something larger, as if giving me permission to bring all of him closer. And so, I did. I pulled his chain downward, bringing Rylan's open lips to mine. Our mouths met in a kiss so tender, it could have melted the universe, and we rolled over in sync, our bodies one.

# Twenty-three

Rylan rolled off me, both of our breaths shallow, bodies soaked in each other's sweat. I rested my palm between my breasts, an attempt to quiet my burning chest, my wide eyes on the canopy above me. I shifted my body to the side, folding a cold pillow under my flushed cheek so I could look at him.

Rylan's eyes were pointed to the ceiling, replaying whatever he just got himself into.

Every single night since our ending, I had tucked myself under covers and turned to the other side of the bed, the empty side, willing his body to appear beside mine. And now, here he was. I wanted to tell him this. I wanted to open my mouth and whisper, *"I missed your lips on mine every fucking day."*

"Hey," was all I could manage.

He turned toward me. I grazed my hand on his arm, his blond hair standing up at my touch.

"I should go," he said, his eyes painfully on mine, as if registering what we just did.

He shuffled off the bed, pulling his workout pants over his

perfect glutes, which was exceptionally rude, seeing as how I was not done taking in the view. I suppose when one crowns herself The Other Woman, light spooning is out of the question. *The Other Woman*. I shuddered at the title, such a nasty term.

Mara was not even a single photo on Rylan's Instagram. Three months ago, I was a framed photo on Rylan's mantel. I really wanted to feel worse than I did about stealing another man's woman, but she was not his, and she had to know it. There was no collateral damage here—no child left to split their life between two homes, no marriage broken, no long-term partnership burned to the ground. The singular weight on my chest was the fact that Rylan was about to sprint out of my hotel room and breeze into another woman's—with the scent of jasmine all over him—*my scent*.

I slowly sat up, knotting my damp and wild hair back into a bun. I pulled the high-thread-count sheet above my chest as Rylan sat on the edge of my bed, shirtless, adjusting his white Nikes. I was inches away from wrapping my arms around his broad shoulders and pulling his body back toward me. I wanted to do nothing more, yet he was not mine. The same way Rylan was not really Mara's, he was not mine to take comfort in.

I desperately needed to know what this moment meant, and I knew if I refused to pose that question, the possibilities of it would snowball inside my mind until I exploded.

"Should we maybe . . . should we talk about it? About us?"

He turned his face back toward mine, calming his hair with his fingers. He started to shake his head, as if visiting Us was the equivalent of starting a horror movie before bedtime.

"I can't. Not now. I can't, Zoey. . . ." he trailed off as he stood up. There was something about the sound of my name on his lips that crushed me.

"Okay," I barely whispered, peering up at him with wide brown eyes.

A nausea settled in my gut as I hugged a pillow to my chest, breathing in his smell of soft cedar. There was the possibility that this moment between us was just that—a moment. There was the probability that I would unwrap this pillowcase and fold it into my suitcase, stick it in a drawer back home, and smell it every day until my heart stopped aching. The scent of him. The smell of regret.

Rylan's eyes could barely meet mine as he grabbed his shirt from the floor and pulled it over his head. I could faintly see the marks of my nails on his back, and I knew they would quickly fade into nothingness, maybe just like us.

*Us.*

I breathed in the pillow again, swallowing back the tears that were forming in my throat. I couldn't just let him walk away. I began to open my mouth, to form the simple sentence *"Yes, I will marry you,"* but instead, I sat with my jaw clenched, breathing in his scent and letting Rylan walk out the door. For the second time.

Somehow, we'd made love through the entire *Lover* album, and Spotify decided to shuffle me back into the rumination of deep regret. The Spotify Gods had found the *Red* album, because . . . *of course.* The lyrics enveloped my chest, and I could almost picture Taylor Swift's pointed blue eyes tilted in my direction with a look of disdain splashed on her face.

*"Loving him is like driving a new Maserati down a dead-end street."*

Taylor knew the kicker: the dead-end street was a road I had paved. If I wanted to soar down the highway of Forever with Rylan by my side, I could. It was that simple. For any other woman, it was that simple. Why couldn't I be any other woman? I looked to my Spotify, to Taylor Swift's red-lipped album cover, as if she held the answers to all of life's philosophical questions—9:15 P.M. *Fuck.* I scrambled, seeing the time on my phone—the incredibly late time. The billiards room night was in fifteen minutes. It took me an hour to tame my curls on a good day, and this was clearly not a good day.

I tossed my naked body off the bed. Lightness shivered up my spine, and I plopped my bare ass down to the carpet. Eyes closed, I reached above my head, snatching the cool water bottle from the nightstand and pouring it down my throat. I exhaled, ready to hold myself in the fetal position, when I felt a sticky wetness between my legs.

Being a woman is magical. Men roll off our naked bodies, use their boxers to wipe any extra cum off their dicks, put those very boxers back on, and then go about their day. The reminder that I had let Rylan cum inside me trickled down my leg as I wobbled to the bathroom like a wounded penguin. I made a mental note to set multiple birth control reminder alarms on my phone for the remainder of the month, sat my ass down on the cold toilet seat, and forced myself to pee so that a UTI would not be the only long-standing result of tonight's indiscretion. I peered down and apologized to my poor vagina. She sat around doing nothing but watching *Gilmore Girls* reruns for three months, and then, without warning, she went full beast-mode and threw herself into a two-hour workout. *Sorry, vagina, you will be in shambles very shortly.* I tacked on another mental note, reminding myself to ask the butler for ice, so I could fasten a cold compress to my labia before I went to bed. Again: fucking magical.

I staggered to the closet's full-size mirror, examining red and purple bite marks on my neck. I angled my reflection to its side, running my sweaty fingers over the scratches above my shoulder blade. My long-sleeved silk blouse would hardly cover the sides of my neck, and I knew I would resort to being that asshole who pops the collar on her leather jacket.

I tugged dark jeans over my bony legs and shuffled into my suede booties as my eyes scanned the hotel room. A lamp lay on its side below the nightstand, the pillows were everywhere but the bed, a small chair was overturned by the balcony's sliding door, the welcome booklet that was once on the nightstand was tossed to the opposite side of the room, and the heavy duvet hung half-off the edge of the bed.

Rylan had showed up at my door, and I let him inside. What a high. This mess was ours, yet somehow, it was just mine to clean up. Emotions clouded my vision as I lifted the gold lamp off the carpet, slowly placing it on the nightstand. I hesitated, and then I tugged the heavy duvet back onto the bed, feeling heat trickle down my cheeks. I moved at a pained pace, the way one might take her time when cleaning a loved one's room after a funeral. What a low.

I closed my wet lashes to find the memory of Rylan down on one knee, the black velvet ring box in his shaky palm, lifted upward toward my stunned face. His hopeful smile.

His high.

His low.

This mess was ours, and it killed me that Rylan didn't want to stay so that we could clean it up together. For a second time, I watched him walk out my door, gutting me with the feeling that I wasn't worth sticking around for.

Suddenly, a realization shifted my drooping shoulders upright. I punched back at my pity party with new evidence. Rylan wasn't perfect. Whether he liked it or not, the moment Rylan Harper stepped into my hotel room, the second he pulled my lips onto his, I became his gray area. I was Rylan's weakness. He was now flawed, just like me.

# Twenty-four

I tightened the messy bun atop my head, unable to pull myself together quick enough to emerge as Cinderella at the ball, as I found the wooden door reading BILLIARDS ROOM off Ashford Castle's sprawling lobby. I stepped slowly into the opulent nineteenth-century man cave, my entire body aching from the last six hours—emotions swirling with thoughts of wild pleasure interrupted by stabs of immeasurable longing. I took in the room, a dark-brown-on-darker-brown color scheme with red accents throughout. It was clearly decorated by a man who was horny for royalty, oak, and leather. A large mahogany pool table sat in the middle of the room, where Graham stood with his college friends, his head tilted back in laughter as his friend scratched on the eight ball.

I smelled tobacco under my nose, and I looked up to see a lanky Ashford Castle waiter holding a tray of freshly rolled Cuban cigars toward my face. I twirled the paper between my fingers, fully aware that if I drank enough, I would be smoking this Cuban later and regretting it when I woke up with a burning throat in the morning. I shrugged, leaning in to regret, and tucked the cigar behind my ear.

I searched for Hannah, finding her in a cream cashmere sweater and black leather pants, cornered by a Division One athletic sprinter, her wide hazel eyes locking onto mine with a *"come join me in hell"* tilt of the neck. I chuckled, mouthing "one second." On any other night, I would have strolled right up to her side and thrown a rope to my best friend, rescuing her from the tiny man showing off his best running times on his iPhone as if he were showing her pictures of his children, but I had no energy left. I needed to put the oxygen mask on myself before the plane went down. Zoey Marks needed a goddamn *moment*. I plopped myself down onto a tufted leather couch by the fireplace, fully prepared to save Hannah after a quick refuel.

"Didn't take you for a cigar girl," an irritating voice sang behind me.

I rolled my eyes, tilting my head back and glaring up at Ezra's smirk. He jumped over the couch, plopping himself down next to me. He was surprisingly dressed down, a faded The National T-shirt tight over his chest.

"Didn't take you for someone who enjoys music . . . or anything at all," I said, nodding to his shirt as he sank down into the couch.

"Speaking of music, nice little song and dance you did earlier. And I'm not referring to Céline."

My face reddened. Did he know? Did I have *"I just came three times while fucking my ex-boyfriend in my hotel room"* written all over my ravished body?

I turned toward him with a fake smile.

"Do you walk into every room like you're waiting for it to disappoint you, or is this weekend special?"

"Just so we're clear, you're *not* planning on telling your best friend that she's marrying a guy who isn't over his ex?"

"All I did was defuse your cowardly grenade," I hummed, but his question sat with me for a moment too long.

Somehow, compartmentalization had worked so well that to my deep shame, I had actually forgotten about the moment at the bar that did not include Rylan's hard body pressed against my breasts. I moved my frame closer to Ezra, our knees now pointed toward each other, as my face widened into a realization: this man was no threat to me. There was no enemy action with Ezra, because the only way Ezra could ruin this wedding was with me as the middleman. I grinned widely.

"What?" he asked, clearly not enjoying my easy-breezy demeanor.

I grabbed the whiskey from his hand, my eyes locked onto his as I took a sip, the peppery liquid gliding down my throat. I kept an ice cube between my lips, letting it linger on my tongue, and then I crushed it between my teeth. Ezra arched his blond eyebrows up to the ceiling, and I realized that what I just did was actually incredibly sexy, and I should not be doing an incredibly sexy thing with my enemy. I took a larger gulp of his drink, refocusing back to a pointed smile and bringing Ezra down to reality.

"You don't like getting your hands dirty. Do you, Ezra?"

He looked down at his large calloused hands, lifting them in front of me and examining them with care.

"Well, they are very beautiful hands."

"You want other people to sling the mud for you. You *could* tell Hannah about Lindsay, right? But you won't. You won't, because you can't be the guy who ruins his brother's wedding, because you know he'd never forgive you."

Ezra exhaled with a smile, taking his drink back from my hands. He leaned in. *Too close.* I moved to arch back, but his eyes held me captive. I was frozen in front of his dimpled smirk, close enough to study the dark thick eyelashes that the man upstairs had wrongly blessed his sparkling blue eyes with. What a waste of a gorgeous man.

"Speaking of unforgivable . . . you prevented your best friend from knowing the shitty truth and making her own decision. It's one thing to not want to throw my brother under the bus, it's another thing to do what you're doing. And I'm going to figure out why."

"Why what?"

"Why you're the worst best friend ever."

I felt stabs of guilt rush to my gut, hating that Ezra might have a point. Was I the worst best friend ever simply because I refused to be the person who popped the lovebirds' love bubble? I covered any discomfort with an openly hateful smile.

"This seems like a whole lot of projection coming from the worst best man ever."

"Well, aren't we just two peas in a pod," he said, smirking.

The idea of sharing any traits with Ezra made me want to hurl a glass ashtray across the room.

My eyes followed the familiar sounds of bright laughter, seeing Hannah lean over the pool table. Graham's body was folded around hers, both of their fingers on a pool stick as he guided their aim toward the far corner of the table. They sank the four ball, and he playfully pulled her in for a kiss. It was a reminder that I had rewired my brain to see the world through rose-colored glasses.

I looked back at Ezra, emboldened. I grabbed the cigar from

behind my ear, twirling it between my fingers in a testosterone-filled power trip.

"Listen, asshole, my friend is happy," I said, equal parts convincing myself and directing Ezra's eyes to Hannah's visible glee.

"So was I once. Happy and completely unaware."

A cloud passed over his face. He was clearly not over the betrayal inside his marriage, nor would he be over it anytime soon. I too lived in the town of Love Fucking Blows, I could empathize, but compartmentalization called for a lack of empathy. The gray area could not exist. Hannah had to get down the aisle, her wounded future brother-in-law be damned.

"And look at you now?" I asked, patronizingly. I made a dramatic frown with my dark red lips. "You're all broken inside?"

I hated myself the second the words left my mouth. I didn't understand why this guy was bringing out the total monster in me. He stared at me, and just as I wondered if I had crossed a line, just as I felt a twinge of guilt creep in, Ezra leaned into my ear. He paused right near my earlobe, and my heart thumped as I felt the heat of his mouth near my neck, orange and coconut in my lungs.

"Aren't you?" he whispered.

He lingered by my ear for a moment too long. I could sense goose bumps forming under my leather jacket, and I told them to *quiet the fuck down*. Ezra slowly appeared back at my face; our eyes locked. He raised the glass of whiskey up to his lips, took a generous sip, and let an ice cube linger on his tongue. He cocked an eyebrow at me and bit down. My chest tightened at the sound of ice cracking between his teeth.

I hated this man. *That's* why he brought out the monster in me.

My hate was interrupted as Ezra's eyes widened. I stretched back to see what he was staring at, and my body constricted as Rylan came into view. His eyes were darkening on Ezra and me.

Rylan was bathed in jealousy, and I fucking loved it. I had never seen him like this. He was always confident and stitched up into perfection, unwilling to let petty emotion get the better of him. But something was tugging at his heart, making one hand bunch into a white-knuckled fist. Apparently, much like myself, Rylan did not hide jealousy well. If this were a predictable nineties teen movie, I would latch on to Ezra like a monkey. Yet, based on the vein threatening to pop out of Rylan's tightened, reddening neck, I knew I would not need to resort to such treacherous measures.

Ezra's eyes darted between us both. Rylan stared at me for a moment, piercing green eyes hardening on my face until I could feel my cheeks burn. The heat plummeted to my stomach as Mara appeared next to Rylan, folding her delicate arm around his waist. He tore his eyes away from me and slid his fingers across the back of Mara's barely-there wool dress. I grabbed the drink back from Ezra's hand, taking a long sip and begging my expression to stay neutral as I watched them parade to the bar. I was fully unprepared for the gut punch of seeing the man who was just inside me order a dirty martini for his girlfriend as she nuzzled her face into his neck. Mara had the audacity to place her hand on his cheek, as if taking ownership of it, and bring his lips onto hers.

Pain swelled in my chest, threatening to spill onto my cheeks. I fought the urge to stand on the pool table, viciously point to Rylan, and roar, *"Those lips were just all over my body!"*

"He's really not worth it," Ezra said, interrupting my bitter desires.

I swallowed the tears in my throat and turned my face to meet Ezra's expression. Gone was the smirk, and in its place was sympathy from the devil. I had seen this look from him once prior, and I sure as hell did not appreciate his mercy.

"He seems like kind of a shitty guy," Ezra said.

I felt my defenses rising.

"I don't think you should be tossing *shitty guy* stones."

"He breaks up with you, and just a few months later brings a woman to the wedding he *knows* you'll be at? I wouldn't even do that to my ex-wife, and she was the actual worst."

"Oh yes you would. You were totally born with that level of petty."

"I'm not petty. I'm a *man*," he said with alarming conviction, staring deep into my eyes, his rough hand taking his drink back from me. He took a sip, his eyes not leaving mine.

I swallowed hard and cleared my throat, cracking my neck to remind my humming body exactly who had control over it.

"Trying to sabotage your brother's wedding doesn't make you a man. It's petty."

"Anything I do here, I'm doing out of love."

"Love? Are you implying that you have a heart under there?"

I put my hand on his chest, which was, of fucking course, rock hard. I could feel the flutter of his heart race under my touch. He clenched his jaw, wide blue eyes tilting sideways at me, and I quickly removed my fingers from his body.

"Felt like a black hole to me," I coughed.

"What he's doing right in front of you, that's a dick move." Ezra nodded toward Rylan, who smiled a perfect row of teeth at Mara as she tilted her slick high-pony back in a crisp cackle. Ezra was not wrong.

It was a dick move.

But I was a dick too.

Sure, Rylan was not innocent. He was not committing a victimless crime. But if one had all the facts and supported eye-for-an-eye justice, he might cheer Rylan on. Rylan was the good one. All he wanted to do was love me Forever. I could feel the tears blanket my vision, and I tore my eyes away from Rylan. Ezra bunched his face up into a ball and pulled his head back, reading me, and apparently not liking what was on the page.

"You cheated on him. . . ."

I looked at Ezra, whose entire gaze had changed, as if he was sickened by the sight of me. I was many things, but I was not a cheater.

"Never," I fumed.

Ezra pulled his drink up to his mouth, eating humble pie. "Sorry," he muttered into the glass.

"Oh go fuck yourself."

I looked back toward Mara, who was engrossed in a conversation with one of Hannah's cousins, who "couldn't get over" how beautiful Mara's dress was. I whipped my head around the room, wondering where Rylan went, until I found him standing tall in the doorway, his brow scrunched in thought as he stared at his phone. I had the morals to never cheat on him, but goddamnit, I wanted him to commit a thousand crimes against another woman. Anguish and longing tore through me, and I helplessly stepped over Ezra, pushing my way through mingling bodies until I found myself inches from Rylan.

His eyes were glued to his phone, fingers scrolling through an email. I casually stood next to him, not so casually letting the back of my hand brush up against his fingers. His eyes widened instantly, staring at me as if I were getting away with murder—

which in all fairness, it felt like I was. I was getting off on the ability to touch Rylan in a crowded room and get away with it. It was electric. It was careless. Suddenly, his body twisted out of the door of the Billiards Room, his fingers locking into mine as he tugged the criminal with him.

Rylan pulled me around the winding hallway and down a stone staircase, reminding me that we were, in fact, in a castle. My throat was too dry to ask where he was taking me, my body was too lost without him guiding it, and so, I surrendered to his pull, as if he was my North Star.

With a slap of cold wind, we were outside, standing on an empty concrete patio, the moon hovering over the lough in the distance. The crisp air woke me to the feeling of two cool hands tightening around my waist under my leather jacket. My stomach fluttered as Rylan tugged me forward. Our faces inches from each other, he stared at me hard, as if he didn't want to be staring at me at all. His warring eyes and strong hands pushed my body against the gray stone, his hand finding the wall before the back of my head could. He gripped the lapel of my jacket and pulled my lips onto his. Rylan Harper kissed me like he couldn't help it. Like he was powerless and even hated himself for it. I kissed him like I wanted validation that we had just made love—validation that our bodies twisting around each other meant something to him. I kissed him tight against me, like I needed the warmth of his beating chest to mend all the cracks on my shattered heart.

Our lips numb, we finally came up for oxygen, our breaths huffing in the cool air. I stood on the tips of my boots, my forehead pressed onto his. We were silent, swaying against each other. It felt like the end of the universe, yet Bruce Willis wouldn't be rescuing us—only I had the power to do that. My fingers moved to pull Rylan's face back onto my lips, to take comfort in him again—but he stepped back, inhaling a long, deep breath.

I could feel my chest tightening as Rylan's mouth twisted in confusion. After a moment, he shook his head at me. I mimicked him, shaking my head back. It was not as if I'd pressed a gun between his shoulder blades and forced him to lead me outside so he could kiss me like the world was ending with the moon as a backdrop. Yet, Rylan stared at me as if I had done just that. Maybe I was a criminal, but he chose to be my accomplice.

"Where's Mara?" I dared, reminding him that he wasn't exactly an innocent party here.

The sound of her name seemed to sting his eyes.

"Don't do that," he said with a clenched jaw.

"Do what?"

*I knew exactly what I was doing.*

"Make me feel worse than I already feel."

"I don't know how you feel. You literally perfected the Irish Exit."

He stepped closer to me, his eyes widening. Apparently, I wasn't allowed to bring up what we did in my hotel room. It threatened his ability to compartmentalize—to pretend he was never inside me.

"That shouldn't have happened."

"Why?"

"You know why."

"Because you finally found someone Protestant enough for your mother?"

I knew better, but I was holding on to a chaotic swirl of emotions, and the vindictive ones were fighting hardest to break free.

"Pretty sure I tried to put a ring on your finger without my mom's approval. But while we're on that subject, she didn't think you were the type to stick around for a lifetime . . . and I guess I should have listened to her."

I felt tears sting my eyes. Regret clouded his face—he knew those last words shouldn't have left his mouth. Rylan took an apologetic step toward me, his jaw twitching. Suddenly, our bodies slid apart at the sounds of distant laughter. I turned around, seeing a wide-eyed Ezra holding the patio door open, with cigars in one hand and a drink in the other. Before I could wonder how much of this conversation Ezra had heard, Graham and Hannah walked through the door laughing. Graham wrapped his jean jacket around a shivering Hannah, and a few more of their friends followed, each holding drinks and cigars.

Hannah buried laughter in her throat the moment her eyes met mine. She took in Rylan and me—steps away from each other on the expansive patio, both doing our best to appear as though we had not just taken knives to our unhealed wounds. Our best was not good enough. The tension in the air was so thick one could bottle it, and Hannah sensed that my heaving chest was about to crack.

"Let's go look at the moon," Hannah sang with a firm smile and alarmed eyes, tugging me away from Rylan.

I stumbled along the grass, turning to look back at Rylan. He put one hand on the back of his head, pacing in a tight circle. Ezra kept his eyes on me, possibly now the bearer of the fun fact that I turned down Rylan's proposal.

I shook off the myriad of sinking feelings as Hannah and I strolled toward the dock, leaving the castle behind us. She took a sip straight out of the red wine bottle in her hand, her knowing eyes staying on me.

"What?" I cracked.

"Nothing," she said, fully aware that *we both knew* it was not nothing.

I walked the plank like the bad, bad girl I was, my boots grinding on the weathered slats. Hannah and I strode shoulder to shoulder along the creaky dock—the sounds of the lough lightly splashed below us. We passed a row of wet and muddy overturned blue kayaks, and I steadied myself on one of them, suddenly seeing stars. Hannah watched me struggle, her eyebrows drawn together.

Instead of continuing to walk, I sat down right there. I sucked in the frigid air until the only stars in my eyes were the ones in the sky. I felt cool glass in my hand and looked down to find the wine bottle now in my possession. Hannah put her arm around me, tugging me close. My body shivered as I poured the rich Pinot down my throat, letting it add fire to my burning insides.

I glanced over my shoulder, my eyes finding Mara walking outside. She tightened a camel coat around her dress as she approached Rylan, wrapping her arms around his waist and tugging him close to her. Could she smell me all over him? Every horrible part of me hoped that she could as I shifted my gaze back to Hannah.

"Second-to-last day of being Ms. Green—"

"Zoey," Hannah interrupted, seeing through my attempt at distracting from the obvious.

"What?"

"What are you both doing?" Hannah asked gently.

"Celebrating our favorite girl," I tried out, putting my arm around my best friend.

Hannah studied my face in an unusually disarming way. My body hummed, walking a familiar tightrope of excitement and shame. I was teetering on the edge of Getting Caught, one of my favorite childhood pastimes.

I was sixteen again, sneaking into my house through the back porch, the screen door slapping behind me, extremely high after smoking my first rolled joint with my high school crush. My mother took in my bloodshot eyes and demanded to know the name of the delinquent who gave her daughter "the marijuana." I had an unconscious need to rub my rebellions in my parents' innocent faces. They never quite understood me, and because of that, I decided to intermittently punish them, letting them see the sides of myself that most teenagers hid from adults. I didn't go out of my way to cover up indiscretions, because a part of me took pride in them. This followed me into adulthood.

Channeling my mother, Hannah folded my jacket's popped collar down, sensing I was hiding something underneath. She shook her head, staring at a bite mark.

"Zoey Ida Marks," Hannah scolded with an alarmed smile. "Zoey, what are you doing?" she asked again, this time with a tone that warned, *"You don't know what you're doing."*

*Well, I for one am trying to get you down the aisle, reverse a curse, and embrace marriage . . . and sure, somehow I may have gotten sidetracked by pheromones.*

I shrugged the corners of my leather jacket up to the moon.

"Love, I think you should figure it out, before someone gets *further* hurt," she said, acknowledging that I was in pain, even though I was terrified of unpacking it in front of her.

Here we were on a mossy dock. Two best friends. Two keepers of secrets.

It felt wholly impossible that my best friend—the once-tiny, blond, freckle-faced girl with an effortless smile—was getting married in two sleeps. I stared at Hannah, now taller, same effortless smile, enveloped in her fiancé's denim jacket.

I glanced back to see Ashford Castle glowing in the night, finding Graham, Ezra, and a couple of buddies lighting their cigars on the deck. My wandering gaze shifted to find Rylan and Mara having a quiet conversation. Their expressions were tame—she was not angry, which of course deeply infuriated me.

I sensed Hannah was watching me. She was desperately trying to respect my feelings and be a good friend, but Hannah craved answers, and she was longing to know my *why*. I had never shared my real fears on marriage with Hannah. A fear of Forever made me seem callous and cynical toward love, and I was anything but that. Growing up, I thought marriage and I just had a strange misunderstanding—I would grow up and grow out of the fears before they blew up in my face. The opposite happened. And before I had the chance to unpack my emotional baggage to Hannah, she had a sparkly ring on her finger.

If I admitted to Hannah why Rylan and I broke up, I would also have to reveal my bridesmaid failures to her, and this moment was not about me. This moment was about Hannah, about getting her married.

*Hannah. Married.*

My inner voice was growing louder, telling me I should be doing my Zoey Thing. I took in my best friend, our legs dangling off the dock. I should be telling Hannah the brutal truth, no matter how hard.

*Hannah, earlier, I discovered that your fiancé might still be in love with his ex-girlfriend. Also, I think it's probably not the best idea to get married without telling your fiancé that you're unable to have your own biological children.*

I should be saying these difficult words to my best friend who needed to hear them. I stared into Hannah's warm eyes, which always let me know I could tell her anything. I opened my mouth—

"Am I the only one getting some serious Capeside vibes here?" Hannah said, smiling.

I exhaled a chuckle, grateful for Hannah's ability to fully chicken out when faced with Hard Truths—hers or mine. Hanna grinned and tilted sideways, our shoulders bumping each other, a bottle of red wine floating back and forth between us as she started humming the *Dawson's Creek* theme song. Suddenly, we were nine years old, two girls lying elbow-to-elbow on my bed, chins resting on our palms, the heat of the WB's Tuesday-night lineup in front of us. Mere children, eager to dive in to situations we did not fully comprehend.

Our thirty-one-year-old selves—now swimming upstream in adult situations that we did not fully understand—swayed together on the dock, singing off-key, neither of us doing Paula Cole any justice. I was unsure in this moment which one of us was Joey and which was Pacey, but clearly neither of us wanted to be Jen or Dawson.

I took in Hannah's beaming reflection in the dark water. "You're getting married. How did this happen? How are we old enough to do adult-y things?"

Hannah sat up straighter, her perfect posture reminding me how horrible mine was. She looked up from her reflection, her tongue searching for the right words, always so careful.

"Zo, I've spent so much energy trying to bend myself into

different shapes just so I could fit next to someone else," she said, twirling the ring on her finger. "Graham sat next to me on a plane, and at some point during our conversation, I realized that I was more myself than I'd ever been with another man before—and I had known him for only an hour. We fit without a fight—as if we were made to understand each other. I think that if I'd never met him, I'd have spent every day clinging to the hope that someone like him wasn't possible . . . because if I knew a man like him existed, it would have made settling impossible."

Hannah smiled with tears in her eyes, gazing back at Graham. He met her eyes from across the lawn, tilting the rim of his glass toward us and taking a sip.

I hated the thought, but I knew it was probably true—Hannah would have settled. My Hard Truths wouldn't have worked on her into her late thirties. She would have presented me with an acceptable version of a man, I would have told her that he was incapable of lighting her world on fire, and she would have told me—with conviction—that she *needed* someone next to her to grow old with.

Society and biology work together to try and put rogue women in their place. It starts with a slow burn, a tiny voice in our ear when we're young—when happily ever afters close out the movies, when relatives ask about our love lives before they do our careers. The voice gets louder, becoming a roar as our eggs casually leave our bodies—90 percent gone by the ripe old age of *thirty*. It's troublesome, when after all those years of shouting voices from both inside and out, a grown woman walks the road by herself—without a partner, or without a baby in her arms.

Hannah was a people pleaser, and she didn't appreciate being alone. She would have latched on to a partner before the societal ticking clock branded her a lost cause. Graham was the rebellious townsman who met the princess and lit up her world, saving her from a life of pageant smiles on the arm of a boring prince. Hannah wasn't just choosing to marry Graham—she was saving her own life.

I, on the other hand, thought societal pressures could go fuck themselves. I was cloaked in armor, my sword pointed to the moon, riding a white horse, shouting "I can save myself" to every strong jawline that came my way. I could save myself, but could someone else ride next to me? I didn't know what it felt like to settle, because it was impossible for me to fake comfort. I was either comfortable in my own skin, or I was crawling out of it. My relationship with Rylan was comfort wrapped in passion. He felt like home, always. If only I could lay down my sword and surrender to Forever, so that he might be my home, always.

I looked back toward the castle. Mara's arm fit snug around Rylan's back as they stepped toward the porch doors. He turned his head around, meeting my wistful gaze, and then Rylan slipped inside, lost for the night to someone else.

*Always.*

What an ambitious word for a fickle world.

# Twenty-five

I awoke surrounded by my usual disaster of pillows—one clenched between my legs and another pressed over my face. I plopped my heavy feet to the ground, shuffling them into velour hotel slippers. I felt my body sting, a reminder of yesterday's activities. All of them.

I opened the drapes in a circle around my face, hesitant to show off my naked body through the window to the men fly fishing out in the lough. The rising sunlight beamed into my dark room as a smile graced my lips. Hannah was getting married tomorrow. My smile fell as my stomach grumbled. I was suddenly all too aware that I had failed to consume any food last night. I had, however, burned a thousand calories fleeing from a falcon and colliding with Rylan.

I was suddenly famished. I needed All The Carbs.

I hungrily scanned the hotel's à la carte breakfast menu, horrified to discover that All The Carbs were gluten free. I did not have celiac, and I refused to be punished. I whimpered with the realization that I would have to pull myself together and go on a hunt for gluten-packed baked goods.

The George V Dining Room was named after a king for a reason: It was bathed in royalty. Tables draped in seamless white linens surrounded by deep-blue chairs, light from Waterford crystal chandeliers dancing on the ceiling, and me, Zoey Marks, wearing my finest oversized T-shirt and sweatpants. I sat in a corner by the window, alone, scooping a berry scone into a bowl of clotted cream and then shoveling it in my starving throat, washing it down with an Irish coffee. Whiskey at ten in the morning. *When in Ireland.*

I leaned back, licking cream off my top lip, a belly full of pastries and pancakes, and my head much clearer. I'd gotten nine hours of sleep, and I was a new woman. My eyes floated out to the lough, knowing that later this afternoon, I would be floating on it. Instead of a normal rehearsal dinner on land, Graham's parents had opted to host a rehearsal dinner on a yacht, coupled with a sunset cruise around the lough. Falcons? *No, thank you.* Yachts? *Yes, please.*

I squinted, seeing a white ferry out in the distance of the lough. I bit my lip with a deep inhale, willing my mind to stay in the present, but nostalgia burned brighter. Before I knew it, I was turning thirty again.


It was our first night in East Hampton, about four hours after Hannah had arrived. At dusk, Rylan's car approached the blue-and-white ferry that would take him and me, inside the car, to Shelter Island, home of that night's dinner spot. Hannah was back at the inn wrapping up a conference call, and she was set to meet us in a couple hours.

I sat in the passenger seat in a deep-ruby off-the-shoulder silk dress, my naturally olive skin a shade darker after a day in the sun. Rylan pulled his BMW onto the ferry, already packed with eleven cars, getting the last spot in the far corner. He shifted the car into Park as I rolled down the windows, giving us a perfect view of the ocean and the setting sun outside.

I felt a jolt in my body and realized we were moving—the ferry had left the dock. I inhaled the fresh ocean air as Rylan turned up the car's volume, blasting our "Best of Bruce" Spotify playlist. "I'm on Fire" howled, and an orange haze dusted the cloudless sky as the high tide wrestled below us.

Rylan reached a strong arm across my lap and rolled up only my window, the tinted glass darkening my view. Before I could wonder why, he'd unclicked my seat belt. I stared at him with a furrowed brow, finding his expression hardened upon my brown eyes. My body lit up as his hands slid under the bottom of my silk dress, reaching my hip and twisting my lacy thong in his fingers. He leaned into me.

"We have seven minutes," he whispered into my ear.

Heat enveloped my body in a fever of excitement, and he tugged my underwear down below my heels and then tightened a grip around my waist, pulling me across the gearshift and onto his lap so I was facing him. I straddled him with my back against the hard steering wheel, my bare knees bent on either side of his denim. He inched the base of his seat back, raised eyebrows taking in my stunned face.

I was bathed in disbelief, staring at the guy I was straddling— the guy who was not into having sex in public places—while total strangers surrounded us. *This guy.*

He pulled my open mouth into a hungry kiss, wiping the shock off my lips as I tasted peppermint on his tongue. I felt him grow hard under me, and I undid his pants, pulling him free and lowering myself onto him with ease. I held on to the lapel of his slate-blue collared shirt, squeezing it in my fingers as he arched himself forward, clenching his hand around my ass and tugging our bodies together. I felt my body tremble as he thrust himself deeper inside me.

I couldn't help but look out the passenger window to see the strangers sitting inside their cars. I couldn't help but wonder if they could see us—a thought so dangerously sexy, I nearly erupted just entertaining it. My mouth dropped open in a moan as he thrust harder inside me, and I felt his thumb grace my lip and settle on the dimple of my chin, bringing my eyes back to his.

I clenched a fist over the back of his hair, pulling hard, heat blanketing my body as I moved back and forth on top of him, my legs buckling around him. I arched my torso backward, moaning loudly, forgetting I was in a public place with a window open, forgetting *everything*. He cupped his hand over my mouth with a wide-eyed grin, muffling my sounds as the ocean mist sprayed inside his window, the water cooling my quaking body as heat blurred my vision. He let his now-trembling fingers leave my open mouth as I caught my breath, and I felt his hands tighten around my hips—pulling our bodies tightly together, furiously until he came.

I let out deep exhales, arching backward and wiping the sweat and ocean from my forehead as I rested my spine on the steering wheel. He caught his breath and then drew my body back to him, bringing my pounding chest against his.

"Happy birthday," he said breathlessly, smiling, giving me a tender kiss. I could taste salt on our tongues, and I felt my knees weaken as our lips parted, neither of us pulling back, our damp foreheads still touching and our hearts racing against each other.

Rylan aimlessly traced a line from my knee to my waist with his fingertip as we stared out the window, watching the sun set on the ocean. Suddenly—a moment before the blue horizon swallowed the burning sun behind the Atlantic—a fleeting green fluorescent light grew on the curve of the sun. Two seconds later, the green sun was gone. It was a green flash sunset—a phenomenon where the Earth's atmosphere refracts sunlight and splits the light into different colors, leaving green visible to the eye. I had never seen it before.

My unblinking eyes turned to meet Rylan's. I soaked him in below me—his breath shallow, his hair tousled, his shirt and my silk dress tangled up in each other and splattered with the ocean. I memorized every line on his face, my finger tracing his jaw as if he were a rare sunset. He was green light enveloping the sun. He was magic, and we were the result of a perfectly strange atmosphere.

"What are you thinking about?" he asked, tucking a curl behind my ear.

I felt a thickness in my throat as the answer tore through my bursting heart.

*"Will I ever love another man as much as I love you in this moment?"*

I was living in a moment I knew I would one day ache for. I was home, and I was homesick. He was magic, but magic was fleeting.

"Nothing . . ." I lied.

It was everything.

R esting my chin on the back of my hand, I gazed achingly past the window of the George V Dining Room, the way one might stroke an old photo. The ferryboat melted into the lough, but the memory of Rylan and me stood heavy on my chest, and I wasn't sure if time was capable of lifting the weight.

Maybe it wouldn't have to.

# Twenty-six

"This is a latke," I said, defiantly holding a potato pancake in my hand.

"Boxty," corrected a cater waiter, with an incredibly thick Irish accent, holding a tray of latkes in one hand.

"I've survived, like, thirty Hanukkahs, and this is a *latke*," I doubled down, berating him as I swallowed a mouthful of warm and crispy potato pancakes.

The cater waiter shook his head at me with a furrowed brow and stepped away. I turned my head as the sun warmed my spine, a backless red-satin dress hugging my body. Ashford Castle shrank in the distance, and I gripped my hands on the railing of the aft deck, leaning forward to take in the expansive view. The autumn-colored Connemara mountains mixed with the tiny lush green islands scattered on the rippling water looked like something out of a fantastical dream.

Thanks to Hannah's future in-laws, I was a passenger on a stunning eighty-foot yacht that was floating down Lough Corrib. Roughly fifty guests were mingling and laughing as the yacht's staff offered up trays of dainty Irish finger food and glasses of cold champagne.

I grinned, letting the fresh air hit my cheeks. All I had to do was get Hannah through this rehearsal dinner and late-night drinks at Ashford Castle's bar. We would wake up tomorrow morning, and this bridesmaid would get her first bride down the aisle—and get Rylan back. My chest tightened, hearing Rylan's distant laugh, as if he were somehow mocking my internal to-do list.

I slowly turned my head to meet the image of Rylan in a crisp navy suit, laughing alongside Mara, who wore a long-sleeved floral wraparound dress, the hues of purple in the fabric perfectly matching Rylan's skinny tie. Rylan's mother, Gemma, stood in between the Instagram-happy couple, holding adoring eyes on Mara and tilting her head back in an exaggerated cackle.

I had to hand it to Rylan. His current commitment toward building castles in the air with Mara made me eager to browse Zillow and purchase an identical model. Gemma shifted her beaming eyes back and forth between Rylan and Mara, likely imagining the potential union of two faultless bloodlines. I angrily stuffed a latke into my mouth, chewing with quiet rage, unable to tear my eyes off the Rockwell painting from hell.

"Enjoying the view?" I heard Ezra's voice sing.

I turned, my eyes meeting Ezra, who leaned back on the deck's railing, taking me in with a smirk.

"Not anymore," I replied with a mouthful of fried potatoes.

A fitted light gray suit hugged his body, doing everything for his broad shoulders. I snickered, the manliness of his shoulders undercut by his white collared shirt—buttoned up to his neck, gripping tightly around his blond scruff. I wondered if Ezra wore his shirt buttoned all the way to the top as a physical reminder to remain uptight at all costs. He was like a mutt wearing a shock collar, dying to escape and frolic in the park, but the weight around his neck kept him on guard in the front lawn, barking at anyone who walked by.

"Can I help you?" Ezra asked, his arched eyebrows pointed toward me, probably wondering why I was staring at his neck.

"Might make you less insufferable if the circulation to your brain wasn't cut off," I suggested, flicking his shirt's top button.

Ezra stepped closer to me.

"Excuse me?"

"It's just cute that your outsides match your insides. That's all." I shrugged, grinning into my champagne glass. It was a lie. His outsides were unfairly gorgeous and his insides were horrible.

"My *insides?*"

Ezra's ocean eyes locked onto mine as he ran a hand over his stubble beard. His fingers moved down to his throat, slowly peeling back his shirt's top button, setting his neck free. He kept going, one button, then another, and another, until his ripped torso was daring to break free. I swallowed hard.

*Mazel tov to his CrossFit instructor.*

"Are you happy now?" he asked in a low voice, his eyes glued onto mine.

I sucked in my cheeks, forcing a cool expression on my face.

"I was wrong. You're still insufferable."

"Ezra?" sang a voice with a slight Irish accent.

I turned, seeing an earthy woman in her sixties breeze toward us. I took in her auburn hair braided to the side, her flowy skirt, and dizzying pattern on a cashmere sweater atop it. She adjusted a bunch of chunky turquoise jewelry clinking around her wrist and peered sideways at Ezra's open shirt. It was a look of amused horror that only a mother could own. This was clearly Ezra and Graham's maker, Fiona. One could plainly describe her as "really fucking cool," a trait only one of her sons inherited.

Hannah had raved about Fiona, branding her "the anti-mother-in-law." Fiona was free-spirited and didn't spend one sleepless night imagining the agony of her son plotting a future with someone who was not her.

"What a darling look for you," Fiona teased, her eyes going to Ezra's open shirt.

Grinning, she took her hand and messily tousled his hair. I watched Ezra's face turn red, and he quickly ran his fingers through his hair and began buttoning up his shirt. Fiona turned to me, studying me and then Ezra with a smile, as if I had just given her a gift.

"You must be Hannah's Zoey."

"That I am. Hannah's Zoey—it's my favorite title. And you must be the mother of the groom."

"One of *my* favorite titles," Fiona said, beaming. "Well, as you were." She hummed, taking her finger and undoing Ezra's top button. She pinched his cheek and sauntered away with a wide smile.

"Wow. The apple really fell far from the tree," I whistled, looking from Fiona to Ezra.

Ezra shifted his focus, taking in Rylan and Mara across the deck.

"I take it back, princess."

"Take *what* back?"

"The part about you not getting a ring."

I felt my chest twist, hating that Ezra held some of the Zoey cards, and terrified of which one he'd play to win the house.

"You got me, congratulations," I said sarcastically, flipping Ezra the bird, as if my middle finger were his prize.

I went to step away from him and find Hannah, but he cornered me with his broad shoulder. "Actually, I *don't* get you," he corrected, brows furrowed. "If you're all pro-marriage, if you're all piney for your ex, then why won't you marry him?"

I stared at Ezra, my tongue stuck in my mouth.

"I have a theory. Wanna hear it?" he continued.

"I've never wanted to hear anything less."

"My ex-wife basically proposed to me." He folded a damp cocktail napkin between his fingers, a tell that divulging this might not be the most comfortable thing for him to do. "You get to be in your thirties, and you're dating someone for a significant period of time, and everyone expects you to do the math, even if you're unsure of the answer."

"You're probably working at a kindergarten-math level, so—"

"I'm a CPA."

"Well, that explains why you're epically boring."

"She wanted a ring, pretty much demanded that we either get engaged, or we end. I wasn't sure if I was happy—*really* happy the way I thought I should have been, but I felt this pressure to do what you're supposed to do after three years together when the woman you're with wants kids, when she's kind, when you've put in all this work and you know each other inside and out. So, I bought a ring. And it turns out, I didn't know her at all. I should have listened to my gut. 'Kind of happy' isn't good enough."

"Nice story, but what's your theory?"

"My theory is that if you have to be *dragged* down the aisle kicking and screaming, you don't want to marry him. You're not in love with him, not the way you should be, because if you were, you'd have a ring on your finger right now. So my theory is that you don't want to marry him, but now you're faced with the idea of him with someone else . . . and so suddenly you want what you can't have, and something that you could've had is something you don't actually want."

This uptight curmudgeon thought he knew me. If only my relationship with Rylan had not been bathed in pure bliss. If only our universe wasn't full of rare green flash sunsets, moments big and small that took my breath away and ripped through my insides like poison. If only I could point to unhappiness and a lack of big love as the reason my ring finger was bare. If only I could exhale an emphatic admission of, *"You're right, he just isn't The One."* If only.

This was not that. If Rylan wasn't The One, then no one would ever be. If it was a no to marrying Rylan, it was a no to marriage. Forever.

I clenched my jaw into a seething smile, stepping up toward Ezra's self-righteous face, as if I were an MTV promo teasing, *"You think you know, but you have no idea."* Ezra tilted his head, trying to peel back my expression.

"You don't know a goddamn thing about me. So, if you feel the urge to generalize about me like I'm some predictable girl ripped out of a Psych 101 textbook, do it in silence."

I blew past Ezra, heading down the yacht's side deck, looking for Hannah. Suddenly, I felt a cold hand full of sharp jewelry etch into my arm. I spun around, seeing Celeste in a crisp linen pantsuit, huge cream pearls around her neck and upon her ears. Her eyes were eager and anxious. Clearly, as we were all gathered upon this boat for an impending rehearsal dinner, her daughter was still getting married, and clearly, Celeste was running out of time to try to stop it.

"So . . . ?" she asked.

"So . . ."

"Did you talk to Hannah?"

I let out an exasperated exhale. I didn't have the energy to pretend I was going to stop a wedding right now.

"Mrs. Green, she's getting married tomorrow. Isn't it easier to just embrace it? Hannah seems to really love him, and he seems to really love her. I don't know what you want me to say. . . ." I trailed off as Celeste pursed her lips with an inhale, dissatisfied with my response.

"You turned down a marriage proposal from my nephew."

"Meaning?"

"Meaning, I thought you would be of greater help here, Zoey."

Was there one person on this yacht who didn't feel the need to tell me who I was? Everybody had a theory about Zoey Marks, and frankly, it was starting to infuriate me. I had enough wild theories to fill the ocean—the last thing I needed was outside noise.

"Well, what can I say? I'm a changed woman."

"She doesn't seem right, Zoey. I'm telling you, she's . . . something's not right."

Celeste's face turned to the lake. She held a distant gaze with her light blue eyes, an expression that for the first time made me empathize with her. Mothers have this way of just knowing. They're like emotional Santa Clauses, hovering from somewhere up above, sensing when you're bad or good. Celeste knew that Hannah was hiding something. She knew it in her soul, and when your only child is keeping a secret from you, it's a reflection on you.

Hannah believed that revealing her fertility news to Celeste would be traumatizing. Celeste would turn Hannah's pain into her own pain of not having biological grandchildren. Celeste would imply that Hannah had not exhausted enough resources, and she would send Hannah different online articles dispelling her diagnosis, or try to get her to different "world-class" doctors. Celeste was not the mother who would just hold her daughter, tell her that she was sorry she was suffering, and ask if there was anything she could do to take away her pain.

As I took in Celeste's weakened face, my chest dropped, remembering my own mother. The thing about mothers is that sometimes you can't tell them anything. I received a call from my mother two weeks after my breakup with Rylan. It was a call that did not begin with asking how I was doing, but instead a call that berated me for not divulging the news that Rylan and I had broken up. My mom *had to find out from Celeste*. Could I *imagine* how that made her feel? She *knew something was wrong* with me when she spoke to me last, and she *could not believe* that I had kept this from her.

I actually could *not imagine* how she felt having to find out about her daughter's breakup from a third party, because I could barely manage to keep food down. It took everything inside me to make it through the workday without crumbling. The thing about mothers is that while they can sense when we're not in a great place, they don't always know how to get us to a better one.

"Dinner is now served belowdecks," a voice said.

I turned, seeing Fiona standing below the stairs with champagne in her hand. Celeste rolled her false lashes, seemingly already pained at the idea of marrying into this hippie-dippie family.

On the dining deck of the yacht, the spacious sunlit room was decorated with half a dozen round tables, Irish wildflowers adorning the center of each, and massive photos of Graham and Hannah on stands around the room. A typical Sunday carvery was on the table, generous portions of roasted meats, gravy, fresh vegetables, potatoes cooked every way. It smelled and looked like an Irish Thanksgiving. I sat next to Hannah, with Graham by her other side, and Ezra unfortunately at my left. Ezra's elbow grazed mine, and I sharply lifted my seat, scooting it a few inches toward Hannah. Ezra smirked, amused by my open hatred.

Across the table, just a reach away, were Rylan and Mara. Mara was engaged in an animated conversation with Graham's cousin, most likely detailing her love of Rylan and her ability to feed the world. My bitter eyes found themselves meeting Rylan's, and I longingly tore a piece of soda bread off the giant loaf in the center of the table, taking him in as if he were the dessert. I had misbehaved, so I was probably going to bed without him.

With my mouth full, I turned to the front of the room, where Graham's parents stood by a microphone, giving their toast, glasses in hand. Fiona cleared her throat, looking lovingly at Graham and Hannah, near tears.

"As you probably know, Graham and Ezra were born a few towns away from here, and we moved to the States when Graham was just five. At age eight, Graham declared that it would be 'extremely helpful with the ladies' for him to have an

Irish accent, and so he asked if we could 'move back to Ireland, just for a few years.' While Graham did not get his wish, as it turns out, my son didn't need the aid of an Irish accent to charm the perfect woman, he just needed to be *in* Ireland."

Fiona nudged her husband, who handed her a floral bag, a little gift with pink tissue sprouting from the top.

"Hannah and Graham, come on up here," Fiona continued.

Everyone erupted into a chorus of applause, and I looked on with a smile as Hannah and Graham scooted off their chairs and stood up next to Fiona.

"So Hannah, my soon-to-be daughter, tomorrow you will walk down the aisle and carry with you . . . this. There's an old Irish tradition . . . oh dear . . ." Fiona shook her head and wiped her tears with a cocktail napkin, overcome with emotion.

"Your mom is the cutest. How did you turn out to be so horrible?" I whispered into Ezra's ear.

"Feels like an odd time for you to throw stones," Ezra whispered back with a knowing smirk, glancing from my eyes to Rylan.

He had a point.

"Go fuck yourself," I said through a smile, as I heard Fiona come back to the microphone.

Hannah held the contents of the gift in her delicate fingers—it looked to be a cloth of some sort.

"My family teases me for being quite superstitious, but I *am* Irish," Fiona continued, having pulled herself together. "You see, this piece of linen in your hand, it's more than just a handkerchief, Hannah. Graham's grandmother gave it to me on my wedding day with some instructions. I was to carry it down the aisle, and then put it away. And one day, I would take a few stitches to my wedding handkerchief, and turn it into a baby's bonnet . . ."

My entire body dropped as Hannah looked down at the handkerchief. I could see tears stab her eyes as Fiona continued.

"I carried this piece of linen down the aisle at my wedding. And then a few years later, my little Graham wore it atop his head as a bonnet when we brought him home from the hospital. And so, the tradition continues with you, Hannah."

Fiona raised a glass to a wide-eyed Hannah and a smiling Graham, who wrapped his arm around his bride, kissing her cheek. "I wish you both a lifetime of love, and of course, a houseful of children. Sláinte."

I heard champagne glasses clink around me, but I couldn't take my eyes off Hannah. I scanned her face, trying to read what was underneath, trying to gauge if her devastating secret might spill out into the room full of wedding guests. I turned, seeing Celeste at the table next to mine, hyper-focused on her daughter, her jeweled frame ready to leap into action. It was as if the princess trapped in the tower had finally beckoned to be saved.

Fiona bent down to look into Hannah's eyes.

"Are you okay, dear?"

"Oh . . . yes, I just . . . It's so thoughtful and beautiful. I get a little sentimental sometimes," Hannah managed, quietly. I silently clapped for my friend, impressed at her attempt to play crippling devastation off as nostalgic wistfulness.

Graham kissed the side of Hannah's blond locks, and they made their way back to our table. Hannah sat down next to me, but her woeful hazel eyes refused to leave the handkerchief in her lap. I took her hand in mine, offering a double squeeze.

Her fingers stayed limp inside mine. Her eyes were lost in a sea of heartbreak.

The room resumed eating and chatting, but Graham's focus stayed on Hannah. He leaned toward her, *knowing* something was not right. He really knew her after all.

"Hannah, what's wrong?" he whispered into her ear, not wanting to make a scene.

My eyes stayed wide on Hannah. My chest tightened. This was it. Hannah looked up at Graham slowly, taking in his concerned face.

"I think maybe the champagne just got to my head," she said with a reassuring smile. "I'm going to go to the ladies' room and freshen up."

"Want me to walk with you?"

"Don't be silly, I'm a big girl. Go chat with your friends."

She kissed Graham's scruffy cheek, stood with a pursed smile, and zigzagged past the round tables like a bullet. I screeched my chair back to go after her.

"What was that?" asked Ezra, now turned toward me, halting my rescue.

I studied Ezra's face, which was radiating some sort of internal joy. A horrible realization jolted through me. This shithead whom I had written off as a non-threat? He was, in fact, the opposite.

"Did you tell her to do that?"

"What?" he asked.

"Your mother and that bizarre fertility handkerchief ritual. Did you tell your mother to give Hannah that?"

"Did I Marty McFly myself into the past and tell my thirty-year-old mom to bring Graham home from the hospital in a bonnet that his bride would one day walk down the aisle with and then give to her baby?"

"*Yeah.* Minus the time travel. But, *yeah.*"

Ezra shifted his body closer to mine, perplexed.

"What's going on here?"

"Don't play stupid—*er* than you are."

Ezra's eyes scanned Hannah's empty seat, the white linen handkerchief sitting on the table, as if trying to furiously unpack a clue in an escape room as the time ran out. I stood up smoothly, eyes on my enemy as I snatched my purse from the back of my chair.

"I'm on to you," I threatened, leaning down toward him.

"You're a bizarre person," he said, loudly enough so that Mara and Rylan looked over.

I did not have time to dissect Rylan's squinted eyes taking me in—I had to find Hannah.

Chest pounding, I left the table and filed past the seated crowd, storming into the bathroom of the dining deck, but finding no Hannah in sight.

I raced up the stairs to the aft deck. The Connemara mountains were in view and Ashford Castle was alive and lit up in the distance as the sun began its descent. The cold wind lashed at my face as I rounded every corner of the top deck, no Hannah in sight. Exasperated, and with no time to revel in the beauty of the setting sun, I filed down another set of stairs, leading me to the stern deck. I froze in my tracks, slack-jawed.

"Hannah, *what* are you doing?"

Hannah stood on the wooden slats of the back deck, which floated a few feet above the rippling water. Her shaking hands gripped a steak knife, and she was trying to cut a thick rope to release a small lifeboat into the water, *Titanic*-style.

Hannah turned to me with shallow breaths, eyes wide open, anxious sweat dripping down her forehead. I had never seen her like this. This was an animalistic panic coming from the woman who seemed to always have her shit together. I stood frozen with open palms at my side, fully unqualified for this curveball.

"I gotta get off this boat! I gotta get off this boat! Zoey, YOU GOTTA GET ME OFF THIS MOTHERFUCKING BOAT," she panted, pointing the knife toward me.

She was cursing, and not just a "fuck," but a "motherfucking."
*This was motherfucking BAD.*

I darted my head back up the stairs, terrified that someone could so easily walk down five wooden slats and see the bride crumbling. I turned back toward Hannah, and I was quickly reminded that the real horror of the moment was that my best friend was having a meltdown while wielding a very sharp knife with a very unsteady hand on the edge of a very large yacht.

"Okay, just surrender the knife, Hannah." I inched my way toward her in a crouched position, as if negotiating a hostage crisis.

"You're gonna cut it down for me?" she asked, her wild eyes darting to the rope.

"Suuuuuure," I offered in a high pitch, delivering the most unsure *sure* of all time.

"NO. You don't get the knife until you *promise* that you're going to CUT IT DOWN."

I pulled back, terrified. Smudged mascara sat below Hannah's eyes, and her trembling face waited for me to assure her that I was indeed going to cut the lifeboat down.

"Hannah. You jump, I jump," I promised.

With shaking fingers, Hannah slowly handed me the knife, her eyes not leaving mine. I gripped the handle of the steak knife, with one glance back toward the stairs—still empty. I stared at Hannah, my best friend who was unraveling at the seams the evening before the happiest day of her life. She didn't deserve to walk around with the silent weight of infertility in a world that assumed all women her age were fertile. I would do anything to mitigate her pain. And right now, the only thing I could do for Hannah was cut down a lifeboat.

My hands moved furiously, attempting to sever the thick white rope holding a lifeboat to our yacht.

"Are you hot?" I heard her ask.

"I mean, I'm working up a sweat filleting this rope, so yeah I'm kind of warm—"

"I think I'm going to take my clothes off," she announced casually.

"You're *what?*"

Hannah paced in a tight circle next to me, blinking her eyes rapidly. She fanned herself with her white wrap dress as her breathing became shallow. The bride was having a panic attack.

"Yeah." Hannah nodded wildly, as if getting naked on a boat full of fifty of her closest family and friends was a super-duper plan.

I froze, knife at my side, watching Hannah peel the pretty dress off her body. She stood staring at me, shivering in a matching set of a tasteful nude bra and underwear.

"Hannah Noa Green. Put your fucking clothes back on—"

I heard a giant splash, and I looked downward to see the small lifeboat now floating in the water. Apparently, my knife skills were surprisingly decent. Hannah stepped toward the edge of the deck, and before I could rationalize with her, she leapt off the yacht. Hannah peered up at me, gripping the inflatable sides of the orange lifeboat.

"You jump, I jump?" she asked, in a shaky but hopeful tone.

"If we end up clutching a piece of wood out there, you better make some goddamn room for me."

I breathed in courage and jumped onto the lifeboat. I was now just an arm's reach from becoming one with frigid Lough Corrib—one fall from Tom Hanksing my way through survival among the sunset-bathed Connemara mountains. I studied Hannah with anxious eyes, my head shaking in disbelief as I took in my half-naked best friend. And then, she uttered the words that would ruin everything.

"I can't marry him tomorrow, Zoey. Not like this, I can't."

*Motherfucker.*

# Twenty-seven

We floated away from the yacht, slowly drifting along with the calm ripples of the water as the sun inched its way toward the horizon. Ashford Castle was lit up far in the distance, and a chill took over the purple sky.

"I can't marry him tomorrow. I can't. I can't," Hannah continued to cry, tears everywhere, breathing shallow.

I quickly pulled my purse off from around my shoulder and began digging inside it. I felt a small chalky object, bringing me a jolt of relief.

"Chew this, *now*," I demanded to Hannah, handing her a small white oval pill. She studied the pill in her shaking fingers.

"It has dirt on it," she whined, with trepid eyes.

"It's my emergency bottom-of-the-purse Xanax! CHEW."

Hannah shut up and crushed the pill with her teeth, swallowing a bit of disgust as it went down.

"Hannah, you're just having a panic attack. This is normal."

"Oh? Normal? IS IT? IS IT NORMAL? Is it normal to not be able to birth your own little baby that you can put your cute wedding handkerchief bonnet on and keep that from the man you're marrying tomorrow?"

"Well, not *specifically*. But look, Hannah, anyone in your position would have gotten triggered from that gift. Even if Graham knew about your infertility, you would have had a reaction to the pain of the moment. You're not a robot. Cold feet, all these big emotions before the wedding day, that's all normal," I reassured her, stroking her arms.

"I don't have cold feet. It's an iceberg, Zoey."

"Okay, maybe enough with the *Titanic* references, given, you know . . ." I glanced down, referring to our tiny lifeboat. Hannah grabbed my hands.

"I love Graham so much. So, so much."

Her chest caved in, and it broke my heart. One thing was certain amid the chaos: she really did love Graham. I squeezed her hand twice, hard, letting her know that I knew she loved him. That she did not have to convince me.

"He's not going to want to be with me like this."

"Like what?"

Hannah started to sob, fully becoming a puddle of a human as her head sank between her bare knees, her body rocking on the wet cold rubbery boat.

"*Broken*. I'm broken inside. I had a picture of what my life was supposed to look like, you know? I had a plan, a map—it was straightforward. And now, it's all—it's messy. I just want to be less complicated. Why can't I be less complicated? I want to be the kind of woman who can give the man she loves the big things. And my body won't let me, and I can't do anything about it. I can't fix this. I feel humiliated and powerless—like I'm a prisoner in this frame that's betraying me. And it's going to drive him away, Zoey. I've ruined my own future, just by existing in my broken body."

I felt her words. I felt them so hard that my stomach sank, as if she had transferred her anguish into my body. Wincing, I put my hands on either side of Hannah's shaking wet face. Like Hannah, I wished I were uncomplicated. My heart beat out of my chest for Rylan, but my mind was a deceptively twisty place for my desires to land. I held back stinging tears as I took in my best friend's face, and I was met with the memory of Rylan's face right before he walked out of his brownstone after I had turned down his proposal. *His wounded eyes.*

I understood the kind of shame Hannah felt, even though mine was wildly different. We both wanted to gift the people we loved with things that seemed effortless for the majority of women to give their partners—babies, marriage. Like Hannah, I was at war with my body. Yet, Hannah had no control over her body's inability to produce children. I had control over my mind's failure to embrace marriage. Accepting Hard Truths is never an easy task, especially when the world tells you your current reality is fucked up. How do you move forward with your head held high when the world tells you you're not living up to your potential *as a woman?*

Ever since I could remember, I had lived by a code of honesty. I was a middle-class outcast in a sea of upper-class Barbie and Ken dolls, and I grew tired of proving myself after I had already proven myself. I grew tired of being looked at skeptically when I was too loud in a room full of well-behaved leaders of tomorrow. I grew tired of being passed over when I eagerly raised my hand in class. I grew tired of trying to suppress the different opinions bubbling inside me. And so, at a very young age, I stopped raising my hand—I let my thoughts roll off my tongue. I glared back at the head tilts. I marched into rooms with my entire personality atop a chip on my shoulder. As I grew older, that chip melted into outspoken confidence. I became the kind of woman who would have been expelled from the Garden of Eden for an inability to be anything but herself: naked, aware of it, and unashamed. I wore my differences like badges of honor. I leaned in to them. I cursed once, someone winced, and I did it again, just to let them know it was my fucking right. I was never inherently ashamed of what was inside my heart—not until it broke. "Fuck-you honesty" was a proud shield, until my differences were no longer layers that could safeguard my soul, but rather knives inside my chest. I could no longer walk around with my truths on my sleeve. I was complicated, and I was no longer proud.

I managed to swallow a throat of tears, refusing to drown in Wallow City. I had to woman-up, strap on my wounded shield, and get this bride to do the same. I turned my body toward Hannah. She was now breathing normally, and I silently prayed this meant the Xanax was taking effect. I gripped my cold fingers around hers.

"Hannah, listen. Graham said he'd move mountains for you to be happy. *Mountains.* If he doesn't want to be with you just because you can't have children the way he envisioned, then he isn't the guy who would move mountains for you. And fuck the guy who won't move a mountain for the best person I know."

Hannah sniffled as tears rolled down.

"This isn't a mountain. It's . . . Zoey, it's a steel wall."

Yesterday, I'd made the decision to lean in to optimism—

trusting that Hannah and Graham's shared love was mightier than the secrets they were keeping from each other—trusting their union would release me from the chains that were holding me back from having a union of my own. I didn't anticipate the curveball of pulling a forlorn bride over a "steel wall" of despair.

"Hannah, if it's a steel wall, then you'll face it together."

"I have to tell him before the wedding, don't I?" she asked, already knowing the answer.

Of course she had to tell Graham. Any rational human knew this to be true. Rationality had left the goddamn lifeboat. If I agreed with her, if I told Hannah she had to come clean to Graham, she might never walk down the aisle. If I told Hannah to keep her mouth shut, Hannah would walk down the aisle tomorrow, her happy union intact. However, keeping this secret until after the honeymoon was a gamble that could end in divorce. Neither option was great for Hannah, and while I personally preferred option B, I wasn't monstrous enough to try to salvage my romantic future by destroying my best friend's.

"You should tell him," I found myself saying.

"Yeah, I have to tell him." She nodded her head in terrified agreement.

Hannah started to take slow breaths in and out, and I exhaled as well, realizing with great relief that her panic attack was waning. I whipped my head around, seeing that we had drifted far from the yacht. Really far.

*Fuck.*

I looked back at Hannah, who was half-naked.

*Also, fuck.*

I closed my eyes, knowing what I had to do, yet not loving

the idea of it. I drew a deep breath, told myself this was for the good of my future, turned around, and put my back toward Hannah.

"Unzip me."

"Huh?"

"I can't bring the bride back onto a yacht with all her family and friends, *naked*, without it being a thing."

"But you can go back in there naked?"

"It's me. I'll just tell everyone I undressed to protest the baby lamb burgers, or something."

Truthfully, Zoey Marks half-naked at a party would surprise no one, least of all Celeste and Gemma, who probably expected much worse from me.

Hannah cautiously unzipped me, and I shuffled the red dress down to my toes. Here I was, in a black bra and black underwear, on a lifeboat.

"You're the best human ever," Hannah said, as she tugged my dress down below her knees and I zipped the side of the dress up around her pale skin.

I was nowhere near the best, but for the first time in a few months, I felt like I wasn't the worst. *Progress.*

"Are you okay?" I asked.

"Not really."

"Super."

I leaned down onto the lifeboat's small motor and tugged at it. *Nothing.* I pulled it again, harder. And again. And again. *Nothing. NOTHING.*

I pointed my wind-chapped face up to the purple sky, closing my eyes and inhaling courage. In building up defensive walls over the course of my childhood, I had become the woman who counted asking for help as a weakness, rather than an act of brav-ery. While personal growth allowed me to grab my cell phone out of my purse, it did not make what I was about to do any less difficult. My numb fingers prepared to dial a number I had not dialed in three months—the number at the top of my Favorites. My shaking index finger hovered over his name.

*Enemy action.*

If I refused to make this phone call, if I refused to ask for his help, then the result would be chaos. The entire wedding party would notice that the bride was gone. There would be a dramatic search and rescue, Hannah would undoubtedly vomit her infertility secrets to Graham in front of a crowd, in the worst way possible, and I would go home unable to say yes to Rylan.

And so, I pressed down hard on his name.

"Hello?"

The sound of Rylan's deep voice echoed in my ear, causing heat to bubble upward in my chest. I inhaled the wind and swallowed hard. Now was not the time for heart flutters. Now was the time for All-Business Zoey. It was shark time.

"So, if you look out the left side of the yacht, you'll see this tiny yellow orange speck, this sort of lifeboat situation just floating on the lake. . . ."

I directed Rylan to our boat, as he confusedly walked up to the deck, looking out and spotting us.

"What in the hell . . . is that you?"

"Yep. And the bride. So I'm going to need you to discreetly find a junior captain or something, and get a lifeboat with a working engine, and have someone come rescue us—"

"Zoey, what did you do—"

"NO. You do not get to ask any questions. *Just. Rescue.*" I hung up the phone, my heart now fully racing. Hannah simply stared at me with a blank face.

"What? Rylan is going to run for office one day. He should get used to rescuing civilians."

I plopped my ass down on the rubber base of the boat, suddenly all too aware of how cold I was, and how little clothing I had on my body. Shivering, I tugged my knees into my chest to keep warm.

"Zoey, what are you doing?"

"At the moment, I'm floating down the lough, half-naked with my best friend." I knew full well that Hannah was not referring to our current state of affairs.

"Why aren't you two engaged? Really?"

It suddenly felt like there was a cold hard gun pressed against my temple. Hannah had never outright asked this question. She had danced around it delicately, respecting my silence, aware that the girl who had never loved before was not ready to unpack loss for the first time. I opened my mouth to see if something clever would come out, but instead, the frigid air floated between us.

"Was it someone else? You know I won't ever judge you. I'll love you no matter what. Always."

"I know you will. I just—Hannah, I'm . . ." I trailed off, unsure of exactly who I was, or who I had become.

"You're complicated?" Hannah offered, filling in the blanks as I nodded. "Yeah, it's the *worst*," she confirmed.

"The *worst*. Why can't we be like Mara? God, she's probably fertile as shit. And marriage? She already has a Pinterest folder ready to go for her modern elegant ceremony."

"He doesn't love her, Zoey."

"I know. But she has something that I don't have, and I hate her for it, and I envy how easy it comes to her."

"What comes?"

"Being an uncomplicated woman."

We stared at each other for a long moment as the orange sun dipped into the water. I looked into Hannah's open hazel eyes, which were now a beautiful blue. I had to tell her this truth. I had to tell my best friend. She deserved to have my truth when I had all of hers.

"Hannah, I turned down his proposal—I turned it down because—"

The crisp air abruptly thickened, darkness loomed over our bodies, and I lost my words. My wide eyes peered up to the sky, where instead of a setting sun, I found an arched wall. Hannah and I were floating under a bridge, through a claustrophobic stone tunnel.

Suddenly, our lifeboat slashed against a jet-black turbulent tide. I tightened a grip around the lifeboat's handle as violent waves spanked us from side to side, water slamming onto our shoulders and onto the boat's floor.

"WHAT IS HAPPENING?" Hannah shouted, trembling.

"I DON'T KNOW," I yelled back, terror enveloping my half-naked body.

Thunder cracked against the tunnel walls. We inched our shaking wet bodies toward the center of the lifeboat—cold lanky bones cowering and clawing onto each other.

"IS THIS HOW WE DIE?" Hannah cried, tightening a grip around my wet skin.

"WHY WOULD YOU ASK THAT?"

The thunder rose, evolving into what sounded like a caterwaul—like a person getting viciously murdered.

"THIS IS HOW WE DIE," Hannah confirmed, nodding her head wildly.

"I DRINK WAY TOO MANY CELERY JUICES TO DIE THIS YOUNG," I yelled—my eyes closed so that I could meet my death without actually facing it.

My nauseous body twisted with the tide—just a monstrous wave away from becoming one with the lough. As the frigid water continued slapping my face, I realized I was inhaling crisp air. I dared my eyes open, blinking back the purple night sky. We were out of the tunnel, but we were not out of the storm.

Hannah and I gripped tighter onto each other, weathering the furious waves hammering against our lifeboat. Suddenly, a vicious sea creature—possibly the result of a bloodsucking demon mating with a SeaWorld attraction—shot up from the water, soaring over our heads. With bloodcurdling howls, Hannah and I clenched our eyes shut, preparing to die young and pretty and with devastating secrets.

And then, silence fell upon calm waters.

Hearts beating out of our chests, we dared our wet lashes open, eyes like saucers, wondering if this was the afterlife, or if we had actually skirted death. The demonic sea creature, the harsh waves, the thunder, they were all gone. The lough rippled back casually as if it were all in our heads. I turned my shaking face to the other side of our boat, noticing air bubbles in the water—the spot where demonic Shamu landed. Before I could entertain the terror of where he went, I heard distant clapping.

I tilted my head up in confusion to see a beautiful gray stone bridge, from which we had just emerged, the bridge that led to

Ashford Castle's grounds. Standing on it and giggling down at us was a group of half a dozen children. They wore goofy grins and ASHFORD CASTLE KID'S CLUB T-shirts. A boyish enthusiastic camp counselor stood behind them, leading their excessive cheering and clapping. I crossed my arms and held my bare shoulders, hugging my trembling body, and hoping that a boob had not popped out in front of small children.

"You see, kids? The Loch Ness Monster *is* real," the counselor boasted.

"Do it again! Do it again!" a little girl in pigtails pleaded, jumping up and down.

"DON'T YOU FUCKING DARE," I roared.

I felt a twinge of guilt for cursing at a child, but *desperate times.* This little slice of horror was a kids' attraction? I hadn't been this close to dying at the hands of an animatronic creature since my Jaws encounter during the Universal Backlot Tour, and at least that ride came with a warning sign.

"See, children, sometimes the Loch Ness Monster can be very unpredictable," the counselor said, winking at me, hoping I would play along with his sadistic game—clearly not picking up on my internal terror.

"THE LOCH NESS MONSTER LIVES IN SCOTLAND. *NOT* IRELAND. WRONG-FUCKING-LAND."

"There have been *sightings*," he countered, seemingly horrified by my childish behavior in front of mere children.

"Umm . . ." I heard a familiar voice say.

Heat shot through my body as existential dread let crippling embarrassment have the floor. Normally, Rylan would be the only man I would let see me like this, but right now, he was the last person I wanted to see me like this. And yet, I had called him for rescuing.

I slowly turned my head, as if I could somehow delay humil-
iation if I simply pretended that I wasn't born with the correct
neck muscles to look sideways at people. The image of Rylan
motoring a small lifeboat by himself in a crisp suit made my
body hum.

"What in the world—" he began.

"I said no questions."

I looked over at Hannah, who was staring out at the horizon,
frozen with a blank expression. She was in shock, and rightly so,
as we had just survived an urban legend. I turned back to Rylan.
His eyes lingered on me for a little bit longer than I would have
expected as he knotted the two boats together with a thick
rope.

"You're naked."

*Oh. There was that.* I had forgotten about my lack of
clothes.

"Half," I corrected. Rylan stepped onto our lifeboat and took
off his blazer, resting it over my numb shoulders. I pulled the
warm jacket tight around my chest, breathing in cedar as my
eyes locked onto his.

Rylan glanced at Hannah, and his eyes darted back to me
in confusion.

"Is she wearing your dress?"

"That's a question."

"I thought I was going to die," Hannah said into the air, to no
one. Her expression was blank, and her hands were trembling.

Rylan bent down to her, concerned.

"Hannah, are you okay?" he asked.

Hannah looked at Rylan, doe eyes welling with tears. "All I
could see was him. I thought I was going to die, and all I could

see was Graham. I have to marry him. *I have to.* I have to be buried next to him."

Rylan smiled at her. "Well, I've got some good news for you, Hannah Banana, tomorrow is just a day away."

Hannah shifted closer to me, her eyes blinking rapidly.

"What if I lose him?" she whispered, her chin quivering with the thought.

I could read Hannah like a book, and *"I'm telling Graham jack shit before the wedding"* was written all over her face. Apparently, my best friend was not the type of hero to emerge from a near-death experience and vow to live her truth. Hannah focused on the fly in the truth ointment: the radioactive fallout. Authenticity came at a price, and Hannah wasn't willing to give the whole truth up for Graham. Oh, how I didn't blame her.

I shifted my attention from Hannah to Rylan, who knotted a second rope around our lifeboat. I watched his calloused fingers, reminded of the night before when they'd knotted inside my own, traced the curve of my neck, tangled in back of my hair. I studied his lips, losing myself in the memory of them open on mine, and I found my own lips parting into words.

"If you don't want to tell him, then don't."

I knew these were the words Hannah wanted to hear, yet a sharp pain in my gut told me they weren't what Hannah needed to hear.

Hannah sucked in air, leaning back onto the wet rubber boat with a full-body exhale. She stared at me with a growing grin, as if the reason we were shivering on this body of water in a broken lifeboat was no longer a factor. She clasped my hand, pointing her body toward me, her eyes brightening as she stared into mine.

*Oh God. Don't thank me. Not me. Don't—*

"Thank you," she said, earnestly squeezing my hand. "Zoey, I almost blew this whole thing up. I almost blew up my future. If it wasn't for you, I don't think tomorrow I'd be marrying the guy I want to die with."

*If it wasn't for me, you wouldn't be marrying the guy who doesn't know you can't have his children and who is still in love with his ex-girlfriend.*

"I love you so much. You're the best bridesmaid ever," Hannah said, beaming, taking me into a tight hug.

*I am the worst bridesmaid ever. Certified.*

Hannah let go, and my body slumped in shame against the cold, wet rubber floor of the lifeboat. I looked down at my twitching fingers, wondering how to garner enough strength to actually be *the best bridesmaid ever*, when suddenly, I realized I had an audience. I lifted my head upward to find Rylan's eyes locked onto mine. There was a light as he took me in, a warmth that I had not been able to fully access since our breakup. A slow smile reached Rylan's ears. His beaming expression was a puppet master, pulling the uneasy lines on my face up toward the sky until they exploded into a smile, matching his. He reached out his hand, linking his fingers with mine and pulling me up from the floor. I got lost in his green eyes—the heat of his body warming my skin as he tugged me tight to his thumping chest, *purposefully close*, leading me to his lifeboat.

"Look at you, saver of unions," he whispered, his gaze not leaving mine.

A couple minutes later, we were on the stern deck of the yacht, all the guests still belowdecks eating dessert. With a plan to tell those who asked that Hannah and I wanted to take a joyride

and have some girl time—something no one could question—
Hannah wrapped her white dress back around her body, and I
tugged my red dress back onto mine. I readjusted my footing,
realizing that the once-anchored yacht had started its return
toward the castle, which by the looks of it, could not be more
than a few minutes away.

Rylan finished tying the lifeboats up on the side of the yacht.
He glanced up, watching me glide my dress past my waist, as if
I were putting on a show just for him. To be fair, I was getting
dressed at a ridiculously slow pace, *just for him.*

"Can I give you a hand?" his voice cracked, referring to my
zipper.

It was actually one of those easy zippers—side zippers were always my favorite, except under unfortunate circumstances where
side-boob got caught up in the metal—but, who was I to say no
to the possibility of his fingers on my body? That would be a
crime.

I nodded wordlessly. Hannah looked over, watching us with
wide eyes, as if searching for any insight that I was unwilling
to share.

I could feel the heat of his mouth nearing my bare shoulder as he arched forward behind me. I breathed in the man
standing unbearably close to my trembling body—warm cedar
swirled amid the musk of autumn. I gathered my hair up into
a high bun, leaving my neck and spine naked, both of which
longed to fall backward onto his strong hold, just a fingertip
away. His lips were close enough to meet my skin as he inched
the zipper up the side of my ribs, as slowly as possible. My heart
hammered against my chest, and I fought to keep my sanity as
my skin prickled against his touch. Sure, he was technically

helping to dress me, but it felt as though Rylan were peeling back every layer on my skin, leaving me helplessly exposed. His fingers grazed my clavicle, and I looked up to the darkening sky, holding my breath. I could have died right there and gone out swinging.

"All good . . ." he whispered into my ear. I swallowed hard, turning to meet his burning eyes. We stared at each other like we were fireworks erupting in purple dusk. We took each other in as if we were the only people on this yacht.

*We were not.*

"What's going on here?" asked a quavering voice.

Caught, we slowly turned, our wide-eyed faces finding Mara standing at the base of the stairs belowdecks, anger and confusion splashed upon her face. Her squinted expression darted from Rylan, to me, and back. Rylan opened his mouth, but before he could defend his completely defenseless actions, Mara slunk downstairs with heavy footsteps. Rylan started to move after her, but he paused at the base of the stairs, glancing back at me. It was a weightless gaze, a flame for me still burning bright. It was as if he recognized that I was not a lost cause. That there was hope for us.

All at once, the spark in his eyes became my escape door in a maze of guilt. I soared through the exit, culpability melting from my body.

# Twenty-eight

The second Hannah and I descended below to the dining deck, all the guests were standing and putting on their jackets. We were a moment away from docking, and Hannah delivered our excuse perfectly, explaining that she and I just wanted some quiet girl time. Everyone bought it without a second thought, except for Celeste, who was still irked by Hannah's previous behavior.

Barefoot, I disembarked from the yacht and found a nearby bench to sit and put my shoes on. In front of me, Ashford Castle was glowing in the distance. A full moon brightened the night, which I prayed was not an ominous sign that the gods would do everything in their power to keep a cursed woman cursed.

"Something isn't right with you," I heard Celeste's icy voice say.

I looked up from my heels to see Celeste and Hannah stepping off the yacht.

"Mom, I'm fine. It's the night before my wedding, can you stop?" Hannah said, scurrying down the dock. Celeste tugged at Hannah's arm, trying to guide Hannah back toward her.

"If not now, then when am I supposed to have this conversation with my daughter?"

"*Stop*," Hannah yelled, edging herself out of Celeste's grip.

I arched back, as did Celeste, whose face widened in shock. I had never witnessed Hannah stand up to her mother. Hannah was a pleaser by nature, especially when it came to her perfect parents. She was a fighter when she needed to be or when backed into a corner, but rarely did she go up against her makers. Rarely did life give her a reason to. She toed the line perfectly. Once, she tripped over the leg of a chair, fell, and broke a glass vase in the living room. Hannah grounded herself for two weeks—not even giving her parents a chance to tell her it was okay, that everyone made mistakes.

I was almost relieved to find Hannah hurrying away from Celeste rather than folding into self-blame for something that wasn't her fault. But even worse, I was relieved that Celeste wasn't able to pull the truth out of her.

I watched as Graham joined Hannah's side, putting an arm around his bride and kissing her head as they slipped inside the castle's doors to get ready for a night of drinking with friends. My eyes scanned the remaining bodies on the yacht's stern deck—eager to know what happened with Rylan and Mara, whom I had not seen since Rylan dressed (undressed) me.

"What's wrong with her?" asked Celeste. She loomed over me, interrupting my masochistic search and glaring at me with knowing eyes—eyes that pointed blame in my direction, eyes that knew I was full of secrets.

"She's a bride," I said with a shrug, hoping that would appease Celeste. It did no such thing.

"She's pregnant, isn't she?"

My mouth stood ajar. Celeste was *so* far and *so* close—same universe, different planet.

"The quick wedding, the reaction to that baby handkerchief. She's pregnant. She's pregnant . . . and she hid it from me."

It was apparent that the idea of Hannah keeping big news from Celeste hit her harder than the idea of Hannah carrying a tattooed man's baby out of wedlock. Celeste edged her body away from mine, strapping on her embossed crocodile boots, her hands trembling from the weight of a realization: she had become an outsider in her daughter's life.

Celeste had never been my favorite person. She was constantly striving for perfection from everyone around her, and she put too much pressure on Hannah to embody this perfection and become a smaller version of herself. But Hannah was wrapped in empathy—there was an openness to Hannah that Celeste did not possess. Yet, as I took in Celeste's weakening face, I was shocked to discover there was genuine vulnerability under her proud exterior—you just had to press a precise button to see it. Celeste felt that if she relinquished control over the hard shell around her, if she softened, she might never be able to put her armor back on again. In disliking Celeste for so many years, I had fully underestimated her. I had underestimated her simple love for her daughter, and her simple, very human need to be loved and trusted *by* her daughter.

I watched Celeste suck in tears, sticking her face up toward the moon. She did so, not in a way that I normally would have written off as snootiness, but in a way that told me she struggled sometimes. The most hardened woman I knew was not impervious to feelings. We all wanted the same things out of life, we just went about it differently: we wanted to be loved and trusted. The thing about mothers? They're complicated too.

A few minutes later, I traipsed down the winding hallway inside the castle to find the warm safe haven of my room. I was exhausted, having just survived the Loch Ness Monster and all. I sandwiched myself under the velvet duvet and snuggled into the bed, my red dress still on my body, my numb extremities prickling back to life under the warm covers. I turned quickly to check the schedule on the wedding welcome pamphlet sitting on the nightstand, confirming that night-before drinks were at nine thirty at Ashford Castle's Prince of Wales Bar. I set a phone alarm to wake me in an hour and a half, and I let my eyes get heavy and my body take comfort in a motionless room.

An hour later, I woke to the muffled sounds of arguing outside my balcony. Groggy, I wiped a spot of drool off the corner of my mouth, and I shuffled out of bed with a furrowed brow. I pulled back the heavy curtain and glanced outside, seeing the quiet moon glisten over the lough. Hearing the voices again, I curiously tugged open the balcony door as cold air hit my face. I shivered, curving my head around the side of the castle, eyes widening to find Rylan and Mara engaged in warfare by a massive firepit. By the looks of it, they had not stopped arguing since she found him zipping up my dress on the yacht. Rylan appeared exasperated and guilty, sitting on an iron bench while he darted glances up at Mara, who paced in an infuriated circle above him.

"You proposed to her *two weeks* before we met?"

*Oh boy.*

Rylan looked down at his fingers, as if they might hold a different answer than the shitty truth.

"I understand it might not be considered *cool* to talk about your ex, but a failed proposal feels like a little nugget of history you should have shared with me, especially before I came *here*."

"I liked you. I really liked you, and I didn't think you would . . ." Rylan trailed off as Mara came down toward his face, an edge to her perfect facade that almost made me like her.

"You didn't think I would jump into it with you after hearing that you'd just gotten down on one knee for another woman? Gosh, Rylan. *Yeah*, your gut was right," she said sardonically.

Mara huffed and plopped down on the other side of the bench, her body turned away from him as she furiously pulled her phone out of her small clutch and typed as if she were defusing a bomb.

"This has nothing to do with who you are. Mara, you're amazing. You're everything I should want in a—" Rylan's attempt at making nice was thwarted with Mara's palm pointed toward his face, her eyes not coming up from her phone.

"I'm already leaving here as collateral damage. Spare me the eulogy. There's a five A.M. flight out of this place. I'm going to pack."

Mara stood up, shoving her phone back in her purse. Rylan took in a pained breath, standing to look at her.

"I'm so sorry—"

"NO. You don't get to feel better about yourself here."

"I'll Venmo you for the flight," he said sheepishly.

"Yeah, no shit you will," she replied, cool as ice, her eyes cutting through him. She shook her perfect hair at him and stormed away toward the castle's side door.

I watch the side door slam shut, my body jolting with guilt. Mara was not the villain in my story. She was not my enemy.

She was not my competition. She was a woman. Mara was intelligent, she had a healthy amount of self-worth, she cared about other people, she was joyful, and she wasn't a doormat. I had treated a blameless woman like she was expendable, and I only had myself to blame for that. Mara deserved better.

I glanced back toward the bench, watching Rylan peer down at his shoes. He ran a hand anxiously through his hair with an exhale, arching his neck upward to study the moon. Rylan lived by a code of conduct that included being honest and loyal. I knew he would beat himself up for hurting Mara in the least-honorable way possible. Rylan Harper was a good man, but heart-break had brought out the worst in him, the worst in us both.

I hesitated on the balcony, unsure if I should go to him, or simply leave it be. I wanted nothing more than to use my lips to melt the worst of us both away, but Rylan and I deserved to sit with the monsters we had become before earning that prize. I stared down at his aching face, those green eyes chipping away at my rationale, until I convinced myself not to conflate a les-son learned with a sentence served. I took myself out of adult time-out and slipped out of my hotel room, as if pulled to Rylan by a chemical force.

I had disappointed absolutely every past lover with an un-apologetic admission that I had only watched the first couple of *Star Wars* films. Year after year I promised myself I would start from the beginning and finally understand the beloved fran-chise. However, this was akin to promising I would start read-ing a book while the writer added a hundred pages to each end. Therefore, I was no expert, but from what I could gather, I was "Force Sensitive." An indescribable energy in the atmosphere bent my free will and pulled me outside to Rylan.

Unfortunately, I was lacking a Yoda. I was entirely unaware of how to use the Force, and I did not have an epic plan for what to do after it brought me to Rylan's body. I was Force Sensitive and Human Stupid. If there existed such a character in *Star Wars* whose death served as a cautionary tale for the real heroes, then consider me, Zoey Marks, most likely this character.

Without a lightsaber by my side, the Force pushed my body outside the side door, led my heels down a stone path, and slowed my steps until I was bathed in the heat of the roaring stone fire-pit. Rylan sat on the bench, staring into the flames, as if willing them to burn him alive.

"Hey," I said.

Rylan's body rose from a slump of anguish as he turned to look at me. I cautiously sat next to him, both of our faces glowing in the orange light. He parted his lips, stammering, leaving me wondering what was going on in his pragmatic mind—a mind that had just let the uncomplicated, perfect woman go. I gave him a moment, and he tore his eyes away from mine, tapping his finger anxiously on the cold iron bench.

"Mara . . . she's . . ."

"I saw. And heard."

I took his tapping hand into mine, knotting our fingers together while I studied them in the firelight. He pointed his body toward me, but his eyes remained down, now watching our hands.

"I shouldn't have brought her here. I know that."

"Then why did you?"

He exhaled, shifting his shoulders, a tell that he was about to reveal something that made him uncomfortable. I usually en-joyed seeing this rare side of Rylan, leaning in to his discomfort with wide eyes, as if daring him to get more vulnerable. But on this bench, I was motionless, as if paralyzed by the possibilities of his answer.

"I couldn't face you, not alone. Having someone by my side when I came face-to-face with you . . . I wouldn't have been able to get on the plane otherwise. I know that's selfish, and really unfair to Mara, but . . . a part of me didn't care who got hurt, as long as it wasn't me again."

*Boy did his rebound ricochet.* Honesty: It wasn't pretty, but he sure did it well.

"You thought she would be a good weapon to use against me?" I asked, wondering if Mara had simply been his lightsaber.

"Maybe an emotional one, so that I wouldn't . . ." he trailed off, untwisting his fingers from mine. He ran his hand over his face with an exhale.

"Zoey, it's easier not loving you."

There was an echo of thunder in my ears—the sound of my heart slamming to the pavement. I peered down at the ground, as if I could somehow pick it up with my eyes. My heart was useless—it was the kind that was hard to hold. I was too difficult to love.

Rylan lifted my chin upward, locking my eyes onto his. Suddenly, I could feel his hand at the nape of my neck and the heat of his mouth on my lips.

"Why do you have to be so damn easy to love?" he whispered.

The question disappeared into my mouth, our lips meeting in a hungry kiss. The kiss deepened as our fingers knotted into each other's hair. I pulled him tight against my glowing body, my heart twisting back inside me and stitching itself together.

Rylan slowly broke, our lips parting, the warmth of our

breaths huffing between us in the frigid night. I nestled my face into the curve of his neck, taking comfort in the feeling of his scruff against my cheek.

I had read Rylan's "it's easier not loving you" all wrong. I was complicated—a difficult person—*and* I was easy to love. Unfortunately, I was not greater than the sum of those two parts. I was a heartbreaker—the woman who would tear down your walls while hiding behind her own. I was every guy Taylor Swift had warned us about. I was the Bad Boy corner of a WB triangle. Rylan had called in reinforcements, a Mara shield, but the armor was no match for this heartbreaker.

I didn't just want to be lovable, I wanted to be uncomplicated when it came to matters of love. My finger grazed the base of Rylan's throat, my palm settling on his racing chest. I was desperate to be the safe place his heart could land.

Suddenly, I felt Rylan's body tense. He pulled back from me, his green eyes scanning every inch of my face.

"Do you want to be with me?"

*I feel like I can't breathe without you.*

"Of course."

"No." He shook his head. "Zoey, not just now. In fifty years, do you want to be with me?"

Rylan wanted my future. He wanted everything. He needed a yes. *Of fucking course he did.* I dug down, shoving past the armor, desperate to emerge with the answer that would wrap us up in a bow and present us to the world in a way that many women would die for. But, there were still walls—still a gnawing pain in my gut that stopped me from undoing my own heartbreak.

I sucked my cheeks in, completely at a loss. Why in the fucking world could I not have practiced patience, for once in my impatient life, and saved this conversation for tomorrow night? Why, after three months, was I still my own worst enemy? I was helpless when faced with the opportunity to love Rylan. But I was not powerless in the face of Forever. I had a lightsaber ready to fight the enemy of *no one*. Everyone cheered for marriage, but here I sat, pointing a weapon with trembling hands at the wrong target, terrified that if I dropped my guard, the enemy of no one would suffocate me in my sleep.

He was waiting, eyes unblinking. Rylan was waiting to see if we would grow old together, *again*. Would I be eighty-one with him by my side? He was waiting to see if I had become friends with my misunderstood enemy.

"Ask me tomorrow night," was all I could say. I felt the words leave my mouth, my stomach dropping, knowing they were not enough, knowing those words were not what he wanted to hear.

"*What?*" he asked, as if he couldn't have heard me correctly.

"Can we just go hold each other and not do this right now—"

"What is tomorrow night going to bring you that the past three months haven't?"

"Confidence . . . confidence in something I don't feel confident in."

He shot up from the bench and pressed his hands against his temples, seconds away from ripping out his own hair.

"GODDAMNIT, ZOEY," he exploded, a vein pulsing on his neck. "You either want to spend your life with me, or you don't! It's *black or white*. It shouldn't be this hard."

I *knew* it shouldn't be this hard, which only made it punch harder. My chin quivered as I choked back tears.

"It's not that simple for me. Please just ask me after the ceremony, okay? There are too many emotions swirling right now, and Mara just left—"

The rest of my sentence disappeared into the night as I watched Rylan's face curl into an epiphany, one he could barely wrap his mind around.

"You need to see Hannah get married before you can say yes to me . . . don't you?"

I could feel my heart pounding. My mouth hung open in the tempestuous air. I was defenseless, utterly exposed. I watched his sardonic smile sharpen into anger.

"Unbelievable. You think Hannah saying 'I do' is going to make you want to marry me? That's not how *this* works. You're not in charge of other people's love lives, and they're not in charge of yours. What's wrong with you?"

My eyebrows folded inward, and I stood up from the bench, tightening my leather jacket around my chest as the wind howled around me.

"Is it asking for too much to see some positivity in the Forever Department before I walk down that road?"

"Your parents have been together for forty years. What more evidence do you need?"

"My parents? They've had their lives planned out since they were twenty. And I haven't. I'm not like them, Rylan. I don't know where I'll be in one year, let alone fifty. Asking for Forever is a lot to ask of someone."

"People have been known to grow together. It is possible," he pontificated, as if I were the only human in the universe who didn't believe couples could stay together and remain happy.

"If they're lucky. And I'm not."

"So that's what this is? Reverse your luck and reverse your fucked-up view of the world?"

"You think the way I see the world is fucked up?" I asked, tears stinging my eyes.

He paced in a small circle, drawing in the wind, as if trying to calm a storm. He stopped in front of me, his eyes narrowing onto mine.

"One month in, six months, one year—*anytime*. You had nearly two years to tell me that we were on a road to *nowhere*, and you chose to say *nothing*."

"I'm not perfect. I don't have everything figured out like you do. I loved you, I *love* you. I didn't want to lose you over something I didn't understand. I still don't."

"Zoey, what do you think comes after living together? What's the *appropriate* next step for two adults who love each other so fucking much? You knew what was coming—you knew I would ask you to marry me."

"I didn't know *when*. It's not like you asked for my ring size, and you definitely didn't give me an ounce of grace to wrap my head around it. I asked you for more time, and you couldn't give that to me. You walked away because I didn't fulfill some instant fantasy for you. You just walked away—" I choked on the memory, stepping closer to him, clutching the lapel of Rylan's jacket, turning his pacing body toward me.

"Don't walk away from me again. I need to see Hannah make it down the aisle. I need—"

"I walked away from you because you broke my fucking heart. You don't want to spend your life with me yet you love me? I don't understand why you're this way. I just, I don't understand you. . . ." he trailed off, shaking his head at me with a furrowed brow.

He studied my face like he had stumbled upon a confusing paragraph in his favorite novel.

It shattered me.

The first guy to look at me like he understood me, to *really see me*, to lean in and love every inch—here he was telling me he didn't understand me, not at all. It was a total betrayal. Yet somehow, Rylan had successfully made me feel like the traitor. His proposal threw me off my axis, and instead of clinging to him and not letting him walk out the door, I had clung to my gut instinct like it was my life raft. Rylan had always been mesmerized by my ability to let my intuitions guide me, until they didn't send me down the road he had paved. He wanted me to betray a part of myself—a part he used to love—and he expected me to do it instantly.

My aching pain grew sharp. It grew raw and angry. Suddenly, I was furious with Rylan for wanting me to shrink so that he could stand tall.

"Why do you only want me on your terms?" I cried, my desperate and wet face inches from his.

"You only want me on *your* terms. There's nothing wrong with wanting what ninety percent of people want. That doesn't make me an idealist—that just makes me a *normal person*. What's so wrong with what Hannah and Graham are going to do tomorrow? What's so damn scary and horrible about it?"

His arms hung in the air as he waited for my answer.

There was about to be "a great disturbance in the Force," I could feel it. The secrets I had locked up inside, they were on the edge of my tongue, punching to break free. And then, furiously, my shield cracked, unable to hold them back any longer.

"THEY BARELY KNOW EACH OTHER. HANNAH HAS NO IDEA THAT GRAHAM IS STILL IN LOVE WITH HIS EX-GIRLFRIEND. GRAHAM HAS NO IDEA THAT HANNAH CAN'T HAVE HER OWN CHILDREN—"

"You can't have children?" I heard a low voice ask.

A chill shot through my insides, punching my gut and strangling my throat. Anticipating the worst, I slowly turned, getting visual evidence of The Actual Worst. Hannah, Graham, and Ezra stared at Rylan and me, all slack-jawed. My body was frozen in shock and shame as I watched Hannah's wide hazel eyes fill with tears, her body shaking. I had uncaged her Truth Monster, and now she was forced to fight it—with no weapon and no training.

Graham turned back to Hannah.

"You can't have children?" he gently repeated, his brow furrowed in confusion, his voice begging Hannah to reassure him that my words—which callously left my big mouth—were untrue.

Hannah's eyes anxiously darted to Graham, then me, and back to Graham. Tears streamed down and her chest caved in. As sobs escaped, she sprinted away, her heels digging into the lawn and her ballerina body disappearing behind the side of the castle wall.

I had to go after her. I had to, but my legs were cemented to the ground. I was once again the stunned opossum, and I could not move.

Graham turned to me, still replaying the words in his head.

"She can't have children?"

After watching Ezra, Rylan, and Graham take my frozen body in for what felt like twenty years, I found enough strength to will my mouth open. I set my wet eyes on Graham.

"So? You're not a grand prize. It's not like you aren't holding on to your own secrets."

"What are you talking about?" Graham asked, his head

shaking. Apparently, he had only heard the part of my violent outburst having to do with Hannah not being able to have children. *Men.*

"Ezra had the band play that U2 song at the bar so that you would get all teary-eyed over your ex-girlfriend while staring at your fiancée."

Graham turned to his brother, confusion now replaced with fury.

"I was worried you were rushing into things," Ezra sheepishly cracked. "That you were just diving into marriage to get over Lind—"

Graham silenced Ezra with a sucker punch at the base of Ezra's jaw. If I weren't currently having a life crisis, this moment would have brought me joy. Ezra inched backward, but he did not fall down. He held his face, spitting out a bit of blood from his mouth. He let his eyes stay on the ground, aware that he deserved to be punched and had no moral grounds to fight back.

Graham turned to me with red-faced anger.

"I used to cry myself to sleep listening to that song, and sure, I did so while thinking of my ex-girlfriend. I'm a sensitive guy, the track came on at the bar, and I got a little emotional. You want to know why? Because for the first time, I heard something that used to crush my insides, and the second I heard it, I felt nothing. I was sitting there, looking up at the woman I'm going to spend the rest of my life with, and I just—"

Graham stopped, overcome with emotion. I watched as tears filled his eyes. He let them fall, not even bothering to cover up who he was, or how strongly he felt for another human being. He sucked in a breath of cold air, and he continued.

"I was thankful for all the shit, all the pain, for all the times

I cried over someone else. I was thankful that it all led me to her." His voice constricted, as if realizing that he might be losing *her*.

"You really love Hannah, don't you?" I asked quietly, my eyes taking him in while my heart ached.

"I put a goddamn ring on her finger," he snapped at me, as if to say, *"Of course I love her, you fucking idiot."*

Graham strode away in anger, shaking his head and punching his way past the side door, which was not the direction Hannah ran off to. He loved her, but he was not going after her. Was she no longer worth moving mountains for? Was he just processing? Had I ruined my best friend's wedding by unearthing her truth before she was ready?

I watched helplessly as Ezra's heavy footsteps followed after Graham. Ezra's usually hardened face was now broken and bleeding, remorse blanketing his blue eyes. Ezra had gotten what he wanted out of this weekend. He was about to win the war, and yet he held an expression reminiscent of a soldier covered in shrapnel, ready to claw his way out of a trench with a white flag.

I scanned the black night, which held no sign of Hannah. I swallowed the gallons of tears ready to pour out, and frantically moved toward the greenery, in the direction Hannah disappeared to, when a strong hand grabbed my arm. I had momentarily forgotten that Rylan and I were in the middle of a fight to the death.

"Zoey . . ."

I looked down at his grip on my arm. I felt anger mounting. I was furious at him, but mostly, I hated myself.

"Don't touch me," I cracked, and I edged my arm out of his

hold, tears falling as I ran across the lawn, my legs moving so quickly that the night air dried my cheeks.

I rounded the corner to the back of the castle. The night was eerily quiet. Autumn leaves rustled on the landscape as a chill blanketed my body. Panic rising, I shoved myself through the castle doors.

I knocked on the door of her suite. *Nothing.* I scanned Oak Hall, the closing dining rooms, the bars, the wine cellar, the billiards room—I swept through every inch of Ashford Castle, and there was no Hannah. She was not inside.

An overwhelming guilt swirled in my chest as I breathlessly pushed the front door of the castle open, my heels scraping down the steps, my wide eyes searching the starry sky. In front of me, the full moon towered above the dark night, casting a glow upon acres and acres of dense woods and Lough Corrib. I helplessly spun in a circle, clutching my wild hair.

Our bride was Gone Girl.

And this time, it really was my fault.

# Twenty-nine

I roamed the castle property as if I were embarking on the world's most deserving walk of shame. I gave up helplessly belting Hannah's name into the night sky after the first hour of navigating the greenery on the front and back lawns, my throat growing hoarse and pained.

I kicked my heels off at hour two, letting nature prickle my bare, swollen feet as I stumbled through the walled gardens—a long, sweeping archway lined with green vines. A thorn slashed my thigh, tearing my dress and leaving a nice red cut on my skin. I winced as silent hot tears fell, but I kept walking. I deserved to break and bleed.

At hour five, I twisted my body up the musty, tight, swirling stone staircase, reaching the top of a lone turret out in the woods. I stood tall, looking out the tiny window, searching aimlessly for my best friend. I shouted her name into the darkness. *Nothing.*

At hour eight, I limped along the drawbridge, my muddy feet growing tired on the paved stones. I leaned over the bridge, hugging my leather jacket tighter around my dress as wind howled in my face. I took in the wedding crew by the castle's lakeside as they unpacked boxes of white roses and began to erect a massive white canopy.

I gave up as the sun came up on Hannah's wedding day. Energy had left my body, nature had bruised my limbs, and my actions had rendered me worthy of dying alone, lying in the middle of a stretch of frosty grass surrounded by dense Irish woods. My teeth chattered up to the sky as I watched swirls of purple and orange cut through the darkness. I zipped my jacket up over my torn dress, my body caked in dirt, my feet numb, mascara tears down my stiff jaw. I edged my AirPods into my ears, letting Lilith Fair inflict further pain upon my dying breaths. If this was how Zoey Marks must leave the world, she should at least go out with a proper soundtrack.

Goose bumps enveloped my lifeless body the moment I heard Alanis's "You Learn" hum into my ears. A fleeting grin moved across my cold lips, taking in the sound of my childhood. I stared up at the cloudless sky as if I were living inside a nineties rom-com. A camera was spinning down on me slowly, framing the girl in red who fucked up the best thing that ever happened to her.

The love of my life, my entire life, *no question.*

I let hot tears roll down my cheeks as I closed my wet lashes, and I was met with the first memory I had of Hannah.

Hannah was three, shy and sweet, and very small for her age. Her stick-straight blond hair clung to her perfect, pale, freckled face as she diligently built a sandcastle at our neighborhood playground.

My chest ached as I thought of myself that young. I pictured the wild, athletic girl with huge curly hair haphazardly jumping into the sandbox with a booming laugh next to her shy best friend.

We looked at each other with innocent smiling faces. Only three years old, already opposites in every way. Our tiny hands dug into the sand, working tirelessly to build an imperfectly perfect castle. My first memory. Not just of Hannah, but of my life. I could not remember a time in my entire life when Hannah Green was not the most important person in it.

Tears rolled down as I longed for that sandbox. I longed to be young again. I wanted to cling to the lie that everything gets better as we get older. That adults are superheroes who know what they're doing. That all great love stories end in Forever. I had spent my youth eager to enjoy the freedom of adulthood, and now, here I was, bathed in adulthood, longing to have the freedom of a child. Life was, by and large, unfair. It refused to meet us in the middle. It refused to stand still in the greatest of moments—the moments where we longed for nothing.

Why couldn't a rare green flash sunset last for years? Why couldn't we spend a century building an imperfect sandcastle with the person we loved?

I needed my childhood best friend. I needed her in my life until the day my twisted road came to an end. I still had no idea how I felt about Forever, but I knew without blinking that she was my Forever. We had grown together and had never grown apart. Thirty-one years. I had come to Ireland dead set on changing my mind about marriage. I had come to Ireland to get Hannah down the aisle. I had come to Ireland, yet like many *Bachelor* contestants, I was here for the wrong reasons.

If I was not Hannah Green's Best Friend, then I did not care what other title life threw my way. Unattached, Engaged, Spinster, Housewife, Married, Bad Luck Bridesmaid . . . it all meant nothing if I was not Hannah Green's Best Friend.

Suddenly, I was ten, peering down at my thirty-one-year-old self. Young Zoey Marks, the girl who raised a fist up to the world when most would hold themselves in the fetal position, tilted her face sideways at the adult version of herself. She saw me the way the outside world did, because she didn't understand who I had become. Where was the girl who had the power to create her own anthem and proudly march to it? Where was the girl who showed her best friend there would always be someone dancing by her side?

It is a proven scientific fact that music can increase levels of adrenaline in the body. Alanis shifted the fears warring through my veins, like a nostalgic anthem, willing me to rise to the occasion. And so, I rose from the grass. I was ten, climbing atop my bed with music in my ears after a horrible day. I would not lie down. I would rage.

I could feel my heart beating in my ears as blood rushed to my head. My eyes narrowed upon a curious black shimmer in the distance near the path in the woods. Blinking back the glaring sun, my bare feet trudged bravely toward it. My eyes widened as I picked up Hannah's black heel. She was somewhere near here. She was somewhere near . . . *fuck*. My face fell as I saw the sign in front of me, a cute white arrow pointing to the School of Falconry.

I arched my shoulders back, held my dizzy head high, and ardently limped down the now-familiar pathway in the woods, a meandering trail of large spruces and redwoods enveloping my battered and bruised body.

I approached the dilapidated cabin. My hands tried to open the shaky door, but it was locked from the inside. I yanked my AirPods out of my ears, tucking them into my purse and sucking in a gulp of air. I unzipped my jacket, turned the side of my body to the door, and kicked my bare foot into it, splintering the door wide open.

I crept into the shed with terrified eyes, taking in the small dusty room with five falcons hanging out in their own individual large cages. I shuddered, finding a separate cage that held live white mice. I turned my head, and there she was. Karen stared back at me, her beady eyes taking in the asshole who almost killed her.

"So, we meet again . . ."

I jabbed Hannah's expensive shoe into the slats of Karen's cage, letting Karen peck at it for a moment.

"This is my Hannah," I told Karen.

I pulled out my phone, finding a photo of Hannah's smiling face from two days ago, and held it out to Karen, as if showing a picture of a missing child to a detective.

"You got it?"

Karen looked at me sideways. I was talking to a falcon. Things were going well.

I grabbed the two worker's gloves from atop her cage, tugging them onto my hands. I stretched my neck from side to side, rolled my shoulders back, and proceeded to run in place. I was a boxer in a ring, warming up before she confronted her opponent. I was basically Rocky.

Panting, I grabbed a live mouse from the cage, holding it in one hand, and then turned to Karen, my opponent. I sucked in courage and opened her cage, letting Karen's claws step onto my shaking gloved hand. I held my breath, slowly leading her out of her cage, and then outside into the crisp Irish air, exhaling sanity and in complete shock that I was staring at a bird and not shitting my pants.

"I'm doing it, I'm doing it, I'm doing it, I'm doing it . . . KAREN, I'M FUCKING DOING IT," I cried with eyes full of proud tears as we approached the open lawn, the patch of grass where Karen almost became a dinner course at the farm-to-table restaurant on the property.

I smiled at Karen, no longer afraid, and I courageously swept my arm across my body as if I were sending her into battle.

"FIND HANNAH," I shouted out into the sky, watching Karen soar above me like a gorgeous majestic unicorn dancing over the rising sun.

"We did it, Ratatouille," I cheered down to the confused mouse squirming in my fist.

It was a moment filled with glory. This was the final scene of every Disney sports movie. This was *Cool Runnings*—

"What are you doing?"

I turned to find Ezra. He took me in with a smirk and a furrowed brow. My eyes widened, blinking back my unrecognizable enemy. He was in the same clothes as the night before, but his white collared shirt was dirty and unbuttoned four buttons from the top, his sleeves were rolled tightly around his biceps, his hair was tossed to the side in a mess of curls, and he had a cut above his lip. It was like staring at a different person. A person you might even *want* to stare at. I blinked rapidly, and then I felt a mouse try to free itself from my hand, a reminder that I had more important things to keep my eyes on.

I darted my eyes back up to the sky, seeing Karen soaring over me in a circle.

"Go away. I'm saving the day."

"*How* exactly?"

I rolled my eyes, turning to Ezra with an audible sigh.

"Karen's handler said that falcons are prey animals. They have keen senses of smell and sight. So, I gave Karen a whiff of Hannah's shoe and a visual, and I sent her off to find the bride. I'm a genius. Go fuck off."

"Let me get this straight, princess. You sent a prey animal—a *hunter*—armed with all she would need to find your best friend?"

"Sure fucking did." I beamed with a high chin. "Karen will find Hannah and do her little circle thing indicating where the bride is, and then come flying back to me and eat a mouse as a prize."

I glanced down apologetically to the rodent in my fist. "Sorry, Ratatouille," I whispered, as he stared up at me with "how could you?" eyes.

"That falcon will find Hannah, do the little circle thing, and then nosedive and attack your best friend."

I glared at his smug face, fighting the urge to sucker punch the other side of his perfectly square jaw. I peered up to the sky, matching Ezra's smug grin, crossing my arms, and reveling in the sight of Karen circling in the distance, above an area behind the thick woods.

"*See.* Told you she would—"

I ate the rest of my words, watching openmouthed as Karen folded her wings inward, aimed her beak at the ground, and dive-bombed into a place I could not see.

"HANNAAAAAAAAAAAH!" I shouted in horror.

I felt my bare feet leave the grass, and suddenly, the sky broke in half. I was sprinting down an uncharted path in the woods, my heart beating out of my chest, as thick rain slapped down upon my body.

# Thirty

I sprinted along the path in the woods as the surrounding red-wood branches scraped the shoulders of my drenched leather jacket. My curly hair was soaked, the thick rain stinging my eyes, and I could hear Ezra splashing at my heels. For once, the idea of having him in my atmosphere didn't feel so horrible. I was my own worst enemy, *not just theoretical anymore*. Even worse, I had become Hannah's worst enemy, and I needed an ally to save the bride.

At each little gap in the woods, I squinted past the autumn leaves to find Karen diving with increased velocity toward something in the distance. My dirt-caked feet splashed through the mud as I breathlessly rounded a corner.

Panting, I froze in my muddy tracks. Above me, Karen un-furled her wings, slowing as her nose-dive was met with the roof of a small wood shack. Karen flew back upward, soared in a circle, and then dipped back toward the roof again. I exhaled relief as I studied the worn ivory shed, where a sign on the door boasted Irish Cavalier King Charles Spaniels—Bred on Site.

I collapsed with my hands on my knees, my wet hair dangling between my battered legs. I knew Hannah was in there. I knew that the girl whose parents banished her from further volunteer work with the Humane Society during our childhood—because she kept coming home begging to adopt every dog—was taking refuge in a roomful of puppies. Ezra stopped beside me, catching his own breath, his hand on the side of his ribs.

I swallowed the wet air and got back up. I turned around, my eyes widening, taking in Ezra and his now see-through shirt. He was drenched. I watched water stream down his body—his curls, the cut on his swollen lip, his shifting square jaw, his chiseled chest. He stared back with hardened eyes, also for a moment too long.

"Can I help you?" I asked.

"I can see through your dress," he stated blankly, as one eyebrow danced upward.

"I'm aware," I huffed, *completely unaware*. I tightened my leather jacket around my very visible nipples.

"No need to cover up now," he said with a grin.

I narrowed my eyes, tugging the worker's gloves off my hands and slapping them into his chest. He stepped forward, putting his palm over the gloves as he took me in, my hand on his pounding torso, the frigid rain between us. He snatched the gloves as I flinched back, and we both shifted our bodies away from each other.

"You deal with that," I said, handing the mouse over to Ezra. Confused, Ezra's eyes darted down to the mouse and then up to Karen, who circled above us.

"I'm getting the bride," I fearlessly announced as I strode toward the shed.

I creaked open the door. It was warm inside the shed, and it smelled like puppies and mud. The dawn left a golden haze inside the one-room cabin, which was fairly large for a space that was occupied by just a tricolor mother Cavalier King Charles Spaniel, who was nursing her five puppies, a handful of weeks old. Lying on the floor across from the mother, her body curled toward the dog with her cheek on the newspapered floor, was Hannah.

Still wearing her white wrap dress, which was now muddied and brown, Hannah was barefoot, with mascara below her eyes. Yesterday's curls had fallen out of her hair, but her blond locks lay straight around her face, framing her angelically. She was crying softly, emotionally drained and defeated, broken and still beautiful, as she brushed her hands through the mom dog's curly mane.

"And you probably didn't even want any babies. Did you? You just had one wild night with some super-sexy dog, and *bam*, you got five babies. Why do you get five babies, and I get no babies? I'm happy for you, don't get me wrong . . . your kids are really cute. It's just . . . it's not fair that women, we spend all this time going to battle with our bodies to not get pregnant, only to wake up one day and find out that the war is over. You know? Of course you don't know. You're a dog . . . *a dog with babies* . . ." Hannah sobbed as she curled her body into the fetal position. The mother dog sympathetically tilted her head at Hannah.

My broken heart emptied itself out through my eyes as I watched Hannah. Tears streaming down my face, I slowly lay my wet, shivering body down behind the mother dog, so that I was an arm's length away from my best friend. Hannah's raw, red eyes widened, taking me in. Her body hardened, her devastation darkening to anger. She was not happy to see me, and I did not blame her. I was not happy to *be* me—I barely wanted to live in my own skin after how I had behaved toward her, so I could only imagine how she felt.

I peered over the mom dog's face, resting my wet dimpled chin on her warm fur. Tears streamed down as I choked on the words.

"I'm sorry," I said with a trembling voice.

"Go away." Hannah sniffled, sitting up and shifting her body away from me as she tugged her legs to her chest.

"Hannah, I'm so sorry. I'm so, so, so, so sorry. I've been the worst friend ever. The worst bridesmaid ever."

"No arguments here," she muttered under her breath. "I want to be alone."

"No you don't," I said softly.

Hannah rocked her body on the newspapered floor, her knees pulled to her chest as she stared at her muddied toes. She was dying to ask me something, but she did not want to give me the satisfaction of conversation. I knew what it was. I could read her like a book.

"He doesn't love his ex-girlfriend."

Hannah glanced at me quickly, eyes wide, tears spilling out of them.

"He doesn't? Then why did you say—"

"That was a misunderstanding. I promise, Hannah. He loves you, just *you*. He loves you in this . . . can't-live-without-you, storybook kind of way. I can see it all over his face when he looks at you, *the way he looks at you,* when he talks about you, any idiot can see how much he loves you."

I scooted closer to her. I could taste salty tears on my lips.

"And if you want to be with him, then I'm your girl," I continued. "I'll fix this, I'll—I'll do whatever I can do to fix this. I will. I'll kill a bitch if I have to." I grabbed her hand, squeezing twice as she looked at me, eyes not leaving mine.

"But Hannah, if you're not ready to marry him, if this is too soon for you, then I'll be your getaway car. I'll get you out of here. No questions. No judgments. You're the only person who hasn't judged me for being complicated. You love every side of me. You're my person Forever. And that's a hard word for me. But not when it comes to you."

Hannah slowly shifted her body in my direction, her hand still in mine. A tricolor puppy crawled onto her lap, and she stroked it as tears fell onto its innocent little body.

"Did you see Graham's face? When he found out I couldn't have kids . . . his face, Zoey . . ." Hannah trailed off, reliving the look of disbelief in Graham's eyes. I moved closer to her, wrapping my arm tightly around her body.

"He was in shock. That was a shitty way for him to find out, through your shitty best friend shouting it—"

And then, out of nowhere, my arm left Hannah, and I started choking on my own hot tears. I cried with frustration and shame, I cried with relief to no longer pretend that there was not a war going on within my soul. I let the tears fall as the words followed.

". . . through your best friend shouting at the guy she loves so damn much, who she can't seem to say yes to because she's scared, and not sure if . . . I'm not sure if I'm made for marriage. I'm not sure if it's made for me. I want to be with him, but I don't know if I can marry him, and if I can't marry him, then I'll lose him, and I don't want to lose him. I wish I was like you. I wish *this* came easier to me . . ." I trailed off into tears, going round and round in a circle game of No Win.

Hannah scooted toward me and we took each other into our arms. I let my chest cave in as we held on, both gripping tighter, both just a little bit betrayed by the world that promised us we could have it all.

"At least your ovaries work," Hannah offered, trying to lighten the mood.

"As far as I know. Can I donate mine to you?"

"I don't think that's a thing."

"But if I could, I would," I said, meaning it. I would give her all my organs.

"I know you would." And she did.

We broke, and I wiped my tears on the sleeve of my wet leather jacket, which was of no help.

The room fell quiet as we choked back our emotions, our hands gripping each other, our wet eyes scanning each other's pages and understanding that sometimes, it just fucking sucks to be a woman. The tiny puppy in Hannah's lap looked up at us, big brown eyes darting from my face to Hannah's, as if wondering if her life would ever become this complicated.

Here we were.

Two complicated women.

Two embattled fighters of Truth Monsters.

A creaking sound at the door cut through the silence, and our eyes moved to the cabin entrance. The door dramatically swung open, bringing in the smell of morning rain, and the groom.

# Thirty-one

Graham barreled through the cabin door. Ezra sheepishly trailed behind his brother, holding the mouse in his gloved hand. Graham was breathless, soaking wet, his face both flushed and hardened. He was wearing a soaked-through white T-shirt, untucked over his dark jeans. He had clearly not slept at all this past night, but there was an energy in his eyes as they fixed on Hannah. Tears streamed down her face as she tried to get a word out. They stared at each other as she navigated a sea of pain.

"I'm sorry," she finally cracked. "I'm so sorry I didn't tell you. I was so ashamed, and I found out right before we met, and I just . . . I was so afraid that you might—"

Thankfully, she didn't have to continue. Graham had words prepared, as if he'd been walking around with them in his chest all night. He spoke loudly and clearly, silencing Hannah.

"I want to have a hundred babies with you, however we have them."

He started to walk toward her as she lost it. Hannah's chest caved in with a mixture of shame and relief, her trembling body somehow managing to find its way upright and fall into the safety of Graham's arms.

"I'm sorry. I'm so sorry—"

Graham shushed her. He held her tight, swaying her body in his as he kissed the top of her head.

"Relax," he whispered into her ear. Her wide wet eyes pulled back to stare up into his. He grinned, letting her know he had a sense of humor, even when the world seemed like it was falling apart. She choked back more tears, burying her face in his chest. Graham lifted her face upward. His hand wiped away the tears on her cheeks, and they stayed there as he took her in, his expression resolute.

"Just know, I'm choosing to go through all the good and all the not so great with you. *All of it.* You have to let me go through it all with you. Even the unimaginable. Got it?"

She nodded with her head still in his hands.

"Got it," she said.

Graham pulled her face into his, kissing her gently.

And just like that, they weathered their first storm.

Ezra and I could do nothing but look on, watching the groom hold the bride while she cried in his arms. Our eyes met each other across the room, two soldiers wounded in battle, and a smirk graced Ezra's lips—a grin. My eyes widened, and I exhaled a silent smile. I couldn't quite place how he saw me now, but I had somehow proven that I was the bridesmaid who fought for the bride, not for the union. For a guy who married a traitor, maybe all he wanted out of the world was loyalty. Ezra didn't want to see other people's happiness through a bitter lens. As his eyes left mine to look at his brother, I could tell that he didn't. He saw two people in love, and it didn't make him want to pick up a sword.

Graham's face writhed in pain because Hannah was in pain—his head bent down toward her face. The fact that Graham now knew Hannah's hard truth made it real for her in a way that it wasn't before. Hannah was breaking all over again, as if being told she could not have her own biological children for the first time. There were tears in Graham's eyes, and I knew that under different circumstances, he would let them fall. Yet, I also knew why he was keeping them in—he wanted to be strong for Hannah.

He would move mountains for her.

He could not move this mountain right now, and it broke his heart.

With tears down my cheeks, I took in the bride and groom on the morning of their wedding day. They held each other— broken and beautiful—and I knew this to be true: Hannah would climb the mountain—she would become someone's mom one day. I also knew this to be true: she would climb the mountain with Graham by her side, and that would make all the difference.

# Thirty-two

Moments later, Hannah pulled back from Graham, having emptied all she had left onto him, her chest no longer heaving. She let out a deep exhale, and she looked up to him with thankful eyes as he cupped her chin and kissed her gently. I turned to Ezra, who was still standing sheepishly by the door, holding the live mouse in his hand. *The mouse. Karen. Oh my God. KAREN.*

"Where's Karen?" I asked anxiously, terrified of the answer.

"Yeah . . . the falcon's gone," he said with a shrug.

"Oh, cool, cool, cool. We lost the Pride of Ashford Castle. *Cool.*" I paced in a circle, anticipating surviving jail time in Ireland.

"*We?* No. *You* lost Karen," Ezra corrected.

"Chain of custody. He who holds the mouse—"

"I went after the groom. Thought that might be more important."

"You went to find Graham?"

"Yeah, and bring him to his bride. Who's the *fucking genius* now?"

I shook my head and grinned at Ezra. Saver of blessed unions.

"You lost Karen?" I heard Hannah say.

I turned toward Hannah, who had her back now folded onto Graham's body with his arms wrapped around her. They stared at us with incredulous expressions.

"So the thing is, I broke Karen out of jail to find you."

"You went into a bird situation, willingly, to find me?" Hannah placed her palm on her chest, touched I would do such a terrifying thing on purpose.

"It's honestly the bravest thing I've ever done."

"Should we get out of here? I'd prefer to not smell like puppies on our wedding day," Graham said to Hannah.

My work here was not done. I knew it. I knew based on my behavior that I was getting off too easy, and I also knew I could not risk myself anymore.

"Wait, before we go . . . I . . . I shouldn't be your bridesmaid," I exhaled.

Hannah looked at me curiously.

"First, I wasn't there for you the way you really needed me to be. I was selfish. And second . . . Hannah, I'm bad luck."

"You're *what?*" she asked, her eyebrows coming together.

"I've been asked to be a bridesmaid in three weddings, and none of them have happened, not one bride has made it down the aisle."

There I stood, releasing one of my Truth Monsters out into the universe so that the person who mattered the most could hear it. This weight that had been warring inside my soul and keeping me up at night was suddenly lighter.

"Huh? Your friend Rebecca never—"

"Gone Girl. I'm zero for three, and I just, I really thought I did everything I could to turn it around with your wedding. I wanted to get you down that aisle, and not for nothing, I did what I did for really selfish reasons. To be able to see that marriage could work, to be able to say yes to Rylan with optimism. And I know you guys are getting married in a handful of hours, I *know* it, but . . . just in case, I love you too damn much to do anything to destroy your union."

Hannah tilted her head at me. I wondered if this was the part in our story where it got harder to read the book. Where we became so complicated that the person who used to finish your sentence had no idea what page you were on.

"Rebecca's wedding was the day before Rylan proposed. That's why . . ." Hannah trailed off, wide eyes on me, reading all of my pages.

I nodded and quickly wiped away tears. Hannah understood me—complications and all—the way best friends just do.

"Zoey, you've never been bad luck. Not to me. You're the reason I got through my adolescence. You're the person who cared enough to pull me out of my shell when no one else would even look twice at me. You're the woman who taught me to stand up for myself, even if it was uncomfortable. You're my person too, and no one else is standing up there for me today but you."

I felt tears stream down as Hannah left Graham's arms and walked toward me.

"Are you sure?" I asked quietly.

"When Graham and I are old and gray, and we're looking through our wedding album, and you aren't in the photos standing up next to me, do you want me to call you crying? Because I will. I'll make you feel horrible about not being a bridesmaid in my wedding, even when we're ninety."

I studied Hannah, in total awe of her for so many reasons.

"You can really do that, can't you?" I asked.

"Do what?"

"Look to the future so easily."

"I guess," Hannah said apologetically, knowing that a part of me envied her for it.

Graham walked toward us and put his arm around Hannah, kissing her head and filing to the door. Ezra arched back, preparing to get hit again. Graham looked at the mouse in Ezra's hand, then back at Ezra. He shook his head and edged his wet shoulder into Ezra's playfully, the man version of *"I forgive you for being an absolute dickhead."* They grinned at each other as they stepped out the door and into the rain.

Men. They didn't even have to say sorry.

Fuck them.

Moments later, after we returned the mouse to its cage and gave up looking for Karen, we walked through the path in the woods, the rain now faded away. We could see the castle yards ahead, and we watched wide-eyed as the morning sun melted the icy frost on the lawn. Hannah and Graham held each other arm in arm, her head finding solace on his shoulder.

I limped along behind them with Ezra to my side. We looked like we had all survived some sort of battle. Emotionally, I think we had. We were physically dirty and bruised and bleeding, but I knew we were all somehow lighter. My war was far from over, but at least for this morning, we had surrendered, let our hard truths live out in the world, and somehow survived.

Ezra's shoulder bumped into mine.

"If I'd known I was in the presence of Bad Luck Bridesmaid this entire time, I really wouldn't have overextended myself."

"*Overextend?* I got stranded half-naked on a lifeboat and survived the Loch Ness Monster. You requested Bono."

"Damn, I really wish my ex-wife had you standing up for her at our wedding."

"Why is that?" I said, eyes rolling.

"She would have never made it down the aisle, and I wouldn't have wasted a year of my life. You would have been the best luck ever."

I slowed my walk as the castle stood but yards away. The rain was gone, and the sun bathed every inch of me. A cloud was lifted not from the sky, but from my soul. My world, for a glistening moment, stopped as I felt a change wash over me. "Good luck" hit me, and it hit me like an epiphany should. It knocked my old world down, and a new one stood tall.

I thought of my three brides. I pictured Chelsea in her London office, finalizing fabrics for her successful spring line. Her face beamed with pride, having become independently successful without someone else guiding her compass.

I thought of Sara losing her shit at the baby registry desk, pregnant and laughing hysterically with tears all over her face as she and her partner realized they had spent the past ten minutes seriously arguing over which organic baby butt rash cream was the best.

I thought of Rebecca and her work crush, Harrison, making out against the wall of a staircase in their office building, fireworks crashing around them.

If Chelsea had gotten married, she wouldn't be happily independent and running her textile company. If Sara had gotten married, she wouldn't be having a little boy with the woman she loved. If Rebecca had gotten married, she wouldn't be seeing the world in vivid color—a lens that Croakie-held glasses could have never shown her.

I turned back toward Ezra, tears in my eyes. I had handed myself a guilty verdict the moment each bride failed to make it down the aisle. I had judged myself based on facts alone, but I had overlooked the context. I was innocent. I was more than innocent.

*I'm Good Luck Bridesmaid.*

"Chelsea, Sara, and Rebecca . . . they would be as hopelessly miserable as you are if they'd gotten married," I said with awe.

"Thanks," Ezra deadpanned.

"I'm Good Luck Bridesmaid," I exhaled to the universe, for good measure.

"You're a fucking weird person," Ezra corrected.

I looked at him, and he stared back with an almost charmed face. A sly grin, a grin that told me he appreciated that I was a weird person. I felt a slow smile forming on my lips as I edged my shoulder into his.

Hannah waited for me by the castle steps as Graham held the door open. I stood next to her, putting my arm around my best friend.

"Oh—one more thing. Your mom thinks you're pregnant," I said, wincing.

"Well, this should be fun," Hannah said, sucking in the morning air. "I have to tell her," she stated, without a question.

I smiled, seeing my friend lean in to the messy world of Coming Clean.

"She's your mom, and she'll love you no matter what, but right now she doesn't understand what's going on with you, and it's killing her."

Hannah tilted her head at me, surprised by my defense of the Ice Monster.

"So, what do we say we get you married?"

"You know, technically you're not just a bridesmaid. You're the *only* bridesmaid, which also makes you the maid of honor."

"Are you trying to give me an anxiety attack? You know I'm all out of my Purse Benzos."

"Big day for Hannah and Zoey: marriage, curse reversals . . ."

"Turns out, I'm not actually cursed."

Hannah stared at me with big hazel eyes, her face and hair wet, standing in her tattered white dress. She moved a few wild curls from the front of my beaming brown eyes.

"I could have told you that," she said, as she kissed my cheek and turned to head up the stairs.

Nearly losing my breath, I tugged Hannah's elbow back toward me, turning her around so our wide eyes could scan the horizon.

A thick colorful arch floated in the air above the lawn. Sunlight had shifted direction as it beamed through the misty rain, creating a stunning rainbow—the result of reflection and refraction, light waves bouncing off a surface and light waves changing direction.

I could see myself, the way I was meant to be. I could feel my soul changing directions.

Reflection and refraction.

Hannah and Zoey.

The result of a perfectly imperfect atmosphere.

# Thirty-three

I knew right before the singer put her lips up to the microphone that I was one for four. I also knew that it did not matter. I stood outside the lakeside tent, peering into the flap to see a crowd of beautifully dressed friends and family members sitting on white wooden chairs. The open-air tent offered a view of Lough Corrib on one side and Ashford Castle on the other. I was in disbelief that this day was here—my best friend in the world was getting married. I closed the flap on the ceremony entrance, letting the November air push the tears back inside my eyes.

Our bride was beaming.

Seeing Hannah in her wedding dress was the equivalent of a young child gazing upon the Sugar Plum Fairy for the first time. Hannah was effortlessly perfect in an ethereal white gown with floral applique over sheer lace—it looked as if she was wearing nothing but white floating flowers, a garden dancing upon her frame. She breathed in deeply, looking at me with wide eyes.

"Can you believe it?" she asked, tears forming.

"I can, and I can't," I replied, smiling.

That's the thing about growing up. You spend your life preparing for the big moments, and when they come, they still manage to take your breath away.

I edged the falling vintage pearl comb up into Hannah's waves, swallowing swirling emotions as she gripped my hand. In unison, we both squeezed twice, as if acknowledging that the comforts of our childhood might not work like they used to, but we still needed them. Hannah slowly shifted her gaze, and I turned around—following Hannah's eyeline—to find her mother standing behind us. Celeste was watching Hannah and me with a weightless gaze.

Hannah confided in me that she sat her mom down right before hair and makeup. Hannah tearfully, with Graham by her side, divulged to her mother that she could not have her own biological children. Hannah told me there was a moment Graham leaned in to stop Celeste from going on a spiral of *"well, what if we . . ."* He took Celeste's hand and assured her, "It's going to be okay, Mrs. Green. Hannah and I? We're going to figure it out by ourselves. We're going to build an incredible life together, with a houseful of kids. I promise you, your daughter is going to be more than okay." Hannah said that she saw something beautiful break across Celeste's hardened face. Celeste stared at Graham, the way one might catch her beaming at Hannah—like he was perfect. She quickly stitched up her armor so as to not give too much of herself away, sucking in her tears and nodding her head rationally as she patted Graham on the shoulder. But there was a little stitch missing, as if maybe she was allowing herself one more moment of vulnerability. Celeste turned to Hannah and embraced her in a long tearful hug.

I took in Hannah's mother with a smile. Celeste wore a deep-blue-and-cream metallic gown with trumpet sleeves. She looked regal, which was no shocker, but she seemed different to me. She seemed stunningly human. Celeste's eyes met mine, and I watched her mouth twitch, as if her lips were fighting her tongue.

"I'm sorry," she silently mouthed.

I tilted my head, amazed. Celeste smiled warmly at me—a genuine smile that asked for nothing in return. It only took thirty-one years, but Celeste Green had finally realized that Zoey Marks wasn't a threat to her daughter. If she could go back in time and do it all over again, I think Celeste would look at me the way she was looking at me in this moment—like I was her daughter's champion. The thing about mothers? They can surprise you.

My smile widened, hearing Irish Only begin a song from the corner of the ceremony tent. Graham's last-minute attempt at charming the lead singer into playing Hannah's favorite non-Irish tune for the processional had worked. Mazzy Star's "Fade into You" charged the air with dizzying romance, and I knew it was time.

I turned my head, feeling eyes on me. Ezra stood next to me at the front of the canopy entrance with a grin, wearing a slick black tuxedo with a white bow tie, his face cleaned up with just a hint of last night's punch on his lips. I smirked, stepping toward him, our faces inches from each other. I adjusted his crooked bow tie, and his strikingly blue eyes took me in. We stood staring at each other, eyes locked as the music swelled, the sun setting behind us.

"What are you looking at?" I grinned, feeling heat on my cheeks, waiting for him to lighten the moment.

He lowered his mouth to my ear.

"You're beautiful," he whispered.

I felt every hair on my body stand up as he pulled back. His dimples folded upward in an effortless way, and then, the best man spun on his heels, disappearing into his brother's wedding ceremony. Wide-eyed, I watched as Graham followed, flanked by his beaming parents.

I studied myself in the reflection of the tent flap, smoothing my hand over my hair, which was pulled back into a tight bun, not a flower crown in sight. I pulled my dress down, running my hands over the daring-but-tasteful front slit on the black velvet gown. I was objectively beautiful, but more so, I felt beautiful—because I felt like myself.

The wedding coordinator nodded at me, and I stepped through the opening in the tent, the room dripping in green vines and dainty twinkle lights. I kept my eyes forward on the smiling groom and the best man who stood next to him at the altar, Ezra taking me in with arched eyebrows.

I turned around at the floral altar, and my heart leapt out of my chest.

There he was. There was the man I loved in a black tuxedo, leaning forward in an aisle chair—just to meet my eyes. He couldn't help but take me in. I couldn't help but love him. It was chemical, a phenomenon that might just never go away.

I heard laughter, and my eyes darted away from Rylan to see Hannah's second cousins, two flower girls, ages two and four, forcefully pelting white rose petals down the aisle. The concerned ring bearer, age three, trotted behind them while diligently picking up the rose petals, trying to clean up. The older flower girl turned around and tugged the ring bearer down the aisle by his arm.

Suddenly, black-tie-invited bodies rose from their seats and turned around. Two hands pulled the large canopy flaps back, bringing in a purple sunset and the beaming bride. Standing between her parents, Hannah gripped the handkerchief wrapped around her white bouquet. She was angelic, her lace veil floating behind her, and she kept her eyes locked onto Graham's with each careful step. I turned to look at the groom, and I watched Ezra sweetly hand him his own pocket square as Graham let tears fall with a grin so big that it melted the room.

Hannah slowed her steps, meeting Graham at the altar. She turned to her side, handing me her bouquet, and she let her hazel eyes stay on mine for a moment—a big moment—the kind you prepare for, but are never prepared for. I held my breath, mystified as I gazed at my best friend, the shy middle-schooler who loved the parts of me others didn't understand, the teenager who thrived diligently coloring inside the lines of a perfect picture, the adult who knew she could handle a curveball. Hannah could read my page, and she knew how proud I was to be her best friend. Tears welled in her eyes, and then mine, in a moment we would remember Forever. It was a moment inside a day that we would tell her daughter about.

Her face stayed beaming throughout the entire ceremony, and, bathed in an orange-and-purple sunset, Hannah and Graham's lips met in a burst of glee, and they were married.

Tears streamed down my cheeks, and as I watched the bride and groom press together for a second sweeping kiss, my heart exploded into a million pieces. I cried because *I knew*. It was more than just a feeling—it was a fact. Hannah and Graham were meant to be.

*When you know, you know.*

I got that now.

Ezra locked his arm with mine, and we watched the husband and wife walk down the aisle, rose petals floating around them in the air. I glanced up at the best man. There were tears in his eyes, which his clenched jaw was desperately trying to will away. I grinned. I think he knew too.

Here Zoey Marks was, Good Luck Bridesmaid, taking part in her first recessional. I felt pride, as if I had raised Hannah. She had grown so much into herself. She had met someone wonderful and unexpected, a person she did not need the outside world to reassure her about—she just knew Graham was her person, she knew it in her soul, and her soul picked right. As I walked down the aisle, I let my eyes float toward the man who held my complicated soul captive. The man who made my heart do somersaults. Rylan stood with a wistful smile on his strong jaw, cheering along Hannah and Graham with the rest of the wedding guests, but with his eyes glued to the woman he loved. I looked into his green eyes, goose bumps prickled my entire body, and finally, I knew.

*When you know, you know.*

# Thirty-four

An hour later, the ceremony space had been transformed into an airy white-and-green garden for the reception. Candles, flowing white flowers, and green vines danced across the interior. The clear walls of the tent surrounded us on all sides, revealing a gorgeous view of the glistening lough, the castle, and the huge full moon hovering above. On the dance floor, Irish Only sang a gorgeous cover of U2's "All I Want Is You," as Hannah and Graham held each other in their first dance. I wondered if they had planned a full moon to go along with this moment, or if it was simply serendipitously perfect. Maybe it had all just fallen together accidentally, the way it was supposed to.

I sat down at a lone table, looking out onto the dance floor with starry eyes, smiling at the bride and groom. Hannah laughed as Graham dipped her and tugged her back toward his chest, kissing her hard, his hand on the back of her neck.

I sat up straighter as Ezra set two Irish whiskies down at the table and pulled out the chair next to mine. He slid one glass my way, and I took the drink in my hand as he peeled his tuxedo jacket off.

The best man. My unlikely ally.

I watched him exhale as he took off his monogrammed cuff links. He arched back and undid his bow tie, letting it hang on either side of his lapel. He stared me straight in the eyes, undoing the top two buttons of his dress shirt. His arched eyebrow danced to the ceiling as his dimples appeared.

I swallowed hard, hiding my widening eyes and burning cheeks behind my stiff drink.

"I saw you fighting tears up there, you little traitor. You lover of blessed unions," he teased.

"Oh please. I saw you wiping your eyes."

"It was just allergies. All the flowers," he deadpanned.

"You know what I don't get? How did you figure out Hannah couldn't have kids?"

He looked at me sideways.

"The handkerchief? C'mon, that really wasn't you?" I asked.

"All my mom. She loves her Irish traditions. But . . ." He shifted his chair, resting his arms on his knees as he looked at me. "I realized something wasn't right after you accused me of handkerchief warfare on the yacht. I was walking back from the dock, and I overheard you talking to Hannah's mom. I heard her say Hannah was pregnant, and I knew she wasn't pregnant, I mean I'd seen her get beyond tipsy the night before."

"And you didn't tell your brother something was wrong?"

"I figured whatever it was, maybe it wasn't my business. But really, I knew that he would have married her regardless. And I guess . . . I guess that's when I threw my hands up. They're in love. I think my brother would turn his entire future upside down just to love her. No army could fight that."

"They've got more than just love," I said wistfully, taking in the bride and groom.

"What do you mean?" Ezra asked, scooting in closer to my chair.

I studied Ezra's expression. It begged to know, *"What could be more than love?"* I went to open my mouth, to explain something that was no longer unexplainable, when I looked up, breathless at the sight of Rylan walking across the dance floor toward me with conviction.

His eyes were locked onto mine, his striking black wool tuxedo hugged his body in all the right places, and his black bow tie sat perfectly under a crisp white collar.

You know that moment you lose your footing, and you're one second away from faceplanting down a flight of stairs? That moment right before your hand finds the banister? That mere second where your heart drops below your chest and everything moves in slow motion? It was that again, the slow fall, the moment where I had to take in every part of this man, just as I had the very first moment I set my brown eyes on him. Rylan stood above me—his strong jaw, his sandy-blond hair slicked to the side, his clean-shaven face, and his impossibly green eyes all sending me to another planet. The smell of woodsy cedar swirled around me.

"Dance with me?" he asked softly.

I somehow stood up, and I let my hand find his—as it had so many times. He led me to the dance floor as Irish Only began to play the Cranberries' "Dreams," and I chuckled, my eyes meeting Hannah's, who was dancing across from me with Graham, both of us acknowledging the nostalgic soundtrack to our childhood.

I gazed up at Rylan as he pulled me close to him, one hand clasping mine, the other on the small of my back. I kept a hand at the nape of his neck—familiar ground. Our fingers pulsed tighter together, both terrified to let go. We swayed with the emotion of the room, and I felt his hand leave mine, now two strong arms around my waist. I let my other hand find the nape of his neck, our arms fully wrapped around each other, our eyes piercing through one another.

A tiny grin softened his jawline. "You got a bride down the aisle," he said.

"Honestly, a giant leap for mankind."

I felt his body tense, his smile fading under a clenched jaw, and it took everything inside of my body to pretend that I didn't—to stay in this perfect moment where the warmth of his beating chest against mine felt like home. My fingers trembled against the curve of his neck, and I swallowed back tears.

"So . . ." he cracked.

"So . . ."

His green eyes hardened onto mine with flickers of fear and hope. I could feel his arms hold me a little tighter, as if bracing for a fall.

"Are you still afraid of marriage?"

"Dreams" swelled as I glanced across the dance floor at Hannah and Graham, the bride and groom wrapped up in each other's arms. *Married.* I looked back at Rylan.

"No. I'm not afraid of marriage. I just know that it's not for me. That doesn't mean I don't want to be with you. I want to be with you more than I think you understand." I swallowed hard, trying to keep tears from spilling out before my soul could get a chance. "I want to be with you, but not the way you want me to. Whether I'm with you for five years or fifty years, I need my road to be open. I want to wake up every day and make a decision to love you, without something wrapped around my finger telling me I'm supposed to."

I took in his pained eyes, and I felt his grip loosen around me.

"And I'm worried that one day you're going to wake up and decide you don't want to be with me."

"Anyone can do that, married or not."

"Without a ring, it makes it easier to walk away."

"I need to feel like I can walk away, even if I won't. I realize that's a lot to ask. I know it's not for most people. But . . . I'm not most people."

I watched his face twist in the light, and I knew the next words that would leave his lips were not leaving his soul easily.

"I want someone who sees a lifetime with me."

All at once, I couldn't bear to look at him. Tears enveloped my vision as my eyes darted around the room. I could still feel my arms around him, but they were numb. I knew I had to look back at him. The truth was best when you didn't say it under your breath. When you said it loudly, clearly. I took a sharp inhale, my chest rising and falling onto his. I dared my face up to his green eyes, tears falling as my mouth cracked open.

"I can't give you that."

I swear, I felt both our hearts break against each other right there on the dance floor.

When I was four, I stared out my bedroom window, thoughtful almond eyes watching the blood-orange sun disappear below the asphalt road. The next morning, I asked my mom, "Where does the sun go at night?" She grinned, and explained that as far as the Earth is concerned, the sun doesn't really go anywhere, but we do—we orbit on an axis. My sunset was someone else's sunrise. I turned away from my mom, eyes like tiny saucers, a weight on my chest as I gazed out the window. The sun stood still just to light up my days. "I'm sorry," I whispered up to the yellow circle beaming down on my vibrant cheeks.

I can't explain it any other way, except to say that the idea of standing still—being someone else's sunrise and sunset until the end of days—made my insides hurt. Marriage only worked with an orbit and an axis. The axis—the imaginary line on which the Earth orbited the sun, always pointing toward the North Star—was like bands of cold metal tight around our fingers—an unwavering promise between a planet and a star. Some days or years you might get to be the Earth, and others, the sun. Why couldn't we just be two untethered planets soaring through the galaxy? Spinning, glowing, darkening, giving, taking, changing—two wild souls finding each other and staying in each other's atmosphere by choice, not by duty.

I came back down to Earth, finding Rylan's eyes had swallowed the room's twinkle lights and leafy plants whole—those irises shone down on me like a green flash sunset. My hands were limp at my sides, no longer around his neck. Everyone around us was swaying, but we were no longer dancing. His hands were no longer even on me, and he took a step back. Suddenly, I gripped my hand around his wrist. Tears were about to spill on his face, his chin was quivering, and I knew he wanted to flee.

"Zoey—"

"No." I shook my head with force. "I want you to know what's inside me before you walk away. You don't have to understand me, but I need you to know what's inside me, Rylan. I owe myself that."

He swallowed hard.

"Okay," he said, his eyes cast down at his shuffling feet. I gently lifted his chin up, so that his eyes were on mine.

"I came here so desperate to fix myself. You walked out of my life, and for the first time, I thought I was damaged. I thought something inside me was missing because I couldn't say yes to you. But, there's nothing wrong with me. I'm not broken, I'm just complicated. I don't see the world the way most people do, and there's nothing wrong with that."

I exhaled with tears down my chin, surrendering to the Truth Monster.

"Rylan, I love you. With every little piece inside me. But sometimes, love isn't enough, is it?"

If only he didn't need marriage the way I couldn't have it. If only I wanted to marry him. If only life would meet us in the middle. It was not fair, but it was honest. I took in his fallen face, memorizing every line on it, knowing I would close my eyes and think about it often, hoping that as time flew by, it wouldn't hurt so damn much. I stared up at the person I was letting go—not letting go because I was broken, but because I was put together.

Suddenly, I watched the most composed man I had ever met lose a battle with his armor. Tears rolled down Rylan's clenched jaw. I had never wanted to hold someone the way I longed to hold him in this moment. But he was no longer mine to hold. Rylan placed his hands on either side of my face, and I knotted my fingers around his hand, gripping onto Us.

"I love you too," he cracked. It was as if he was stitching up a scar on his heart that he would have for the rest of his life.

I had longed to hear those words from his mouth, *I love you.* They filled me up and tore me in half. There was too much love left for each other underneath our breaking hearts. I wish we could have used it all up before we broke. But we wanted different futures. Love, no matter how great, was not always enough.

My vision blurred with hot tears as our foreheads pressed

together, his tears on my face, and I breathed him in one last time.

"Bye," he whispered.

His lips pressed hard against my forehead. He pulled back, and we both tried our hardest to smile through the pain. His fingertips slowly left mine, and all I could do was love him madly as I let him go.

I stood amid the swirling crowd of couples holding on to each other, alone on the dance floor of my best friend's wedding, watching the man I loved walk away.

I could not move, but I did not buckle to the floor. I had broken my own heart, because I knew exactly who I was. It was no longer a fear, no longer something to fix: Marriage was simply not for me. I wanted love, but I wanted choices. I wanted to run through wide-open spaces. If my forever person existed, we would be eighty, and one day we would look at each other with puzzled expressions, remarking how strangely wonderful it was that we were still by each other's sides. Forever would be a happy accident.

A part of me still hoped that one day Rylan would show up at my door with a realization that he wanted to be with me whichever way he could. Maybe I was just clinging to hope to keep from falling down, but sometimes, life hands you a green flash sunset. And sometimes, you just need a little hope to help get past something that's not meant for you.

# Thirty-five

Irish Only began playing Enya's "Only Time" as I found my body swaying alone on the dance floor, slowly empowered by my own broken heart, empowered by the willingness to love the sides of myself that others might not understand.

I felt hands take mine, and I looked up to see the bride pulling me into her open arms. I wrapped my arms around her, and we held each other on the dance floor. I tried my best to keep heartbreak in my throat, rather than letting it spill onto Hannah's very expensive white lace wedding gown.

"You're married," I announced as I felt my vision enveloped in hot liquid.

Hannah pulled her glowing face back to study me. She took her fingers and wiped the mascara-stained tears from below my eyes. I shook my head, holding a smile as our eyes locked, our arms around each other's hips.

"You're going to be okay, you know that, right," Hannah said gently, not asking a question but rather stating the obvious.

"I mean, I might hard-core sob into my pillow tonight, but . . . I know I'm going to be okay. Weirdly, I'm . . . I'm relieved."

"Relieved?"

I stared at Hannah for a long moment, wrapping myself around the newfound fire in my belly, until it twisted off my tongue, and I shared a rewritten page with my best friend.

"I think that too often, women take pieces of themselves they have no reason to hate, and they carry those pieces around like failures. If enough women stopped apologizing, then maybe there'd be less of an expectation for us to always burn bright and stand still. Maybe our complications would become our backbones instead of our scarlet letters. Hannah, it's a relief to stand tall in my own body, rather than shrink because I'm not the woman someone else expected me to be."

Hannah was quiet for a while, studying me with a growing smile.

"You know what I've always envied about you?" she asked.

"My ability to use the word 'fuck' as a verb, interjection, adverb—"

"You've always been happy dancing on your own. You never needed someone else. I'm not like that."

I peered through the open end of the tent, my eyes widening. Hannah arched her neck, following my gaze to see Rylan's tall frame walking away from the reception.

"Sometimes, a dance partner is really nice though," was all I could say. Because it was the truth.

Rylan's strong gait disappeared past the castle doors, and my heart slammed against my ribs. I sucked in the smell of burning wax and flowers around me. Hannah turned my quivering face toward her.

"A wise woman once told me, 'Fuck the guy who won't move mountains to be with you.' You're worth moving mountains for too, Zoey."

"I know." I smiled, my body exhaling into the comfort of trusting its own worth.

I knew I was worth moving mountains for. I had always known it. But when the world tells you you're difficult, at some point, a little voice creeps inside and you start to ask yourself, *"Am I the mountain? Am I the very thing standing in my own way?"*

I wasn't a mountain. No part of me would smooth my complicated terrain so that I could be easier for someone else to conquer. And I wasn't the sun. I wouldn't stand still for someone else. I was a woman who was on her own path, and that terrified the shit out of almost everyone.

I grinned, looking at Hannah, who wasn't scared of me at all. Her hazel eyes squinted past me.

"Okay. New topic," she said.

"I welcome one with open arms."

"Ezra is staring at you."

"I do not welcome that with open arms."

"He's staring at you . . . all . . . *sexy.*"

My cheeks blanketed in heat, and I followed Hannah's gaze. The best man was sitting at a table, staring at me with those piercing blue eyes . . . all . . . *sexy.*

"He's probably just constipated," I deflected.

"I think that's his smoldering face," Hannah offered, with arched brows.

"Why are you doing that with your eyes? Stop that."

"You *are* sad. And he is *extremely attractive.* And sometimes when you're sad, and there's a beautiful man nearby—"

"Hannah Green . . . *Hays,* are you kidding me? I have mascara down my cheeks, I just felt what remained of my heart shatter into a million pieces. The last thing I need is to get tangled up with . . ." I trailed off.

I slowly studied Ezra—his dimples turned upward in a playful smirk, his square chin shifting, his disarming eyes unflinching as they took me in. He was gorgeous, sure. But I had shown him sides of myself that were less than perfect, he had seen the rough terrain, and yet nothing about the way Ezra looked at me told me that I scared him. My Truth Monsters didn't intimidate him. And to me, that was wildly sexy.

"I guess if you look past his personality, Ezra's okay looking." I shrugged, not wanting to give too much of myself away.

Hannah glared at me, reading my page.

"Okay, *fine*. He's very fucking attractive," I conceded.

"I knew it! Oh! Sisters-in-law . . ."

I narrowed my eyes at Hannah with a death stare. She grinned back warmly.

"It's the maid of honor's duty to dance with the best man," she said, and I felt her hands spin me around and nudge me off the dance floor.

I put one heel in front of the other, my body inching toward Ezra. His eyes locked onto mine and widened with my every step. I studied the bow tie undone around his neck, the cut on his full lip, the sleeves of his dress shirt rolled up tight against his biceps. He sucked in air, as if indicating that I had the power to bring him to his knees. Tears were still in my throat, and it was wholly strange to walk tall with a breaking heart. To allow myself to feel pain and excitement. To grieve and grow. What a brave new world.

Complicated women. We sure are fucking magical.

I reached the table and stood over Ezra.

"Hi . . ." I said, twisting the mesh lace on my sleeve, stammering.

"Hello."

I explored his ocean-blue eyes as if they held the tide. I wanted to jump in and catch a wave. I wanted to be anywhere but in the room where my heart broke. And I wanted him to come with me.

With my eyes glued to his, I grabbed the cold champagne bottle and a couple of glasses from the center of the table, raised my eyebrows, and spun around. Heart racing out of my chest, I strode away from the table, excitement itching away at pain. I felt a calloused hand grip mine, squeezing tightly. I looked up to find Ezra sauntering past me, pulling me with him through the crowd. My pace quickened, and we raced shoulder to shoulder out of the reception tent, wide grins on both our faces.

The cool night bathed my body, and I slowed my pace, my lungs taking in the chilly air as my breath huffed up to the full moon. Ezra slowed next to me, squinting back at the bright circle in the sky.

"The moonlight is really showing off tonight," he mused.

"The moon only looks like it's glowing because it's reflecting light from the sun."

"So moonlight is sunlight?"

"Exactly." I nodded.

"Well, that's a betrayal of every poem I've ever read."

"You read poems?" I asked.

"Sometimes."

"That's . . . unexpected." I smiled, enjoying that so much of Ezra was a mystery to me.

"You have a thing for the moon?"

"Sun. I have a sun-thing."

"Can I ask why?"

I held a grin, enjoying that so much of myself was a mystery to him.

"I felt bad for the sun once."

Ezra furrowed his brow. He shook his head at the night, seemingly mesmerized by the moon, the sun, and the woman standing next to him. I started to exhale, but Ezra tugged my hand, leading us toward the gardens in the distance. There was an unmistakable glimmer of magic in the air, my chest pounding with the excitement of not knowing where we would land.

My heels found solid ground, meeting the walled garden's pebbled floor. I took in the bushes of white roses behind me, the reception tent glowing in the night in front of us. Ezra untwisted the foil from atop the champagne bottle, and his thumb sent the cork flying into the night. Here we stood, two enemies who went into battle and emerged as allies, partying on the other side of the trenches. All we had to do to win the war was put down our swords.

He tilted the bottle toward me, and I took it out of his hands, grinning into the glass as I let bubbles float down my throat, gazing out at the reception tent, and soaking in the romance of the couples swaying on the dance floor. A moment later, I felt the bottle lift out of my hand, and I heard it clink onto the pavement as he set it down. Suddenly, I could feel the heat of Ezra's body pounding next to mine, his eyes scanning my profile.

"Can I help you?" I dared.

I turned toward him, my breathing quickening as his piercing blue eyes came into view just inches from my face.

"I think so."

He clasped his hand around my flushed cheek, setting flames to my entire body. I swallowed hard against his touch, and my mouth parted as his thumb traveled to my lower lip, grazing it like a question. His hand settled around the curve of my neck, and I cupped the side of his face in my palm, my fingers exploring the soft stubble on his cheeks, giving him the answer. His hand tightened around the back of my head, and he pulled my open mouth onto his.

It was like walking into a fairy tale. Surprisingly tender, as if all the volatile words we'd thrown at each other were actually just a cover for how helplessly exposed we would become after the venom left our veins. I tasted the warmth of whiskey and cinnamon on his tongue—a gift from the hard candies in the lobby. His hand stayed on the back of my neck, mine on the back of his, and our mouths parted briefly just to find each other again, and once more, until I carefully broke from his lips, stretching my shoulders back.

We stared wide-eyed at each other, as if to make sure we were allowed to find this kind of comfort amid two broken hearts. He lowered his mouth to mine, top lip dancing upward in a mischievous grin, and I knotted my fingers tightly around his thick hair, hungrily pulling his body against my aching heart. His full lips fought for air against mine, our kiss deepening, surrendering to something less tender, more raw, as if acknowledging that the Fairy Tale wasn't made for either of us. My chest thumped against his pounding torso—heartache and hunger splintered through every inch of our bodies, until I could taste the salt of my own tears on my tongue.

I pulled back, still in his arms, silent tears streaming. It was incredible how my heart could break one minute and race the next—how so many possibilities lived inside one person. Ezra gently tucked a strand of curls away from my face and settled his palm on the curve of my neck, staring at all sides of me and not flinching from them. He took in my pain with a sympathetic smile, as if to tell me that he'd been there, and it didn't scare him. He studied the fire in my wet eyes, arching his brows, as if to say, "*Yeah, me too.*"

He shot me a warm grin as he nodded to the iron bench next to us.

I sat down beside him, our shoulders pressed together. My wide brown eyes inhaled the full moon above, and I exhaled the past few months. I exhaled heartbreak. I inhaled hope. I let my cheek settle on Ezra's broad shoulder, and he took my hand in his, his fingers tracing the lines etched into my palm. Suddenly, his grip tightened, and I followed Ezra's wide eyes up to the sky, where Karen soared past the moon in a circle over the reception tent. We watched slack-jawed as our runaway falcon danced over the trees and disappeared behind the dense woods. Ezra and I slowly turned our faces toward each other, sharing shocked laughter.

Maybe Karen was a little bit like me. Maybe she needed wide-open spaces.

I grabbed the bottle of champagne at my feet and took a sip, surveying the reception tent, just yards away. On the dance floor, Hannah Hays wrapped her arms around her husband. She rested her head on his chest, and as their bodies turned with the music, Hannah's hazel eyes found mine. She smiled an impossibly perfect smile, and I leaned in, basking in the afterglow of her bliss.

Here we were. Two complicated women living their truths.

I tilted my head up to the sky, drawing in the dusty galaxy above me with a wide smile, and a rush of excitement prickled every inch of my soul.

My security blanket is the spark of the unknown. For many, it's the comfort of forever. But I like maps without destinations.

Always have.

Always will.

There's a term for a complicated woman who embraces the parts of herself that others might not understand.

A force of nature.

That's me, forever.

# Acknowledgments

I did not have *"embarking on line edits during a global pandemic with your two kids at home"* on my First-Time Author bingo card. The amount of encouragement and support I received so *Bad Luck Bridesmaid* could become a reality was overwhelming.

Thank you to my children, Max and Zoey. Nothing and no one is more important than you two. Max Ezra, my big thinker, your empathy is a gift to all who know you. While you are wise beyond your years, the answer is still *no*: you cannot read Mommy's book (yet). Zoey Noa, my little artist, you are sunshine and happiness on a rainy day. Keep creating rainbows.

Mom and Dad, thank you. Your unwavering support has allowed my wildest teenage dreams to become adult realities. I am so lucky to be your daughter.

To my book agents, Cait Hoyt and Alex Rice, thank you for your guidance and for enthusiastically transforming this screenwriter into an author.

Thank you, thank you, *thank you* to Alexandra Sehulster.

You are the most thoughtful editor and partner in crime. Let's do this again.

Thank you to everyone at St. Martin's Publishing Group and Macmillan for believing in Zoey Marks, right from the start. Thank you to the production team at SMPG, the creative services team, and the sales team at Macmillan. Thank you (and I'm sorry) to Susannah Noel—I will never type "towards" again. A big thank-you to Mara Delgado Sánchez, Anne Marie Tallberg, Brant Janeway, Jennifer Enderlin, Kelly Moran, Marissa Sangiacomo, and Monique Patterson for all your support. Thank you to Maja Tomljanovic and Kerri Resnick for making this book beautiful.

Thank you to Austin Denesuk, Olivia Blaustein, and Berni Barta for fearlessly championing the *BLB* short story (and all that has come after). Austin, you've always been good luck to me.

Thank you to rock stars Ashley Silver, Darian Lanzetta, Brett Etre, Laura Rister, and Jason Weinberg. Also, to Jennifer Au and Jamieson Baker for your early support, thank you.

Thank you to my dear friends Liviya Kraemer and Tamar Barbash. Your confidence in my work made this book possible. You have both changed my life.

Thank you to my friends/early readers. To Allie Greenberg and Randi Blick for your invaluable eagle eyes. To Azita Ghanizada, Breanne Duffy, Julia Duffy, Nicolette Robinson, Stacey Rothberg, and Christine Laskodi for your thoughtful reads. Thank you to my friend and photographer, Talitha Kauffman. Thank you to the rest of my lifelines: Brook Soss; Dana Rifkin; Emily VanCamp; Eugene Kim; Gavin Werbeloff; Jessica Gorman; Jodi Sonenshine; Jonny Umansky; Lauren

Rickoff; Lauren Schultz; Molly Silver; my brothers, Aaron and Zachary Greenberg; and my nieces, Emmy and Hannah.

To all the complicated women who love the sides of themselves that others might not understand, from the bottom of my heart, thank you.

# About the Author

ALISON ROSE GREENBERG is a screenwriter who lives in Atlanta but is quick to say she was born in New York City. While attending the University of Southern California, Alison took her first screenwriting class and fell head over heels. A journey from screenwriting led to marketing jobs, before coming full circle back to her first love. Alison speaks fluent rom-com, lives for nineties WB dramas, cries to Taylor Swift, and is a proud single mom to her two incredible kids and one poorly trained dog. *Bad Luck Bridesmaid* is her first novel.